THE CREEPYPASTA
COLLECTION
VOLUME 2

20 Stories. No Sleep.

THE CREEPYPASTA COLLECTION

VOLUME 2

20 Stories. No Sleep.

Edited by MrCreepyPasta

Adams Media

New York London Toronto Sydney New Delhi

Adams Media
An Imprint of Simon & Schuster, Inc.
100 Technology Center Drive
Stoughton, MA 02072

First Adams Media trade paperback edition MAY 2017

ADAMS MEDIA and colophon are trademarks of Simon and Schuster.

For information about special discounts for bulk purchases, please contact Simon & Schuster Special Sales at 1-866-506-1949 or business@simonandschuster.com.

The Simon & Schuster Speakers Bureau can bring authors to your live event. For more information or to book an event contact the Simon & Schuster Speakers Bureau at 1-866-248-3049 or visit our website at www.simonspeakers.com.

Interior design by Heather McKiel
Interior images © Clipart.com

Manufactured in the United States of America

5 2022

Library of Congress Cataloging-in-Publication Data has been applied for.

ISBN 978-1-5072-0303-3
ISBN 978-1-5072-0304-0 (ebook)

DEDICATION

For those who wish to grow.

CONTENTS

INTRODUCTION

Hey there kids it's me! MrCreepyPasta.

I see you've stumbled upon the second book in our little series. I hope that means that you've survived the first book. In the first creepypasta collection, I had tried to bring you a wide sampler of some of the greatest authors that the Internet community had to offer and this second installment is no different. There are a few names that you will recognize from the past and some new ones as well. All of these stories will be a wonderful introduction to horror for those that are new, and open a new chapter of horror for those who have stuck around.

The Internet has always been a horrible and terrifying place. Anyone that you speak to, read from, or see can come from any walk of life. This is why Mom and Dad always told you not to trust people you meet online. The blogger that you follow, posting those adorable pictures of puppies and kittens, could be a schoolteacher. That schoolteacher could live a perfect life and love animals and children. He could donate to charities and volunteer at soup kitchens. He could be the ideal human being. But on the other hand, he could be the darkest and most deranged person on the planet. This man could be a murderer, cannibal, or monster. He could be using his blog to lure in unsuspecting victims, get close enough to taste them, and strike when they least expect it. He could drag people from their homes kicking and screaming in the middle of the night to god knows where, and it's all because of a little interaction over the Internet.

That same fear is built into the very DNA of a creepypasta. These Internet horror stories are exactly what Mom and Dad used to always warn you about, and yet the addiction to fear stayed with you.

Horror doesn't die, kids.

Stories, such as the ones you find in this book, are all seedlings. They will take root in your mind and your imagination where they can haunt your dreams and nightmares. They hide in your home around every dark corner, ready to grab you if you don't move quickly enough to the light switch.

Horror is growing and organic. As I've seen over the years, horror changes from person to person and from day to day. What was scary once may not be scary when the next phase in your life comes along. Part of the lure of this book series is that it is made to hold this moment in time. The monsters trapped here will always be here every time you open the book. That's what makes these books so special. Hold on to them and revisit them again in a year. Paintings coming alive might not terrify you like it once did, but the chills down your spine will still be there. The demons you unleashed from reading this book will still creep around in the back of your head.

This is your last chance. If you put this book back onto the shelf, you'll be saving yourself from the demons of memory. You'll be safe.

But if you think you're brave enough, turn the page.

Just remember.

I warned you.

YOUR SECRET ADMIRER

CreepsMcPasta

I am writing you to tell you how I really feel.

You probably didn't notice, but for the longest time I've always been there for you. I want you to know what I've done, and I hope by me opening up to you like this you will feel the same way for me! And we can be happy together . . . forever.

I remember when we were both thirteen years old, when you first transferred to my school. As soon as you walked in I thought you were the most beautiful girl in the world. When your tranquil blue eyes crossed mine, even though it was for a brief moment as you scanned across the strange faces in the class, I wanted to be with you, forever. I was heartbroken straight away, though, when you were paired off with some other guy to show you around the school.

You didn't really notice me much. You were always with your group of friends who were so, so different from mine . . .

Who am I kidding. I never really had any friends.

The one thing that got me through all those years of loneliness in school was watching you, admiring everything you did. The way you gracefully went through your day without faults simply left me in awe, day in and day out.

As the years went by you seemed pretty popular with both the guys and the girls. You were sought after by all the popular guys in the school, even by some of the older ones. But you shrugged them off. The girls loved how you looked after yourself. You always had your makeup and hair perfect, which made you admired, but hated. It's sad, but it's human nature to get jealous, and we are all guilty of this crime. What they ended up doing however was far out of line.

I saw, as they pushed you when the teachers weren't looking. They would shove you into any nearby object, which more often than not was the wall. When you stumbled and slammed into the wall, the teachers would simply turn and say, "Watch where you're going, dear," and go about their business, blissfully unaware of what actually happened.

Witnessing it happen every other day burned me up inside; seeing you have this torment for being better than them . . . It was painful to watch every time it happened. I hoped it would die down, but it got worse. I saw when the bullies would knock your drink over when you weren't expecting it, just because the most popular guy asked you out. I was there when they set your bag on fire in the woodwork class because they thought you were being condescending when you tried to help them with their work. And I caught a glimpse of the one time they actually threw you to the ground outside the school gates and kicked you until you cried, simply because you tried to tell the teacher about what they were doing.

After that incident they followed you home. Usually they wouldn't do anything but yell abuse at you. The worst part was never knowing when they'd snap and suddenly attack you. It tore me apart to see the girl I loved feel so vulnerable. I wanted to fix it.

I knew there were three main bullies that were consistent; I knew of more but they seemed to only do it out of peer pressure. The main culprit was that narcissistic whore Bethany. Beth was jealous of everything about you. All the things I mentioned that made you great burned her up inside. She used to be the center of attention, and my gosh, did she love it. All the guys wanted to be with her, and all the girls wanted to be her. The only difference is that she used it for her own personal gain, and ultimately abused it. She slept with most of the guys who showered her in gifts that their mommies and daddies paid for. She only hung around with girls she deemed lower than herself, and demeaned them so they wouldn't be a threat to her God complex. But slowly over the years of you being in the school she eventually lost her reputation, because then all the attention was on you.

The second deviant who had a disgruntled grudge against you was that asshole Chris. He asked you to go to the school's annual dance in front of both his friends and yours and you simply rejected him, like the many others. But what made this instance different was that he ran off crying. He was publicly embarrassed, which in school meant a lot. He denied liking you and lost his friends and reputation, so he took out his frustrations on who he thought caused all of it—you.

The last person was Julie. She had it bad for you ever since the guy she liked always talked about how amazing you were while not paying attention to her, even after she performed some . . . well, let's say desperate deeds for him.

During the last week of school I knew they had something "special" planned for you. So I took it into my hands to deal with it, because I love you, and I didn't want your last few days at school to be ruined.

The first person I "convinced" not to mess with you any more was Chris. Now, he was much stronger than me, being into all the school sports—plus the alleged steroids meant I would not be able to take him in a simple one-on-one fight. But in the end, that would be his downfall. I knew where he kept his steroids—it wasn't hard to figure out, since our school's security and reputation were so low there was no need to hide it. I got his locker's combination by saying I forgot mine. The teacher handed over a list of everyone's combination. Yeah, that's right, they have no sense of security in this school.

I cracked open his locker with ease, leaving no trace of it ever being opened. I found the next shot he was going to use and squirted a little bit out, then pulled the plunger back out to where it was leaving a considerable-sized air bubble. I figured Chris was no doctor, nor does he have a clue how things work. He simply injects himself, then trains in the school gym. I bought a pass for the gym and watched as I pretended to train. He eventually came in the gym laughing hysterically with his friends. *Enjoy it while you can, it's not going to last long* was the thought that cropped up in my head. He went to his locker, and not long later came out dressed up in his training attire with a determined look on his face. He was ready to start. He was fine for a while but eventually slowed down. He had a puzzled look on his face as his body slowly gave up, and eventually the cardiac arrest set in and he was on the floor. People tried CPR but there was no defibrillator around since it was a school full of teenagers—who would expect a heart attack in a place like this? I smiled, and walked out before the paramedics arrived; it was already too late for him.

Working my way down the list, Julie was next. She was always jealous of the way every guy liked you. I silently slipped through her window without her noticing. I knew her parents were out so if she made a noise, no one would immediately come to her aid. I pounced on her while she was sleeping and pinned her down. I tied her hands to the bedpost, and then her legs. I pulled out several jars from my bag, each one almost black. Upon closer inspection, if you looked carefully at the gaps you would see small movements. They were full of all the creepy crawlies one would typically find in the bottom of anyone's garden. I took my time filling these up with every insect I could find. I wanted her to understand the pain you must have felt all that time she was shouting abuse at you, hurting you, making you feel lower than you really are. I propped her mouth open with one of those plastic rings a dentist would use for a long procedure. I slowly poured each jar down her throat. Every time her screaming was muffled a little further by the buzzing and scuttling noises the bugs were making as they adjusted to their new home. Tears streamed down her face as I repeated how all of this was for you.

A few jars in and I could feel the bugs in her stomach where I was sitting the whole time. By this time she had pretty much passed out from the pain. When this happened I'd wait, pour water on her face and slap her until she responded. For punishment I'd take off the ring from her mouth and pour the water down her throat making her swallow the insects and causing them to go on a frenzy of panic. Eventually during the fifth jar, the pain of all the insects burrowing into her internal organs plus all the internal bleeding caused her to pass away, but not peacefully of course.

I saved the worst until last. I had something "special" planned for Bethany. She was by far the worst to you. She made your life a living hell and this was unacceptable. No one as perfect as you should ever have had the displeasure of even knowing these people. So I carefully set the pieces and waited. One day I skipped my last class but no one noticed, not even the teacher. This shows how much attention I got in school. By this time I had memorized her route home. I waited in an archway I knew she walked past every day. I waited and thought about what I was going to do and how it was all for you. When I caught sight of her I grabbed her and pulled her to the ground. She was kicking and screaming, but at this point in her journey home there was no one around. The archway was to an abandoned derelict church.

I dragged her away from the path and toward the building so no witnesses would intervene and no one would find her body any time soon. I did my routine of tying her arms and legs to secure posts so I knew there wouldn't be much of a struggle. I also gagged her as I knew she would be making a lot of noise for what I was about to do. I slowly pulled out my knife, making sure she caught sight of its shiny glimmer. I placed the point of it on her lower leg and smiled as she reacted to the sharp point of the blade. I slowly pushed down making sure the wound was clean as it slipped into her flesh. It took a while but eventually the knife's handle was touching her skin. I took my time pulling it out making sure the wound did not rupture with that easily recognized crimson liquid. That would have meant her death and that would be too easy. As soon as the tip of the knife exited her body I immediately wrapped the split up with a bandage applying enough pressure to cut down the bleeding to a minimum. I then placed the knife a little higher up her leg, doing the same thing. I stared into her eyes as she helplessly watched me do this over and over, all over her body. After every stab I would say a remark about how you didn't deserve what she did to you. Eventually her whole body was nothing but red bandages. She was barely conscious as I slipped the final blow through her heart.

I can imagine you're screaming about now. In fact, I know you will be, and I will be close enough to hear. And by you stopping I know you've gotten to this point in my letter. So I'll start making my way in. It's pretty easy to get into your house now after doing it so many times. You probably thought it was your parents who left this letter in your room in the first place. No . . . it was me. Don't be afraid of the noise downstairs, it's only me. Put down the phone, I know by now you've got it in your hand. I cut the phone line. Don't bother calling your parents. I've already silenced them.

You can stop your screaming now. I am most likely right outside your door. Unlock it now and soon it will be just you and me together, forever.

Lots of love
—x—
Your secret admirer

BUBBLES

Max Lobdell

I was getting my hand stitched up in the ER last night when a series of rapid beeps sounded on the intercom, followed by an announcement of "ABD, code A, bay 1." Every doctor and nurse in the area stopped what they were doing and rushed to the main ER entrance. They got there just in time to meet the ambulances.

I couldn't see anything, so I waited. I figured there had to have been a serious accident. My phone rang. It was my Lucy, my wife. She asked how my hand was. I told her they were still stitching it up. I apologized for getting blood all over her bagel, and she laughed and reminded me that she'd told me not to cut it that way.

There was a pause while Lucy answered one of the kids' questions in the background. Then she came back on the line and asked if I saw that really bright light about a half hour ago. I didn't know what she was talking about, so she went on.

"It was crazy bright—the whole sky was this weird, pastel pink color. Then it turned white. It almost hurt to look at it, it was so bright."

"Huh," I replied. "Maybe it was a UFO." I craned my neck to see over the mass of people still huddled by the ambulance bay. Still nothing.

Lucy laughed. "Yeah, must've been aliens." She said something to one of the kids again, then came back on the line. "Okay, I'm gonna go. Joey said he's about to throw up."

17

I said goodbye and ended the call. The commotion on the other end of the ER was growing as more people from other parts of the hospital arrived. Something smelled terrible.

I covered my nose and mouth with my shirt and stood up. I walked over to the window so I could get a better look at what was happening. The crowd had thinned slightly. I saw a few nurses running off, probably to pick up supplies. At the end of the hall were two gurneys with medical personnel hovering over them.

The smell got worse and I gagged inside my shirt. One of the gurneys began to move as someone pushed it down the hall.

I stood in the doorway and watched. As the victim came into view, my eyes widened. It was a young woman, covered from head to toe in what I could only describe as bubbles. Some were as small as a pea, others were the size of a grapefruit. They all throbbed and pulsated from some pressure inside them, and every so often, one would tear open and weep yellow fluid onto the gurney. The smell was overwhelming.

They pushed her into the room next to mine. I could see everything from the window in the wall. They didn't bother closing the curtains. I heard the other gurney being pushed by and glanced over at it. A girl, maybe twelve or thirteen. I shuddered. I directed my gaze back at the person in the adjacent room. The doctors were popping bubbles to insert an IV. Fluid oozed onto the floor and I used every bit of self-control I could muster to avoid throwing up.

The woman's eyes were wide and darting back and forth. It was an expression of terror. Terror and agony. As if sensing my stare, a thin stalk slid from the center of her left eye. The doctors shouted and backed up. The stalk elongated a little over a foot, and its tip grew a bubble of its own. The bubble expanded and the weight caused the stalk to droop. When it was the size of an orange, it stopped growing. It hung like an obscene fruit. There was a yell from the room where they'd brought the other victim. I assumed it was for the same reason. On the other side of the window, more stalks emerged in a cluster from the woman's other eye. All of them produced bubbles like a bunch of grapes.

My phone beeped. It was a text from Lucy. "Can you go look outside? It's that light again!"

As if on cue, every light in the hospital went out. The emergency lights clicked on for half a second, then they went dead. There was nothing—nothing but the stream of pink light coming in from the open ambulance bay doors.

I stepped in the hall and asked, to no one in particular, what was happening. I doubt anyone heard me, because the light shifted from pink to white, accompanied by a blast of noise I can only describe as static. It caused me to clasp my hands to my ears and retreat backward into the room, where I cowered in the corner.

I saw shadows passing in front of the white light reflecting off the floor. Bizarrely-shaped shadows. They moved in a way that was both jerky and fluid, like jelly suspended on bone. The shadows darkened as whatever was making them got closer. Doctors and nurses in the next room shrieked, and then there was a flash that silenced them. Then, 2 feet away in the hall, harshly illuminated from the back by the piercing white light, I saw it.

My initial thought of jelly suspended on bone wasn't very far off. Six ossified tubes carried heavy, segmented portions of sloshing, semi-transparent sacks. The first thing that came to mind was the body of a jellyfish. Bubbles and waving stalks decorated the entirety of its trunk and it walked by, either not noticing me or not caring about my presence. It reached the room of the other victim. Just like before, there was a scream, a flash of light, and then silence.

The light outside went dark. The sound stopped. The emergency lights in the hospital clicked on.

I scrambled to my feet and looked through the window at the room next to me. The doctors were writing on the ground with burns on their exposed skin. The burns didn't look life threatening.

But the woman on the gurney was gone. Nothing was left but the sticky, yellow fluid on the floor.

"What the fuck was that?!" I yelled, and banged on the window. The person who'd been stitching me up got off the floor, came back into the room, and asked me to sit down so he could finish. A nasty burn on the bridge of his nose wept tears of lymphatic fluid down his mouth and chin.

"ABD code," he said. "Abduction. We've trained for them, but it was the first one I ever saw.

They're not supposed to come back for the abductees, though. I wonder why they did that."

I sputtered and asked, "You . . . you people have dealt with this? How isn't this going to be on the front page of every paper?"

"Well, you'll forget about it in a couple hours. Everyone will. Better write down what you remember so you can tell your friends. You'll recall something happening, but you won't remember what it was."

I looked at him, stupefied. "So how could you train for something like that? And how do you know it was your first one if you can't remember?"

He shrugged. "It's just what I was told. And good point about that other thing." He paused and I saw a series of nearly invisible, faded scars around his hairline. He smiled and nodded. "Very good point."

MARSH BAYWOOD SHIRTS
TalesOfTim

My mother left me when I was young, leaving me with my over-worked father and younger brother, Brandon. It's not like I didn't understand why my father had to work all the time, but I didn't like it. So many times I'd get home with my little brother to find a note on the fridge, "Working late again. Feed your brother and be in bed before eight."

We had recently moved to New Jersey, a street called Havens Cove Road. Our house was the last one before the street took a sharp turn and hit a dead end. The house was surrounded by woods—well, I call it woods but in truth it was the edges of the Marsh Baywood Swamp, an expansive wilderness that my father kept telling me not to play in.

It was a Tuesday. I arrived home with Brandon and found another note. Grunting, I tossed it into the trash. I flicked on the television, grabbed a bag of Cheetos, and vaulted onto the couch—and then I noticed it.

The back door was wide open. My father's shoes, the only pair he had, were sitting on the back porch. I jumped up and walked to the back door, spilling my Cheetos in the process.

"Dad?" I remember calling him, but whether that was all I said escapes me.

Receiving no response was surreal; while my father did work a lot he never once ignored us while he was home. I shivered, even though the weather was hot and muggy. I walked into the yard and waved to Brandon to follow.

A crumpled pair of pants lay nearby, and I knew they were my father's. He had a bad habit of scuffing the pant legs. Once again I called for my father but got no response. I picked up Brandon. When I stepped through the foliage separating the yard from the swamp, I found my father's hat and tie.

I walked on for maybe fifteen minutes before reaching a part of the swamp where I could go no farther. The swampy water had become too deep and the risk of drowning was too high. I would have to turn around and call the police. My father was out there somewhere and my calling was doing nothing. All it did was just scare my younger brother, who was by now sitting on my shoulders.

This area of the swamp was peculiar, but I didn't notice it until I looked up to see how late it was getting. About 20 feet above us hung men's dress shirts. I counted sixteen white, pressed, and clean shirts, nailed to trees deep in the Marsh Baywood Swamp. It was one of the most disturbing things I'd seen and I immediately decided to turn and head back.

I tried calling out once more, and this time I got a response. Once again I can't be sure of the exact words, but I'll try my best.

"She just wants to decorate her new home. I'll be okay; go home and make your brother some dinner."

I spun to see my father climbing a tree a little distance ahead, in the area I couldn't travel to because of the water.

"Dad, come on. Let's go home. You're scaring me." I watched as the skin of his leg caught on a branch, leaving a long scratch that immediately started to bleed. My father ignored it as he kept climbing.

"She's going to get mad if you stay. You need to go. Go home. I'm just helping her decorate." He reached into a knot in the side of the tree and pulled out a long metal nail. He leaned against the tree and pressed the tip of the nail to his chest with a smile.

"That is good? Oh, I'm so glad." It was as though he was talking to someone, but no one was there except us. "They're leaving. It's okay, you don't need to." He paused. "All right."

My younger brother gripped my head and pointed to the water that had begun to bubble. The swamp began to get darker even though I swore we had another hour of sunlight left. My skin began to crawl as the bubbling became more violent.

"I told you she'd be mad. You should leave. Go." My father's voice became more frantic and urgent, though it still had an air of calm happiness. It was like he wanted to yell, but couldn't.

My younger brother started to cry as we stared at the bubbling water. A lone hand reached up from its depths; a hand attached to an arm long enough to reach branches higher than I was tall.

"Run." My father's cheery voice again.

Another hand burst from the water, followed by another and another. Each of them grabbing branches. Whatever was down there was pulling itself out.

"Run."

A low gurgling scream emitted from the water, growing in volume. I watched transfixed by the number of hands that were sliding out from beneath the dark waters of the swamp. My younger brother was yanking on my hair; he wanted to run, but I couldn't move.

"RUN!" This time my father's voice was different. It was urgent, it was frantic, and it was a yell. I immediately snapped out of my trance and turned to run. I could hear the thing behind me trying to give chase through the dense trees. I burst into the backyard and slammed the back door behind me. I put Brandon on the couch, grabbed a kitchen knife, and opened the door to the backyard.

Nothing was there, aside from my father's shoes arranged near the door. My father was never found. When I took the police back to where I had found my father the only thing we found were the shirts. The sixteen that were there before, twelve new ones, and my father's, hanging by an iron nail.

FOR LOVE AND HOT CHOCOLATE

K. Banning Kellum

Tragic Encounters with Moving Cars

It was a dark evening when Blain Kellerman lost control of his car, with his wife in the passenger seat. They had been invited out to a friend's house in the suburbs, and thus ventured into the darker wooded areas that surrounded the city of New Orleans. Both Blain and his wife Christine were lifelong residents of the section of New Orleans known as Mid-City, and although both of them were in their early thirties, they had little experience driving in the darker, more rural areas that made up the suburban section called the Northshore.

It was a Friday night. Neither Blain nor his wife really desired to drive forty-five minutes out of the city just to sit down and hang out with friends that they'd known most of their lives. However, the invitation had been sent, and since it was a Friday, no work the next day, the Kellermans agreed to make the short-long drive out to Covington, Louisiana, where their old friends Jessica and Tim had moved.

Blain had groaned more than his wife. He worked long hours in a cramped office building downtown. Christine worked farther out from the hub that was the New Orleans Central Business District, so she couldn't exactly share his pain. She worked at a small store, with lots of parking and plenty of street space. Blain worked on Poydras Street, in the Harrah's Casino legal department.

Poydras runs directly through the heart of the CBD, and therefore he had to fight traffic coming and going to work, as well as park in an overpriced garage.

It was worth it though. Blain and Christine had been married for eight years now, all of them amazing. Sure, there were fights here and there, but at the end of each day, Blain was always pleased beyond words at where his life had landed him. Good job, great marriage. There was nothing that Blain could complain about . . . until that Friday night.

The dinner with friends had been fun. There was a mediocre home-cooked meal, which of course both Blain and Christine raved about to their hosts. There were drinks served, but both Kellermans refrained from overindulging. A couple of board games were toted out after the eating and drinking were complete. Christine and Jessica clucked on about old times, old friends, and old places. The men went outside on Tim's back porch to smoke cigars and also tell stories about old times and old crimes.

Midnight rolled around quickly, and general laughter was replaced by yawns and stretches. It was time to leave.

Jessica insisted that they spend the night. Christine was game for it; the couch looked much more comfortable than spending nearly an hour in the car. Blain, though, wanted to get home. This very want has become a constant source of guilt for the man, but we'll get to that soon enough.

Blain was a stubborn homebody, something that Christine found joy in teasing him about from time to time. He liked to go to sleep and wake up in his own bed. He was never a fan of spending the night with friends. Hotels he was fine with, since it was his own space, but staying with friends, or even family, was something that Blain Kellerman simply disliked.

"I don't like feeling like a guest," Blaine insisted to his wife on Tim's porch.

"Honey, we're both tired. Let's just sleep here tonight and head home in the morning," she replied.

"We have plans tomorrow, babe, and you already know what's going to happen if we spend the night. Tim and Jessica are going to want to do stuff, and before you know it, our entire Saturday will be spent in Covington."

Christine smiled and caved in. "Okay, but you're driving, and no getting mad if I fall asleep on the ride back," Christine conceded.

So goodbyes were said, hands were shaken, and hugs were issued out. By the end of the whole affair, even Christine was about ready to get back to the comfort and privacy of her own home. She loved her friends, but Blain was right about privacy and such; she valued it as much as he did.

The accident happened about ten minutes after leaving Tim and Jessica's home.

The fatigue really set into Blain while he and Tim smoked cigars. He didn't want to admit it, though. After all, he had been up since 6 A.M. and had put in a nine-hour workday at the office. However, he knew if he gave in, he'd be spending the night, and he didn't want to sleep on Tim's sofa.

By the time he and Christine were pulling out into the street, he was running on mental fumes. Christine looked over and offered to drive; Blain brushed it off. Perhaps had he let her drive . . .

His next decision point came when they pulled into one of the few twenty-four-hour gas stations in Covington. He went in and bought a Red Bull, even though, based on his daily caffeine intake, he knew the energy drink was more for the flavor than the energy.

The main drag that runs through Covington is called HWY US-190. Covington at 1 A.M usually had almost no traffic. Blain knew this, so he was paying more attention to digging his can of Red Bull out of the plastic grocery bag than he was to the road. Still, on any other night, this wouldn't have made a difference.

The car that hit him was driven not by teenagers breaking curfew, nor a drunk driver. Nothing so easy to blame. It was just another driver out late in a small town, who probably thought the same thing that Blain did, that there would be no one else on the road.

The traffic light was out. There was not even the flashing yellow light that sometimes came on. There simply was no light at all. Because of the lack of development in that area, there were no street lights to warn Blain that a side street was approaching. Something as simple as a stop sign may have changed everything.

There was no stop sign, though, and thus fate enforced its will. The other driver, a man named Martin Bendles, struck Blain's car on the passenger side, directing all of the force of metal and momentum onto Christine. Blain's head struck the steering wheel, with the airbag deploying and possibly saving his life. Christine was not so lucky.

Her airbag did not deploy. Her head struck the dashboard, then snapped backward, jerking her back into the seat. Her neck and head took almost all of the force.

The Coma of Christine Kellerman

Blain woke up in the hospital many hours later. Doctors came in and explained what happened.

"Where is my wife? Where is Christine?" Blain demanded to know.

All would be revealed, and the terror was still unfolding.

Christine was knocked into a coma. The doctors did all they could, but her brain showed no signs of life. Machines were doing her eating and breathing.

Several months passed. Blain slowly recovered. Physical therapy did its job, and by the time six months passed, he was pretty much physically whole again. Martin Bendles, the hapless driver who struck Blain's car, died in the hospital. Blain considered his passing to be no great loss.

Christine, however, did not wake up. She slept on in her coma. Blain went to her bed each and every day. He brought in her favorite foods and drinks; they had picnics in her hospital room. Some days he would wake up and just know . . . know without a doubt that his wife was going to wake up that day. He would race to the hospital, even bringing her a new change of clothes, as though she was just going to jump out of that hospital bed ready to change out of her gown and head home. That was Blain's illusion of the situation, anyway, and perhaps the only thing that kept him sane.

He had sued the car company for the defective airbag. There was a huge settlement out of court, with the automotive corporation agreeing to pay for any and all of Christine's medical bills. Blain ordered the doctors to keep her alive on the machines because he was convinced that one day she might just wake up.

With the settlement money, Blain was able to take a substantial amount of time from work. His boss would call him from time to time and ask when he planned on returning. Blain would usually brush this off. In his heart, he knew he couldn't go back to work until Christine returned to him. Perhaps he could have lived like this for years, too. He would spend each and every day with her, talking to her in her coma, massaging her muscles, watching television next to her lifeless shell. He would tell her about his day, and with each passing week, with each advancing month, he would become more and more sure that any time now, she would just wake up.

The doctors explained to him the full extent of her injuries. They told him that the odds of her waking up were almost nil. Blain would hear none of it. Even Christine's family eventually let their voices be heard. They wanted the machines turned off.

"It's wrong for her to live like that!" Maggie, Christine's sister, screamed at Blain over the phone.

"It's wrong to kill my wife, too, to just turn off the machines and watch her choke to death, or starve to death, or however the process works!" he shouted back.

"We have legal recourse Blain, and if you won't end her suffering, we will bring the law into it!" demanded Christine's mother.

"You'll have to kill me before I let that happen. How can you sit there and lobby for them to kill your daughter? She is alive; she is still in there. Would you allow her to die if she might wake up the next day?!" screamed Blain.

"Blain, you know how much we love Christine, and you too. But son, have you been listening to the doctors? She isn't going to wake up. Her brain . . . her brain is dead. What's laying in that hospital bed . . . that isn't our daughter . . . that isn't your wife . . . please, let's do this with dignity, don't force us to bring in the law on a family matter."

That particular logic bomb was being delivered by Fred, Christine's father. He was a level-headed family man, but he was a fool if he thought for even a second that Blain was going to allow them to just kill his wife. He would fight them to the end.

This argument raged on for weeks. Blain was perfectly willing to continue this verbal joust, but things moved a lot faster than he was prepared for. Legal papers were filed, and for the first time, when Blain actually found himself standing in court explaining to a judge why Christine should be allowed to live, he realized that he could lose her. Christine's family made valid points in court. They had medical papers, testimony from doctors and other medical professionals, all outlining exactly how pointless it was to keep her alive on the machines. Blain began to feel small and weak in the debate. They had facts and statistics. He was just a sad and broken man, begging a stranger in a black robe to allow him more time with his wife. For the first time since the accident, he began to feel truly helpless in the situation. They were going to take her away from him, with the power of the law to do it. He would have no means by which to stop them.

Legal wheels do turn slowly though; everyone knows that. Almost a year went by. Court was held; opinions were voiced. Pro-life groups rallied for Blain's cause. However, these were the same nuts that wanted to tell women what to do with their bodies. They were Bible thumpers at best, a faction of society that Blain would have never associated with before this. Now, they were his only hope.

Toward the end, the final days in court, Blain already knew which way the judge was going to sway. He knew enough about court procedures to know he was going to lose. He couldn't watch her die. He couldn't be a part of it.

"I love you so much, Christine. You are my life, my everything. They want to kill you . . . and there is nothing I can do to stop it. In a week the judge is expected to rule, and even I know . . . they've made a better case. I am so sorry, my love . . . I am so sorry, Christine . . ." Blain wept long into that night. He finally went home around 11 P.M. Things weren't better there. He broke down into tears that simply wouldn't stop flowing. Everything in their home reminded him of their lives together.

Photos on the wall . . . their wedding, their anniversaries. How happy they were together. Emmy, their pet cat, would jump into his lap. She was an old cat now, but he still remembered the day they went down to the animal shelter together and brought her home.

"I will love you forever and forever," he mumbled to himself. It was what he said to her the day they were married.

"But will you love me forever, forever, and forever?" she responded later that night, when they were alone in their hotel room.

"Take all the stars in the sky, multiply them by forever and add in a few more forevers, and you still wouldn't be close."

They had laughed and made love. Forever and forever . . . Blain was starting to realize just how short that theoretical time frame could be.

Talking to Astrid

It was the thought of the stars that next inspired Blain. During the course of his marriage to Christine, the stars had played a big part, at least in lore, to their success. The night that Blain decided he wanted to ask her on their first date, he had been standing in his front yard. It was twilight, and the very first star had appeared that night. On a whim, he had invoked that old child's nursery rhyme about wishing on the stars.

"Star light, star bright, first star I see tonight, I wish I may, I wish I might, have the wish I wish tonight."

He had recited this little astral ritual, followed by wishing Christine would agree to go on a date with him. That night he called her, and she said yes. Blain had made this same wish again on the night he intended to propose, and on that same night, his wish was once again granted.

Now, Blain was a smart man and didn't believe in much superstition, but still, the double success of this little tradition did strike him almost as fate at work. Years later, he told Christine about his little twilight wishes. She laughed about it, but they kept the tradition going.

Before they bought their first home, they did a star wish. They got their home at an unbelievably low interest rate. Almost, some would say, a miracle.

Christine, who was the art major of the marriage, began calling this tradition "Talking to Astrid." Whenever the couple needed a real long-shot of luck, they would wait until dusk, sometimes even checking online to see what time the very first stars would start to appear that night, and they would go out into their front yard and sit on the grass and wait. When the first star became visible, they would make their wish, and as luck would have it, each and every time they talked to Astrid, their desire would be met.

"We should wish for a million dollars," Blain had mentioned one night.

"It won't come true that way," Christine corrected. "So far, our wishes have been for unselfish desires, things that we need, rather than millions of dollars. Plus, I feel like if we made a wish like that, it wouldn't come true, and that might break our streak of luck with Astrid."

Christine made a great point, and she and Blain had never abused their crazy stargazing methods. In Blain's mind, he always just assumed these things would have happened either way, and the star wishing was really just more of a morale booster than an effectual process. He was pretty sure that Christine believed the same. Still though, it was something that was fun, and something that was theirs.

Tonight, as Blain paced his small home, a home that felt somehow even smaller without his wife there to share the space, he decided to try once more. In his heart he knew it was just a stupid child's fantasy that something would actually come from wishing on a star. However, he had tried all of the adult methods of saving his wife, from medical to legal, and now it seemed as though nothing would work.

Blain stepped out onto his front yard at dusk. Being in the middle of the city always meant that there weren't a ton of stars to be seen, especially early in the evening. One usually had to wait until later, once all traces of the sun were gone, to really see the diamonds light up the sky. He sat on his porch, smoked a cigarette—a habit that started just recently—and waited until the sky was mostly darkened. The sky at twilight in the city always had a neon glow, something that used to bring him comfort. Tonight, the lights from the street lamps and the nearby downtown high rises just seemed to weigh down on his mind.

He scanned the sky for the first star, and quickly found Venus, in her usual spot near the moon. Venus was a planet, though, and tonight he wanted to talk to Astrid, not just some non-twinkling rock in the sky. He looked over and saw Mars, apparent by its reddish glimmer. It never occurred to him that he was picking out a lot of heavenly bodies for this time of night in New Orleans. The sky seemed to be opening up for him as never before.

Then he saw it. A real star, apparent by its shimmer. He almost thought he was looking at Mars again, because there was an unmistakable red hue. He looked back and saw the non-glimmering Mars, right where it should be. So what was he looking at?

He was no astronomer, so seeing this tiny, slightly rust-colored star shining in the evening sky didn't exactly throw him into overdrive. It was a star, a rather unique one at that. He decided that as far as wishing goes, this one was as good as any other.

"Star light, star bright, first star I see tonight, I wish I may, I wish I might, have the wish I wish tonight," he recited as always. Tears were falling down his face now. "Bring back Christine . . . please . . . star, God . . . whoever . . . please, I can't live without her. I am broken without her in my life, she is everything to me . . . I will do anything . . . just please . . ."

Blain stood there a moment longer, allowing himself to weep. Thankfully, none of his neighbors were out. He didn't care if they saw him cry, but he didn't feel like answering the always lovely "Are you all right?" question. This was his and Christine's connection. He had talked to Astrid.

He returned to his home, slamming the door behind him.

"Wishing on stars . . . yeah, I am on top of the world . . ." he mumbled to himself, before collapsing on his couch.

Mr. Pinkerton

That night, he was awoken by a knock at his door. It was a gentle and restrained knock, as though the person knew he would be right there on his couch, instead of upstairs in their bed, where he most certainly would have slept through it. Blain rolled off the couch and looked at the clock on his cable box: 11:04. Who the hell would be knocking this late?

The knock returned in the same restrained manner. However, there was a strange persistence in it, something that said the person wasn't going anywhere. They could wait.

Blain grabbed the baseball bat that he kept for just this sort of thing, and peered through his peephole. On the other side was a small man, probably about 5'6" at the most. Blain could only make out part of his face, as he was wearing one of those old flat brimmed hats, the kind that old Southern politicians were always seen wearing back in the 1950s. The round brim cast a shadow over his eyes and nose. The hat was blue and white striped.

"Who is it?" Blain replied in a gruff voice.

"Mr. Kellerman, oh Mr. Kellerman . . . my name is Mr. Pinkerton, but my friends all call me Mr. Pinky. I would just loooove it if you called me that too. I am here to speak with you on a very personal business matter. I do believe you reached out to me and my associates this very evening."

Whoever this Pinkerton man was, he was almost a walking cliché. He had a Southern accent that was practically a caricature of the "Southern dandy." He pronounced Blain's last name "Kellerman" and really threw out a lot of his words for emphasis.

"What business do we have, Mr. Pinkerton?" Blain inquired through the locked door. He still sounded gruff, but Pinkerton seemed to pay no mind.

"Mr. Kellerman, if you could be ever so gracious as to open your door, we could discuss the matter at much greater detail, and in far more human comfort, I would imagine."

"You show up at my door at this hour and expect me to invite you in for coffee . . . whatever you're selling I am not buying. Piss off, Pinky."

Blain observed a small smile whisk across Pinkerton's face. However, he did not move from his position on the porch.

"Mr. Kellerman, know two things. If you turn me away now, I will never return. You will never see me or hear from me again. But also know this, your precious Christine will die."

Suddenly heat rushed through Blain's face, a rage so sudden and so raw that he almost felt faint. He flung the door open.

The sight of Mr. Pinkerton just about deflated his anger. The man was indeed short; he had a potbelly and was wearing a blue and white suit that matched his ridiculous hat. He had a bow tie around his neck, tied loose. His skin did have a pinkish hue, as though to match his name. Blain realized it was no doubt sunburn. Pinkerton looked like a very delicate man, a true dandy if ever there was one. Blain wouldn't have been surprised if the moonlight on this very night had given Pinkerton his burn.

His eyes however, told a different story. His eyes looked sharp and cunning. A dark blue, piercing stare. His eyes made him look a little dangerous in the dim glow of his porch light.

"What did you say about Christine?!" Blain demanded.

"Well now, Mr. Kellerman, does this mean I may enter your humble domicile?"

"If this is a con . . . I will fuck your world up!" snarled Blain Kellerman.

"Sir, if this is a con, I will gladly offer you my body to enact your every primal desire of revenge. However, once you hear what

I have come to say, I do believe harming me will be your last impulse."

Blain backed up and allowed Pinkerton to enter his home. He removed his hat, revealing a perfectly bald head. "May I sit?" he asked.

Blain gestured to his couch. Pinkerton sat, and placed his hat neatly in his lap. "I would so love that coffee you mentioned before, Mr. Kellerman, if you would be ever so kind. And if I may venture to be so bold as to make a suggestion to the man of the house. I would implore you to make yourself a cup as well; you're going to want to be awake for this."

Blain was in sort of a waking shock at this little man, who had invited himself in, ordered himself a cup of coffee and even suggested one for Blain. Pinkerton had a certain energy about him that Blain was hard pressed to identify.

Blain returned a few minutes later with two steaming cups of coffee. Pinkerton requested his black, same as Blain. "Okay Pinky, you got in, you got your coffee, now tell your story. What do you know about Christine, how can you possibly help me?"

The small man sipped his brew and smiled. He licked his lips and began speaking. Blain was entranced from start to finish.

"Mr. Kellerman, tonight, at about 7:45 P.M., as you know time, you ventured right out there into your front yard and called out to the very stars for help, did you not?"

Blain nodded.

"Over the years, this was a bit of a tradition of you and your wife. Let me tell you, there was no magic in those wishes; you simply had good luck. However, your belief, your honoring of such old and glorious traditions, certainly did catch the attention of my superior. It is indeed a thrill to see a young man such as you, in this here modern world, still holding true to ways and days that have long passed by."

"What do you mean?" Blain asked.

"Picture this, Mr. Kellerman, and really, I do mean, picture what I say in your mind. Eons and eons ago, there was a kingdom among the stars. A floating castle, as you would no doubt imagine it. In that castle sat a very powerful king. His name . . . well, he has many. King Tobit is the best for your tongue I do believe. A few of his other names are a bit . . . let's say, twisty. Anyway, Tobit sat in his castle in the stars, granting his favor to those who called out to him. For centuries he would bestow his kindness onto mortal creatures, small critters like yourself, scampering through your ever so short time on this level of existence.

"For some time, this pleased Tobit to no end. People would speak his name, glorify his image, he of the goat's head and man's body. Then things changed. People demanded his favor. Blamed him for their problems. And unlike other powerful beings that your kind know, Tobit did not forgive so easily. He shifted his favor to those who deserved it. Those who were willing to earn it.

"Those that would risk it all.

"He even came to earth and built a city, just for his most loyal. Oh, and what a paradise it is, but the cost to reside there . . . well, that doesn't concern you. I am not here to invite you to his glorious city in the frozen lands; that's a different ritual altogether. What I am here to offer you, Mr. Kellerman, is your wish, the very desire that you cried out for tonight in your yard, when you gazed upon King Tobit's star. That star revealed itself to you, Mr. Kellerman, because King Tobit believes in you. Oh yes, he does. He believes that you may be worthy of his favor. However, sir, you will have to prove it."

Blain spoke up for the first time in what seemed forever. "You mean, you're telling me Pinky, that this Tobit character can bring Christine back from her coma?"

Pinkerton smiled, and snapped his fingers, as if for emphasis. "Just like that Mr. Kellerman. At King Tobit's whim, your lovely bride will simply awaken, as though she has just been in a long slumber. There will be no brain damage, no physical problems. As far as she will know, it will be as if she simply fell asleep after one too many mint juleps. And won't that just amaze her family, who seem to be in such a rush to see her demise?"

"This has to be a trick . . . you . . . you can't be serious," Blain insisted.

"Answer me this, Mr. Kellerman. Are you prepared to gamble on that? Let's say I am just some crazy man, some individual that has been following you and your problems, just some lunatic out for a good time? You could thrash my tender hide at this very moment, or you could call your local police to come on over here and haul me away, but you haven't. No, you sat here and listened to me talk about god-kings in floating castles, magical wishes and bringing your wife back. Tell me, do you doubt me, or just doubt yourself?"

"Prove it then! If you really are magical, prove it!" Blain shouted.

"Now, now, Mr. Kellerman. Faith is of the utmost importance in such matters. If I went around doing parlor tricks for everyone who beckoned upon my Master, well, this whole operation would turn into a travelling carnival . . . and me, I guess that would make me the clown. Mr. Kellerman, like wishing on those stars, you must go into this with faith. The proof will be given to you in the form of your beautiful Christine waking up and calling out for her husband."

"What do I have to do then?" Blain asked cautiously.

"For now, simply sleep; you will need your strength come tomorrow. I will see you at my place of business, where all rules will be explained and all contracts will be agreed upon. Should you succeed, you will have your wife back with you again, happy and healthy."

"Wait now, if I succeed? Does this mean it isn't guaranteed?"

"Mr. Kellerman, nothing in this sad, fragile world of ours is ever guaranteed, now is it? However, what I can promise you is that

THE CREEPYPASTA COLLECTION, VOLUME 2

there are rules that will be followed, and any and all participation will be fair and impartial. I am not here to see you succeed or fail; I am simply here to make the offer and ensure that all aspects of the agreement are upheld at the conclusion of our arrangement."

"So, if I succeed, Christine wakes up. What happens if I fail?"

"Well now, Mr. Kellerman, at the risk of sounding cliché, if you fail, King Hyraaq Tobit gets your soul for all of eternity."

"Okay, enough of this shit! Get out of my house, you're fucking nuts!" Blain said, raising his voice with each word.

"Very well, Mr. Kellerman. You did invite me in, and you did serve some very delicious coffee. So for you, I will make a small exception." Pinkerton pulled out a card from his suit pocket.

"Be at this address tomorrow. Come by yourself. I will wait for you until nightfall, and at that time, I will pack up my lovely little operation, and move on to the next town. There are always people in need of favors. As I said at your door, you will never see me again, and yes, your wife will most certainly die. If you want me to perform a miracle, allow me to predict the future for you real quick. Your wife's mother and father are going to win. The judge has already decided in fact. They are going to allow the plugs to be pulled, and your sweet wife will fade out, but not before suffering greatly. Pulling that plug doesn't bring instant death, but rather a very slow and deliberate suffering. And since her mind isn't capable of conceiving time in her current state, her suffering will seem like an eternity, as she chokes and gasps, reaching for a rescue that will never come."

"Just get out of here!" Blain screamed.

Pinkerton showed himself to the door and stepped out to the porch. He turned and made one last comment before leaving.

"Be the hand that rescues Christine. She is reaching for you even now, Mr. Kellerman. Should you meet her one day on the other side, do you want to tell her that you allowed her to die a horrible death, rather than spending one day with me to wake her back up? Come to the address tomorrow before sundown or live in your misery forever."

With that, Pinkerton quickly stepped down the porch to the sidewalk. Blain, consumed with rage and emotion, grabbed his baseball bat, intending to take out his aggression on the small chubby man. He charged into the street to find Pinkerton gone.

Blain's Nightmare

Blain didn't sleep the rest of that night. He sat up and twirled the card in his fingers, looking down at the address. It was a spot way out in the country, in a small town called Madisonville, Louisiana. Oddly enough, Madisonville was not that far from Covington, where all of this began.

Blain was almost sure that this Pinkerton asshole was just as full of shit as any one man could be. All of the information he presented Blain was readily available if someone really wanted to dig a little. The newspaper ran an article on the accident last year. The hospital records were sealed of course, but Blain knew all too well that Christine's sister kept a pretty updated blog. He had read it himself a few times; it detailed all the secrets of their lives, comic and tragic alike.

Blain was thinking out loud.

"So let's say that Pinkerton is a con artist, and all of this is just a scam. What does he have to gain?"

Blain was directing this set of questions at Emmy the cat. Emmy gazed at him with her sleepy eyes, as if to say, "Humans . . . so many stupid questions."

"Maybe he wants to get me out there in the middle of nowhere and kill me, did you think about that?"

Emmy stared back, silently. Blain answered his own question.

"Well, if he wanted to kill me, he could have just done it right here. Why would he leave me the address on a card, knowing that

I could just call the cops, or have someone wait around for me to make sure I was all right?"

The cat looked back. She seemed to be bored with the situation.

Blain waged this internal debate until almost sunrise, when fatigue finally caught up to him. At that point, he fell asleep, and dreamed.

He was at home, but it was different. The house was lit up, bright with life. Emmy was purring, music was playing from the television, and the smell of hot chocolate filled the room. Of course it did, though; Christine loved hot chocolate. She didn't drink coffee; no, she drank hot chocolate, almost all the time, even in the summer. Blain walked into the kitchen and saw the cup of hot chocolate, but no sign of Christine.

"Darling, will you bring me my drink?" came Christine's voice.

Of course, she was upstairs in bed; it was early. She must have come down, made the cup, and then gone back up to snooze until he came home.

Blain grabbed the cup of warm fluid and began to take it upstairs.

"Here baby, it's nice and hot . . ." The sight before him stole his words.

Christine was in their bed, but she wasn't the Christine he knew. She was wasted, dying. Her face was too thin; her arms were nothing more than sticks. There were machines hooked up to every part of her body. A large black pump was jutting out of her chest. It sucked in air, and Blain could hear a thump, her heart, before the pump would deflate again. Each time it did, blood would splash out onto the bed. A device that looked like a car radiator was dug into her stomach, belching out black smoke. Tubes ran from her eyes, ears, nose . . . everywhere.

"Blain . . . it hurts so bad . . . please, I can feel this . . . all of it . . ."

"Christine! What have they done to you?" cried Blain.

"This is what I feel . . . every second on the machines . . . oh God, Blain, please, make it stop!"

Suddenly Christine's family rushed in. Her mother and father, their faces set and stern, like an executioner before he throws the switch of an electric chair, or a hangman before he drops the platform. They began to rip the devices from Christine's body, and as they did, the life in her eyes slowly vanished. Her family backed away and began to weep softly. Christine was gagging, choking on air. Her stomach began to sink in, becoming further emaciated. She looked at Blain, mouthing pleas, begging him to stop the suffering.

"This will go on for weeks, Mr. Kellerman." A voice— Pinkerton, standing directly behind Blain.

"I have to stop this—she is suffering—please," Blain begged.

"If you leave her on the machines, she suffers; take her off the machines, she suffers. Salvation, Mr. Kellerman, salvation is yours to claim. There is no freedom from King Tobit; there is only freedom through King Tobit. Vie for his favor, show your worth. If you truly love her, if you are capable of expressing that love . . . well, just imagine."

Pinkerton snapped his fingers, and Christine was standing in the room. Healthy, whole.

"Blain, I feel so amazing, so much better. Thank you for bringing me my hot chocolate. You always know how to help me wake up."

The room vanished again, and Blain was standing in the dark. Pinkerton was near him, whispering in his ear.

"Bring your wife her hot chocolate, Mr. Kellerman. Help her wake up."

The room suddenly lit up, and Blain saw an image before him. A being standing at least 40 feet tall. A massive masculine frame, with the head of a goat. Behind this being burned a red star. Its light and heat bore down on Blain.

Hyraaq Tobit.

The Grove in Madisonville

Blain snapped awake. It was late morning, at least according to the amount of light coming in through the window. The card was still in his hand.

Without any thought, Blain cleaned up, got dressed, and started driving.

The trip to Madisonville was normally a long and boring ride. Blain left the city by way of Lake Pontchartrain over the Causeway Bridge. He touched down in Mandeville, a small town on the edge of the lake. Up ahead was a small green interstate sign announcing the exit for Madisonville.

A few miles in, he found the turnoff for Bannister Road. It was just a mud strip leading down into some thick woods. The mud right now was as hard as iron, but Blain had an idea that when the rainy season came through, Bannister Road would be converted into a clay pit that not even a Range Rover could muscle through.

Now the real question came. He was on Bannister Road, but as far as he could tell, there was nothing at all here. He drove down for a mile until it dead ended into a thick grove of trees. Blain couldn't help but think this scene would be beautiful if not for the circumstances that brought him here. He stopped his car at the dead end and climbed out. He lit a cigarette and leaned against his trunk. He gazed around in all directions, and at first, it seemed that he was simply sitting in a deserted grove.

Then he saw it.

About 20 feet into the woods on his right, barely visible through the leaves and bushes, he could make out a roof. There was a building back there. It was bright red, which is what caught his attention. He peered harder through the trees, and could gradually make out more features. It looked almost like a small circus tent. Perhaps a leftover remnant from a long-past carnival.

Then something Pinkerton said to Blain occurred to him. He had made a comment about the carnival, and being the clown, something like that. Was that a hint? Was this the place?

Blain pushed through the woods and came out into a clearing. The tent was old and ragged. Its once bright red and yellow design was long gone. What stood before him was a destroyed artifact, a reminder that once there was fun and laughter here. Now this place was simply dead.

Then Blain noticed the single pink balloon tied to a nearby tree. The balloon was still inflated; it was put here recently. Blain knew he had the right place. Drawing on his courage, which was small, and his love for Christine, which was large and noble, he gathered his nerve and stepped into the tent.

The Trials

"Mister Kellerman!" shouted Pinkerton, full of glee, as Blain entered the tent.

The inside of the tent had a wrong feel to it that Blain would be hard pressed to describe. It was totally hollow inside. If this place ever did house happy, cheering people, those days were long gone. Now there was only Pinkerton, standing in the center, wearing his blue and white striped suit. He was vigorously wiping at his forehead with his handkerchief.

"By the Saints above, today is a hot one, is it not, Mr. Kellerman? I do say, such climate is not suitable for refined gentlemen like ourselves."

"I came, Pinkerton. Now tell me how to get my wife back!" Blaine commanded.

"A man who gets right to the point. You are a dying breed, Mr. Kellerman, indeed you are. Why, if more gentlemen thought like you, perhaps your breed would have landed on the moon a thousand years ago, as was the plan. Oh, the treats that King Tobit hid for you there. Such a shame you all missed it."

"No more games, no more riddles. You told me that you could save Christine, that is why I am here. Please."

"Well, your manners are commendable. Yes, you are here to save your wife, and I am capable of facilitating that very desire. However, before we begin, I must cover the rules. Do be a good ambassador to our beloved Dixie and sit quietly as I explain."

Blain obliged and sat on the ground. His exterior almost appeared patient, but inside . . . inside he was burning.

"Now, as I said before, King Tobit has become, well, disenfranchised with mortals and their constant wants. Still, though, in all of his glory, he desires to shed his favor upon you. However, now it comes down to a test—a wager, really. You will complete a few . . . tests of will, let's say. Like Hercules, you must demonstrate that your strength, your will, is both pure and stoic. Once you demonstrate these qualities to King Tobit, he shall bestow upon you your heart's desire."

"What are these tests?" Blain asked.

"Well, Mr. Kellerman, they vary. Once the trials begin, you will be at the whims of King Tobit himself. I will be here to sort of . . . nod you in the right direction, but in the end, this is your test, your rules, and your duty to complete them.

"Now, as I stated back at your home, the name of the game here is fairness. Our mighty lord is nothing if not utterly lawful. Even when he imposes his will on his servants, things that you might consider . . . ghastly, it is never out of trickery. Everyone is given a fair chance, especially in the court of wish fulfillment.

"The rules, as they are, are very simple. No cheating. Follow the instructions as they are presented. In order to claim any prize— your wish, in other words—there must be a wager. Remember, Mr. Kellerman, your word will be a direct reflection on how King

Tobit perceives your actions. Whatever you say, you must be prepared to follow through. Be very careful when choosing your words."

Pinkerton stopped speaking long enough to gesture in the direction of another tent flap when a ragged, rough-looking man stepped through.

"This is Mr. Peaty. He is under my employ, and is here to provide a balance to your actions during the trials."

Peaty looked like a mix between a pirate and a biker. He was dirty with a scruffy beard, a black bandana on his head, and a denim vest. He was wearing ragged pants that tore off toward the shins. He stood sort of hunched over, which really hammered home the pirate look. His arms were no joke, though; Peaty looked like he lived at the gym, even though the idea of a man like this working out among preppy gym members seemed almost laughable.

"Is this the bastard pansy that couldn't take care of his wife?" Peaty grunted. His accent sounded like someone trying to do a London accent for a cheap stage play.

Blain tensed and prepared to reply, but Pinkerton beat him to it. "Mr. Peaty, we will have none of that. Your poor breeding and sub-par upbringing is no excuse to speak to Mr. Kellerman in such a manner. He is our guest, and I have personally sought him out. You will behave in my presence."

"Sorry there, boss. You know I got a stupid head sometimes, just goes off on its own. Won't happen again, I say."

Seeing this hulk of a man backing down to someone like Pinkerton actually unnerved Blain more than it comforted him. It produced more questions, like who was Pinkerton really, and how did he keep such a brute in line?

"Now, Mr. Kellerman, Peaty will be in and out of some of your trials. He is simply here to ensure that everything is legal. King Tobit wants you to succeed, but he wants you to earn it."

Peaty spit on the ground in Blain's direction and crossed his arms. He was clearly ready to do whatever his task was in all of this. Blain didn't like it.

"So, what do I have to do?" Blain asked.

"Ah, yes, we should begin soon. Even as we speak, your wife's family is making legal moves to try and lock you out of the decision making. So, do you understand the rules Mr. Kellerman?"

"Yes."

"Are you sure?"

"YES!"

"Very well. What are you willing to do to save your wife?"

"Anything!"

Peaty smiled at that.

"Mr. Kellerman, I fear you weren't paying attention. I warned you about the rules. Had you just answered that question with something like, let's say, eat an ice cream cone, then that perhaps would have been your only test. But, like so many before you, you said 'anything.' King Tobit holds us to our words after all."

"You mean, the trial has already begun?"

"Mr. Kellerman, the trials began when I visited your home. Now you're playing for keeps. Your contract was struck when you answered my question; your soul is now on the betting table. Ante up, Mr. Kellerman!"

Blain felt a panic seeping in. Yet, somehow this still felt made-up. This Pinkerton freak talked a good game, but so far, all he's really shown is his ability to hide out in a tent with some freak named Peaty. Blaine felt his confidence harden a bit.

"Okay, fine, what's the next trial?"

"Mr. Kellerman, I sense that you are still not playing your best game here. Now, King Tobit would not be happy if you were simply . . . what's the term, Peaty?"

"Half-assing it, sir."

"Yes, that. You are wagering your very soul here. So, in the spirit of fairness, allow me to relieve you of all doubt, since it is far too late for you to back out now anyway."

Pinkerton produced, from what appeared to be thin air, a curtain hanging on a rod. He released the rod, and the whole apparatus simply hovered in the air.

"Neat trick, is it not? Now observe."

Pinkerton slid the curtain to the side, revealing a tiny altar behind it. On the altar was a small stone statue, a goat-headed man. Blain recognized it from his nightmare the previous night. It was Hyraaq Tobit.

"Now, Mr. Kellerman, allow me to show you where your soul will be delivered, should you fail to gain King Tobit's favor."

Pinkerton waved his arms, and suddenly the walls of the tent collapsed. Blain gazed around in utter horror. As far as his mind could comprehend, he was in the pits of Hell.

Fire burned everywhere; even the sky itself seemed to blaze with flame. People lay here and there, wallowing on the ground, moaning, crying out. Blain strained his eyes to the horizon, but the orange flame and the pitch-black sky were all that he could see.

"Convinced yet, Mr. Kellerman?" The voice of Pinkerton filled the sky.

Blain strained to look directly above, and the entire sky was the face of Pinkerton. Only now he looked less like a portly Southern dandy, and a lot more like a demon from the darkest corners of the abyss.

"You're not in Hell, Mr. Kellerman. No, that is a different playground for a different religion. You are on the red star, the wastelands where those that fail Hyraaq Tobit find themselves, for all of eternity. However, it does relate to your backward concepts of damnation, in the fact that this is eternal. There is no hope, there is no escape."

Blain dropped to his knees. "Please, get me out of here . . . God help me!" he screamed into the darkness and fire all around him.

"King Tobit is your God now, and I would suggest you avoid such blasphemy in the future. Now, have you seen enough, Mr. Kellerman? Or do you need further proof that this is not a con?"

"Please, I believe you, for the love of . . . for the love of . . ." Blain caught himself before he said "God."

"Very well, Mr. Kellerman."

In a flash of light Blain was back in the tent. Pinkerton and Peaty were in their original positions.

"What the fuck was that?" Blain gasped.

"That'll be your home if you fuck this up," grunted Peaty.

"Yes, Mr. Kellerman. Mr. Peaty's words are far from gentle and are barely grammatical, but he is correct. Should you fail to appease King Tobit, you can expect to spend all of eternity there, on the red star. And imagine this—you were just there to witness it. You didn't feel the pain, the fire or the thirst. You didn't feel the loneliness and desperation for freedom. Please keep all of that in mind as you complete your trials. For if you lose, you will be shown no mercy."

The contest began.

"Mister Kellerman, we will begin this easily enough. Tell me, where did you and Christine spend your first date?"

Blain gathered his wits as quickly as he could. He was now terrified, but he was determined to let his love for his wife guide his mind.

"Okay, okay, that's easy. Algiers Point. I took her across the river and we sat on the bank of the Mississippi and had a picnic."

"Sorry, Mr. Kellerman, that is wrong," replied Pinkerton with a frown.

"No, I know where I took Christine on our first date, I planned the whole thing out myself," Blain demanded.

"You're playing this selfish, sir. Your first date, in her eyes, was a simple hamburger at a little shack called Bud's Broiler. As I recall, you took her there after work one day."

"We were just friends then! That wasn't a date!"

"To her it was. How can such a doting husband have missed the look in her eyes at that simple little meal? She was already falling for you. Sad, really, and that was the easy, warm-up test."

Blain once again tried to center himself. Clearly this game was rigged, at least to an extent. Trick question right from the start. He would have to do better if he was going to save Christine, and himself.

"Let's try again, shall we?" invited Pinkerton.

Blain nodded. He would be ready this time.

Pinkerton waved his arms, and three items appeared before Blain.

A silver locket. A wedding ring. A small personal mirror.

"Mr. Kellerman, which of these items is the most relevant to Christine as a symbol of love? Choose wisely."

Blain did think long and hard on this. The locket, that was an anniversary gift. He had spent a fortune on it, and Christine had scolded him, lovingly, for using most of his annual bonus on a gift. The mirror, he remembered it also. He and Christine had gone camping in Alabama one year, and he bought her that mirror for the trip. He made some joke about how she could still spend an hour on her make-up even at a campsite. She had laughed about it, but did in fact end up using it for most of the trip. And the wedding ring, the symbol of their love. He had placed it on her delicate finger the day he swore to love her forever and forever. He knew it was the ring; his confidence was solid.

"Her wedding ring, of course. The symbol of my eternal love for her."

Pinkerton frowned again.

"Oh, Mr. Kellerman, what a shame. The correct answer was the mirror. Had you taken the time to pick it up, you would have seen your own reflection. You are indeed a stronger symbol of love to her than any jewelry could ever be. Or do you think of her in such a shallow light?"

Blain felt that air leave his body. He was down two strikes already, and on such easy questions.

"Let us move on, Mr. Kellerman, for the longer we linger on your failures, the more difficult it will be to return to the track of success."

Pinkerton waved his arms again, and a mug of dark liquid appeared before him.

"Hot chocolate, Christine's favorite—am I correct, sir?" asked Pinkerton.

"Yes . . . she loves it; I would bring her a mug almost every morning," responded Blain.

"Of course, sir, and now you simply must bring the mug to me. Allow King Tobit to witness your affection. Simply grasp the mug and bring it to me."

Blain nodded. At least this one wasn't a trick question or anything. A simple task. Blain grasped the mug and began to walk it toward Pinkerton.

"That's it, Mr. Kellerman, that's it. Right to me."

Blain actually allowed himself to relax a bit, and immediately paid for it.

A sharp pain suddenly inflicted itself into Blain's side, followed by another hard thud to the center of his back. He fell to the ground, spilling the hot chocolate into the mud.

"What the fuck . . ." Blain had time to choke out, before Peaty delivered another hard kick to his ribs. The diseased-looking fucker was smiling through his yellowed and rotting teeth.

"Mr. Kellerman, I warned you before all of this began that Peaty was here to challenge you. I know for a fact that each morning, you would ever so carefully bring Christine her drink, stepping wisely to ensure you didn't spill a drop. Do you mean to tell me that you were more concerned about tripping over your rug at home than you are about a thug like our Mr. Peaty here? What a sad state you're in sir. Another failure, and on such a simple task."

"You bastard, he sucker-punched me . . . How the fuck is that fair?" Blain grunted, trying to catch his wind.

"It's fair because I warned you about it well in advance. Is it my fault that you are such a simple man that you had to apply all of your cognition on carrying a mug? Mr. Peaty didn't vanish and appear behind you. He walked to your blind spot right out in the open. You were the one who failed to see such an obvious ploy. Do not shift blame here, Mr. Kellerman, or I will happily declare this contest over. Is that what you want? Are you finished, sir? Two simple questions and a task that a blind child could perform . . . is that all it takes to defeat your will? Is that all the love you can muster for your wife?"

"NO! I am not done, I will never stop fighting for Christine!" Blain shouted back.

"Then prove it!" Pinkerton answered sharply.

The world flashed again, and Blain was in a moving car, behind the wheel. He didn't know where he was, but the road was dark, and tall pines lined the sides.

"Where am I?" he shouted.

Pinkerton's voice answered from nowhere, and everywhere.

"You are in the car that was once owned by a pathetic little sod named Martin Bendles. Remember him, the man whose car struck yours. The man who caused your wife to fall into her coma. You are in Mr. Bendles's position now. Since I know that you feel it was all his fault, that he caused all of your problems, let us see if you can do any better."

Blain suddenly recognized the environment. This was Covington, that dark side road where Bendles had emerged. Up ahead, Blain could see the intersection. He didn't want to believe what he was witnessing. He slammed his foot on the brakes, but the car continued to move forward. He honked his horn and flashed his lights, trying his damn best to warn his past self of his approach.

The intersection came into clear view. Ahead he could see . . . he could see his Jeep Patriot, or at least, his former Jeep Patriot, before the accident. He slammed his foot on the brake over and over again, honked the horn, but nothing changed.

In that horrifying moment, he saw Christine's face, awake and aware for the first time in over a year. It was not the wonderful moment he had imagined, though. He saw the fear as she turned to look, he saw that fear turn into utter horror, he saw her mouth open to scream, her eyes widen, her arms fly up to shield her face.

Then the impact. He saw her beautiful face smash into the dashboard, as the airbag failed to deploy. He saw her head snap back against the seat from the impact. It all happened in slow motion for him.

He was back in the tent again, on his knees, weeping.

"Mr. Kellerman, what happened? I gave you the chance to change it all. To prevent the accident. You wasted it."

"No, no . . . I tried to stop, I hit the brake, the fucking car kept going." Blain was almost begging.

"Sir, you could have turned your car off of the road. Your steering wheel worked just fine. Sure, you would have been injured, maybe killed, but Christine would have been spared. How sad it is that you were still selfish, even in the moment that could have changed all of this."

"No, it was a trick. Bendles's brakes didn't fail; I remember that from the accident report, he just wasn't paying attention. You . . . you rigged it!"

"Rigged it? Is that what you dare say, Mr. Kellerman? Nothing here is rigged. You said that you would do anything, ANYTHING, to save Christine. Am I to believe that running a car into a tree falls outside the realm of anything?"

Blain gasped, but no words would come out of his mouth.

"Mr. Peaty, I am beginning to think that our dear friend Mr. Kellerman doesn't want to save his wife. Have we not played fair with him? Have we not presented the rules to him in the most transparent means possible?"

"Well, boss, I knew this little runt was a failure when he walked in. Little softy is all he is, ain't he, boss? I bet that little wife of his went into that coma just to get away from him," replied Peaty.

"You shut the fuck up!" screamed Blain, as he rushed Peaty with all of his rage.

Peaty side stepped and delivered a hard knee into Blain's abdomen, followed by a fist driven into the back of his head. Blain collapsed.

"Now, now sir, none of that. If you cannot even abide Mr. Peaty's foul and uncultured sense of humor, how can you possibly hope to gain the favor of King Tobit?" scolded Pinkerton.

Blain gasped and finally found air in his lungs. On legs that felt far too weak, he brought himself to his feet.

"Mr. Kellerman, when I met with you at your home last night, I felt that you were a champion of your love. Why, I even remarked to Mr. Peaty here that this would be a short trial; I simply knew you were going to succeed. It pains me to be so harshly corrected by you. Why, I do believe you have been wasting our time."

"Told yer so boss, told yer this guy was a chump," Peaty chimed in, happily shedding misery on Blain.

"One more test, Mr. Kellerman. I do implore you to try on this last one. It is of little secret at this point that you have utterly disappointed King Tobit. However, in his infinite mercy and wisdom, he will grant you one final trial. However, it will not be simple."

Pinkerton waved his arms one more time, and Blain found himself in a hospital. Not any hospital though, rather, the very hospital where his wife was silently wasting away in her sleep. Standing next to him was Peaty.

The voice of Pinkerton filled the halls.

"Gentlemen, this is a simple foot race. The finish line is Christine Kellerman. Now, Mr. Kellerman, it is your simple trial to reach your beloved wife before Mr. Peaty. In your hand, you will notice a cup of her favorite hot chocolate. Bring it to her, help her wake up. After all, your wife's very words professed that she can simply never wake up without her drink. Should Peaty reach your wife first, well, let's just say you don't want that to happen. He is a very nasty man, and I doubt a woman in a coma would deter his more, let us say, primal urges. Gentleman, we shall begin when Mr. Kellerman; declares that he is ready."

Blain gathered all of his concentration. He knew there was a trick here. Regardless of how fair Pinkerton swore this would be, every single trial had been rigged. He knew that. This one would be no different.

He looked down at the cup of hot chocolate, and that was when inspiration hit.

"Okay, I'm ready!" Blain shouted.

Without hesitation, Blain turned and slung the hot chocolate into Peaty's face, causing the large man to drop to his knees and grasp his face. Blain didn't wait to enjoy his suffering though; he bolted down the hall toward the stairs.

"Mr. Kellerman, what about her hot chocolate?" the voice of Pinkerton echoed.

"If you really knew me as well as you claim to, you would know that every day I visit her hospital room, and every day I bring a packet of hot chocolate mix. There is plenty of it in her room!" Blain shouted, almost laughing as he ran.

"Finally, the noble husband is playing to win!" the voice of Pinkerton answered.

Blain made a sharp turn into the stairwell, but could hear the heavy footfalls of Peaty only inches behind him.

He was halfway up the first flight when a hand grasped his ankle, pulling him down. Peaty. Blain wasted no time smashing the mug over Peaty's head. The large man grunted in pain, and Blain delivered a swift kick to his face, causing him to tumble down the short flight of stairs.

"Why, you smashed the mug Mr. Kellerman; however will she drink it?"

"What, you think I bring hot chocolate packets without a mug? Her favorite mug has been sitting in her hospital room for months now!" Blain announced, feeling, for the first time, hopeful.

"Well now, Mr. Kellerman, perhaps we have all underestimated you."

Blain made it to the fourth floor. Peaty was hot on his trail, but he knew his wife's room. Room 416. Through the door and to the right, directly past the nurses' station. Blain was now running with all of his might. Christine was so close now, all he had to do was round the corner and he'd be there.

Then disaster struck.

A sharp pain, far too intense to be anything other than a blade, slashed into his hip. Peaty, wielding a knife. Blain collapsed. Blood quickly caked his pants. He attempted to stand but could put no weight on his leg. He was cut deep.

"I'll crawl to her . . ." he grunted, but was quickly planted on the floor by Peaty's boot.

"So sorry there, pal. You thought you were cute with the little hot chocolate in my face, but ol' Peaty is in this to win," the burly man spoke directly into Blain's face, his sour breath and body odor seeming to hammer in his taunts.

"Yer wifey in there is going to make a great little prize, now isn't she? I promise you, though, ol' Peaty is going to take real good care of her, until they pull da plug anyway. Enjoy the red star."

With that, Peaty walked into Christine's room, and Blain found himself back in the tent. Peaty was standing next to Pinkerton, who no longer seemed charming or cultured. Now he looked hungry.

"Well, Mr. Kellerman, I do believe that concludes our trials. You did your best, as pitiful as your best turned out to be. However, the contest was presented and delivered in a fair manner, with all rules enforced. You simply failed. Now, prepare yourself."

Blain's world began to fade. He began to smell burning flesh; the heat of the burning star began to grow. The world phased between the tent and the red star. Reality shifting. Blain had time to cast his final thoughts to Christine. How proud she was of him. How much they loved each other. Their first date; their wedding day. She even supported Blain when he worked in dead-end jobs, such as when he was a legal copywriter for Harrah's Casino. That job paid barely enough to keep the lights on, but they always had their love, and what more light could anyone need?

And to think, a man whose entire career was once built around proofing contracts and finding . . . loopholes. Loopholes . . . are legal, loopholes are . . . bending, a bending of the rules. That's how Blain had risen in the corporate ranks, got moved up to the executive wing of the casino's legal depart . . . winning . . . with loopholes . . .

One Final Appeal

"WAIT!" Blain screamed.

"Oh, what now, Mr. Kellerman? Are you going to tell us how you deserve another chance, because of love or faith or some other pathetic mortal platitude?"

"No, I am going to tell you how I won," Blain stated, in a very matter-of-fact voice.

"By all means, Mr. Kellerman, do tell."

Pinkerton had cast aside the Southern charm. He now had the spite and tone of . . . well, damn it all, he sounded just like a lawyer.

"You told me at the beginning of all of this, that in order to claim the prize, a wager was required, correct?"

"Of course. Do hurry along with this," answered Pinkerton.

"You also insisted that successful and motivated attempts at each of the trials were necessary in claiming the prize, correct?"

Pinkerton didn't answer, but simply twirled his finger in that "go on" gesture.

"Finally, you stated that terms in this contest were of the most literal sense, correct? That what we say in this contest directly affects the rules and guidelines, correct?"

"Yes, Mr. Kellerman, I am well aware of the rules of the very contest that I—"

Blain stood, cutting him off. "Then Peaty lost. Peaty goes, not me."

"WHAT! You little shit, you little cunt, how dare you try and—" Peaty was cut off this time.

"How did Peaty lose in a contest for your heart's desire?" demanded Pinkerton.

"On the last test, when we were in the hospital, Peaty told me that he would claim Christine. By your very own policy, one must play the game in order to claim the prize, and the wager in the game is always the person's soul," Blain announced.

"Mr. Kellerman, you are rambling now, trying to avoid—"

Blain cut him off again. "Peaty didn't participate in half of the challenges, but even if all of that is void, even if only the last challenge mattered . . . Peaty . . . Peaty didn't bring my wife her hot chocolate! He failed, and since there is a wager on the board, there must be a declared winner. Since Peaty failed at the contest, since he disqualified himself, that would make the runner-up the winner. That would be me."

"Nice try, Mr. Kellerman, but do you recall, you had hot chocolate in the room, along with her favorite mug! You said so yourself!" shouted Pinkerton.

"But did he make the chocolate, did he complete the task?" Blain demanded.

"Of course he did, he knows that such—" Pinkerton was cut off one more time.

"I am not asking you, Pinky; I am asking him!" Blain, bolstered, pointed directly at the small statue of Hyraaq Tobit.

"King Tobit, you called for a test, you called for true will and strength. I delivered. Surely you do not care about watching a mortal remember a first date location, or pick out an item, or even race through a hospital with a mug of Swiss Miss. You wanted to know if I was worthy. Well, I wager it all now. I will wager my soul that Peaty is lying. He never made her the drink; he failed. If I am wrong, I give you my soul willingly. And since your honest agent, Mr. Pinky over there, was so quick to vouch for Peaty, I am quite sure that he will happily wager his soul that he is telling the truth. So how about it, King Tobit? Can a simple mortal stand on his convictions and truly be willing to give anything for your favor?"

Pinkerton fell silent. He knew that he had been bested. Should he bet against Blain, he knew that he would lose, as he knew that Peaty never made the chocolate.

"Goodbye, Mr. Peaty, enjoy eternity," Pinkerton mumbled, sounding very defeated.

"What, no—No, you little fuck—You can't do this to me—I have been loyal to you—you're letting this little piece of shit manipulaaaaaaaaaa . . ." Those were Peaty's final words as he vanished into the fire and suffering that was awaiting him on the red star.

"Well now, Mr. Kellerman, well done. Well done indeed. It took you until the very end, but you finally understood what it was to risk everything. You honored your words; you were very willing to do anything, give anything, to have your wife again."

Pinkerton sounded totally deflated. Perhaps he had hoped for Blain to lose, or maybe he was just attached to Peaty. Who knew?

"So . . . is it over? Is Christine going to awaken?" Blain uttered.

"My word is my bond, Mr. Kellerman. You have gained Hyraaq Tobit's favor; your wish is granted. Enjoy the rest of your life."

Pinkerton placed his hand over Blain's face, and Blain collapsed to the ground.

The ringing of his cellphone brought Blain back to reality. He was on his couch. He was having some sort of nightmare, something about an evil little man playing games for souls.

He reached over and picked up the phone. It was Maggie, no doubt calling to tell Blain that she had won another legal battle to hasten Christine's death.

He pushed the receive button on his phone.

"What do you want, Maggie?" he asked, with little emotion.

The excitement and squeal of her voice caused Blain to hold the phone away from his head for a moment.

"Oh my God, Blain! It's Christine, you'll . . . you'll never believe it. She opened her eyes today, just . . . opened them up. She sat up and stretched and yawned and . . . she's back . . . I don't know how it happened, but . . . she's awake and talking and . . . she just thinks she's been asleep!"

Blain was floored; his hands were shaking.

"Are you serious, Maggie? You're not fucking with me here?"

"Never, never about this. Oh, Blain, thank you so much for defending her! I mean, Mom and Dad nearly fainted when she woke up. I mean, to think . . . we wanted to . . ." Maggie was now weeping.

"Anyway Blain, hurry up and get your ass down here! She's been asking for you all morning!" Maggie exclaimed.

"Of course . . . my God, of course . . . let me get in my car! I'll be there in a few minutes!"

Blain hung up and bent over to get his shoes. He noticed they were already on his feet. Did he fall asleep with them? He didn't have time to care. Nor did he notice that there were bits of grass on his shoes and mud stains on his pants. He had no memory of the tent or of Mr. Pinkerton. He only had a vague feeling of a strange nightmare, but now he was filled with far too much joy to think of anything other than getting to the hospital and seeing his wife again.

Blain climbed into his car and began to back out of his driveway, when he noticed an item sitting on the passenger seat. It was a mug. A simple white mug. It had a few cracks running through it, as though it had been shattered at some point. Inside of the mug was a folded note. Blain read it:

"Don't forget the hot chocolate, Mr. Kellerman, and don't forget that you are one of the few men in the world that can say he did everything for the one he loved. Enjoy your life; love your wife, Hail Tobit."
Yours,
Mr. Pinky

Blain examined the note a moment longer. Tobit, Pinky . . . it sounded like something from a childhood daydream. Either way, he had no time to dwell on it. He backed out of the driveway and drove to the hospital to see his wife.

THE CRAWLSPACE

Madame Macabre

Um . . . hi there. I guess you could say I'm writing this as a cautionary tale to those who plan on studying abroad in future. I don't mean to discourage you from going in the first place, it's more like I just want you to be aware of this so that something like this doesn't happen to you too.

I guess I should explain a little bit. Last summer I was selected to participate in the study abroad program that would be centered in Rome for several months. Like anyone would be, I was elated. I had never been out of the states before so this was going to be a real adventure for me.

In the weeks that followed I happily packed anything and everything I could fit into my suitcase. (I will be the first to admit that I had way overpacked for this trip.) I was nervous about leaving my parents for the first time but I was also excited for the newfound freedom I would have while in Europe. Before I knew it, my parents were dropping me off at the airport and I was boarding a thirteen-hour flight to Rome.

Despite being long and tedious, the flight wasn't all that bad. When I exited the airport I was greeted by the program supervisor and several other students who would be studying with me. They were about the same age and all looked just as excited as me. From there we went to our mandatory orientation meeting, and afterward we went to pick up our apartment keys.

In the months that preceded the trip, we were responsible for getting to know our would-be roommates as well as finding a place to stay that we could all afford. There were three girls I would be staying with. They were all nice enough and made an effort to make me feel welcome, though I will admit it's a bit hard to get close to a group of preformed friends. But despite my slight alienation, it seemed that things were all going to work out well. All of us were on a similar budget plan, and by that I mean none of us really had much money to spend. Because of this we were all on the same page while searching for the cheapest apartment we could find.

After several days of searching we stumbled across an ad for an ancient apartment located above the Campo de Fiori. That was a prime location and we couldn't believe that it was still available, no less listed for an unbelievably low price. This immediately set alarm bells off in my head. The place was enormous yet the rent was cheaper than for much smaller apartments in a far less desirable part of town. However, reason never really wins out in a group of excited young women. They had already made up their minds and if I would be staying with them this was my only option.

We each received our own set of keys as well as a map with walking directions. Because of the prime location it really didn't take us long to get there. The Campo was amazing. During the daytime it was filled with a vibrant market, while during the evening it was lined with lively street performers. All of the apartments surrounding it looked to be ancient, so ours really didn't stand out all that much. After circling the square three or four times we finally noticed the number nailed to the front of a massive old wooden door. This would be our home for the next three months.

I fought with my keys for a moment until there was an audible click of the heavy old lock. The thick old door swung forward with a screech. We were then met with a long winding staircase. We all looked at one another and groaned. None of us had accounted for the fact that the building had been constructed before elevators were common. So three sets of stairs and countless complaints later, all four of us, with luggage in hand, stood outside our new front door. Once again I reached for my set of keys and fought with the stubborn lock. As soon as the front door was opened there was a stampede of young women trying to claim the best rooms. Being a three-bedroom apartment, it meant that two of us would have to share. I personally didn't really care so I let the others battle it out. When the dust had settled, I found that I would be sharing a room with a girl called Stephanie. That was fine with me. Stephanie was nice enough and she was also very quiet, my ideal feature in a roommate.

Over the course of the day we ran around exploring our new home. There were two bathrooms, a full kitchen, and a living room with an ancient TV. Once again I began to feel uneasy. Just how was it that we were able to get all of this for such a low price? But before I could finish the thought I was interrupted by a fit of loud squealing. My initial reaction was to panic; however, I soon learned that all the noise was from excitement. Down at the other end of the apartment near the front door, apparently there was another part of the flat we had missed. I followed the noise until it led me to a long dark hallway. There at the end, behind the group of squealing women, was a washing and drying machine. For those of you thinking, "What's the big deal?" I should explain that these things are incredibly rare in Rome. Generally exchange students have to wash their clothes by hand in the sink before hanging them up to dry. What was a luxury item like this doing in such a cheap apartment?

Just as the screaming quelled it picked right back up again as the girls noticed a door adjacent to the washing machine. Beyond that door was a master bathroom. It had a balcony, a claw-foot tub, and even a bidet. The girls immediately started fighting over whose bathroom this was going to be. I didn't really see why we couldn't share, but apparently the others were dead set on having ownership. As it turned out it ended up being my bathroom. Stephanie had made a logical argument that because she and I had to share a bedroom, while the other two each got their own, it was only fair that she and I got to share the master bath. And I'll admit that at first I was actually kind of excited—it was, after all, a really nice room. However, over the course of the next several weeks I began to grow more and more wary of the room. I don't know how to put it into words. It's like every time I went into that room I could feel eyes on me. And the voyeuristic element wasn't really what had me so unnerved. It felt like whatever was watching me was angry, that it didn't want me there, and that it wanted to hurt me.

I began doing everything in my power to avoid the room. I asked Alisha if she would mind if I were to use her bathroom occasionally. I made up a lame excuse about how it was far more convenient since her room was so close while my bathroom was at the other end of the flat at the end of the very long hallway. She happily agreed when I told her that she could use my bathroom anytime she liked. This worked well for a while. For the first two months of my trip I was able to completely avoid the eerie room. It wasn't until the final month that everything began to unravel. One night as I prepared to brush my teeth, I found that Alisha was already occupying her bathroom. I could hear giggles coming from down the hallway; it was clear both Stephanie and our other roommate were both getting ready for bed in the master bath. I decided that since there was strength in numbers, it would be all right just for tonight.

So I made my way down to the large bathroom where I joined the boisterous girls in brushing my teeth. They were in the midst of some conversation when Lindsay, our other roommate, had broken into such a furious fit of laughter that she had to lean on the wall for support. But suddenly she jolted upright as if she had been shocked. We all looked at what had been the cause of her reaction: there on the wall, about the same level as the bathtub, was a tiny door just small enough for a person to squeeze through. None of us had noticed it because it was the same color as the walls. The landlord had even painted over it. Naturally this made me a bit nervous. Whatever it was, the landlord clearly didn't want anyone opening it. But throwing all caution to the wind as usual, Lindsay reached for the handle and began tugging with all her might. Stephanie clucked her tongue in disapproval before pulling out a small pocket knife. She began delicately carving along the seam of the door. I wanted to beg her to stop, but I really didn't have the energy to argue that night. So within a few minutes, Lindsay had yanked the little door open with a loud crack.

It was . . . a crawlspace. It was fairly large. My guess would've been you could have fit at least three or four people in there. I was rather curious as to why the landlord would've sealed up an empty little room. Stephanie and Lindsay began calling for Alisha to come see their new discovery. She was just as excited as they were when they first discovered it. However, as could be expected, this excitement waned over time and eventually the crawlspace was just turned into storage for a few towels and laundry baskets.

In the following days after the unsealing of the crawlspace, things started to go from eerie to downright terrifying. Annoyingly, Alisha had changed her nightly routine so that I could no longer use her bathroom in the evenings. Once again I was back in the large bathroom; all the while, the feeling that I was being watched grew worse and worse. I began to get so paranoid each time I went into that room that I would literally jump at the slightest noise of pipes settling, and as soon as I was finished I would run at full speed down the hallway and close the door behind me. For some reason I seemed to be the only one feeling this way. It's not like I could've told the other girls either. I was already enough of an outcast as it was. So I just kept to myself and hoped it would go away eventually.

Unfortunately that wasn't the case. One night as I was getting ready for bed, I found myself alone in the bathroom. As I stood in front of the mirror brushing my teeth something set the hairs on the back of my neck straight up. There was a faint rustling noise. Not the kind that could've been caused from my roommates at the other end of the flat. Any noises caused by them would have had to be quite loud to reach me all the way at the end of the long hallway. No, this noise was very faint, the sound of someone gingerly shuffling things around. I stood completely silent, terror filling me. The soft rustling noise was coming from inside the crawlspace. I turned on my heels and ran down the hallway to grab the attention of my roommates. I tried to explain to them what happened, but all that came out were incoherent murmurs.

Eventually I managed to stutter, "S-something—something's inside the crawlspace!"

They looked at me with fear and confusion in their eyes. As a pack we moved together down the hallway into the bathroom. I nearly fainted when I saw the tiny door hanging fully ajar. Though this discovery filled me with horror, Alisha immediately pointed to the balcony's sliding door. Stephanie had left it open to air out the bathroom after having taken a shower several hours ago. She peeked her head out the door and pointed to the slanted rooftop adjacent to ours. There was a pigeon's nest occupied by a few birds. The girls surmised that a pigeon must have found its way in and was the cause of the disturbance. They all had a good laugh as we made our way back to the living room. I pretended to shake it off but I knew it was not a pigeon that caused the rustling noise. First off, the tiny door had been shut tight all day. None of us really cared to leave it open because it smelled quite musty inside. And secondly, the door had been shut when I left the bathroom, I am certain of this, yet there it was wide open when I returned. You're not going to tell me that a pigeon knows how to and is able to open and close a door all by itself.

It was at this point that I began to suspect that something was terribly wrong with the apartment. When I got back to my room I pulled out my laptop and called my best friend via Skype. She had always been the skeptical and methodical type; however, she also kept an open mind toward things that were hard to explain. I decided that out of anyone she was probably the best to talk to about my situation. As I expected, she was initially quite doubtful, though she also agreed with me that a pigeon was quite likely not the source. She asked me if I had any photos of the crawlspace. She said that if she could see it, that would help her to understand a little more clearly and possibly help her to come up with a more logical explanation.

Relieved at her willingness to at least hear me out, I reached for my camera and made my way back down the eerie hallway. When I arrived I found, to my relief, that the door was still closed. I stood in front of it for a moment, gathering my nerve before finally pulling the little door open. Other than the clutter left inside by my roommates, it was now empty. I snapped a quick photo before closing the door once more and running back to my room. I immediately plugged my camera into my computer and uploaded the photo. When I finally opened the image, I was petrified by what I saw. There in the upper right-hand corner was a face, baring its teeth at me. My whole body began violently shaking.

"Dear God—that thing is in our home!" I muttered to myself. Fear began to overtake me. Someone had sealed whatever it was inside of that crawlspace, and we had let it out. I was so absorbed in my panic I didn't even notice when my roommate returned. She was so blissfully unaware of the imminent danger we were in, yet even if I tried to warn her she would not believe me. I was at a loss about what to do, and finally decided that I would deal with it in the morning. Though not by a large amount, I did feel braver in the sunlight. I attempted to get some sleep. For the first time since being there, I closed and bolted my door before getting into bed. Stephanie eyed me suspiciously while I did this, but I just told her jokingly that Lindsay had been sneaking into our room the previous nights and had been stealing my Nutella. She laughed heartily, shaking her head before settling down for the night. I will admit that the only reason I was able to find any sleep that night was because of her presence. Something about not being alone can give one a sense of false security.

It was about two o'clock in the morning when the sound woke me. I had always been a light sleeper so the faint noise was enough to stir me. It sounded like a door being pushed open at the other end of the flat followed by footsteps. But these weren't normal footsteps. They were far too fast. It sounded like someone was running at full speed from the foyer to the living room and all about the apartment. But these weren't heavy footfalls like the kind you would expect from a running person. They were very light, almost unnaturally so. My initial reaction was to assume it was either Alisha or Lindsay, so I got up and stuck my ear to the wall behind me that separated Lindsay's room from mine. I could hear her faint but steady breathing. She was clearly asleep, so it wasn't her. I then crossed over to the other side of my room near the door and once again stuck my ear to the wall. Alisha's snoring was quite audible, so there's no way it was her. I slowly began to grow fearful as I turned in a last resort to see if Stephanie had perhaps gotten up, but I could plainly see her resting form silently rising up and down. A shiver went down my spine and I nearly screamed when I realized that the footsteps had come to a stop outside my door. Despite all the lights being out, I could see the looming dark shadow of a form through the tiny crack at the foot of my door.

I dared not move. Whatever it was, it was just standing there. Waiting. Then to my horror, my doorknob slowly began to jiggle—gently at first, but then growing violent at the realization of it being locked. The noise of it eventually woke my roommate. She sat up, blinking in confusion. That instant the jiggling of the doorknob stopped. She asked me just what the hell I was doing and if I knew what time it was. I told her it wasn't me. I told her that whatever had opened the door to the crawlspace the previous day had come back. But she just furrowed her brow at me and said that I needed to get more sleep.

The next day I made an appointment with my program's supervisor. I told him that I just needed to go home. He tried to tell me that I was just homesick and that it would pass, but I insisted. He eventually gave up and let me call my parents. They were confused but understanding. They were able to change the date of my return flight to the following morning. I really wanted to get out of there that day, but understandably that was the soonest they could manage. Unfortunately this meant that I would have to stay one more night in the apartment.

When I returned I tried to tell the others about what had been going on. I knew I was going to be getting out of there and would be out of danger, but I was still worried for their safety. But none of them took me seriously; they looked at me as if I was a madwoman. They didn't say anything, but I was sure they all thought I was going home because of some sort of mental breakdown.

THE CREEPYPASTA COLLECTION, VOLUME 2

At that point there was nothing I could say that would convince them. So that night I locked my door and hesitantly went to bed. And right on cue, once again around two o'clock in the morning I was awoken by the rapid footsteps scampering around the apartment. I could hear the door to the bathroom begin to creak open, followed by the door at the end of the hallway. The footsteps grew louder and faster as they moved through the apartment. And finally, once more they came to a pause outside of my door. I could hear breathing this time, slow and heavy. I sat up in panic, and to my horror I saw that Stephanie had forgotten to lock the door behind her after getting up to use the bathroom.

It was right outside my door and I did not know if I had time to jump up and try to lock it before the thing realized there was nothing blocking its way. I hesitated a moment too long and by the time I had sat up straight in my bed, the handle slowly began to turn. I froze in terror as the door cracked open, revealing my tormentor. It stood there ominously in the doorway, staring me down. Its eyes protruded slightly from its skull and gave off a very faint bluish light. It didn't appear to have a nose, only slits where the nostrils should have been. It had the teeth of a man, but had no lips, giving it the impression of an eternally toothy snarl. Its grayish white skin was waxy and stretched tight over its bony face. The rest of its skeletal form was hard to make out, as it was almost entirely enveloped in shadows.

After pausing for a moment in the doorway, it began to head toward me. As it moved, its body let out sickening cracks. I sat there, still petrified by fear, until it had made its way to the foot of my bed. Its heavy breaths were deafeningly loud. I don't know how Stephanie slept through it. The air had begun to smell sour and stagnant.

With frightening speed, it jolted to the other end of the bed, mere feet from me. I gagged at the smell of it, like sulfur and rotting flesh. Slowly it unfurled one of its long gnarly hands and proceeded to reach for me. Not until it was several inches away did I finally find my voice. I screamed as loud as I possibly could and it halted in its tracks. Stephanie shot up from her bed, visibly frightened. The creature hunched over on all fours and fled from the room with unsettling movements that recalled those of a spider. A moment later Stephanie switched the light on and looked at me furiously. She demanded to know what the fuss was all about. I told her exactly what had happened, but she just called me a nutcase.

The taxi came to pick me up very early the next morning. The sun had not even risen by the time it arrived. None of the girls came to see me off, but I expected this. After loading my luggage into the trunk I climbed into the back seat of the old cab. It had driven right through the square and was sitting at the base of my apartment. When I leaned to look out the window I could see where my room had been. My face contorted into a mixture of panic and concern. There, looking out of my old window was the creature. Its unblinking eyes bore into me and its lipless mouth curled into a snarling grin. Before I could say anything, the cab driver took off, leaving that hell house far behind.

I tried to warn them. I really did. I did everything in my power to try to warn them of the danger that they were in, but none of them listened to me. There was no way I could've stopped what happened after I returned home. You see, several weeks after returning to the United States I received a phone call from the program director. He informed me that a day before the program ended, all three of my past roommates had been reported missing. The authorities had no idea just how long they had actually been gone, as they were only recently discovered to be missing when the program director went to check on them after none of them made it to the end of the program wrap-up meeting. They assumed it had been at least a week or two, since all the food in the apartment was expired. There was no sign of forced entry, and no valuables were missing. The only notable detail mentioned in the report was that when they arrived on the scene, there was a strange little door hanging ajar in the bathroom. And when they approached it, they were met with a powerful odor coming from no visible source. The official report has them declared as missing, but I know that they're all dead.

I know that I'm incredibly lucky to have made it out with my life. I think the only reason I'm still alive today is because I fled thousands of miles and across an ocean. Despite their unwillingness to listen, I still feel an unimaginable amount of guilt over what happened to those girls. That's why I'm writing this now. I may not be able to go back in time and save them, but maybe I can prevent this from happening to you. Please, PLEASE heed my warning. If you ever get the opportunity to study abroad, keep this in mind: if it seems too good to be true, it probably is. And WHATEVER you do, don't stay on the third floor of the ancient yellow apartment complex above the Campo de Fiori. There's something there. Something evil.

THAT THING UP THERE

WellHeyProductions

There it is again . . .

That slow high-pitched metal rattle followed by a soft whimper. It is really starting to freak me out at this point. I know there is something up there, but I'm too scared to look.

I have been hiding here all night and it just stays up there. If I could only see the clock from where I am. I would feel much better knowing how much longer before it leaves. It always seems to leave in the morning, but stays all night long; always above me. It is relentless.

I loathe it.

That rattle creeps through the air once more followed by an even louder whimper, almost a sob this time, and then . . . a gasp. I look out and see something pink and furry bounce in front of me. I recoil back to safety at this thing's attack, but after it comes to a stop, it refuses to move. I look again and I can see its cold, black, lifeless eyes gaze into my soul, tempting me to come out, but I cannot.

I am too afraid.

The sob is now followed by what sounds like crying; the rattle becomes much louder as whatever is up there is much more agitated than before. The rattle persists and the crying gets louder. Whatever is up there is just attempting to coax me out of my hiding spot. But I cannot. It will hurt me. It will kill me. I am trapped under its constant torment for the entire evening. I exhale as I come to terms with my fate.

As I do, the rattling suddenly stops. The sobbing stops. The movement . . . stops. I realize that whatever is up there now knows that I am down here. It is only a matter of time before it comes for me. I need to act quickly. I need a plan. I need to think. But it is too late. As quickly as the rattling and crying has stopped, there is one more rattle as the creature up there makes a very quick jerking movement and all I can do is wait for the inevitable. Then, in a high-pitched squeal, the creature screams at the top of its lungs:

"MOMMY! MOMMY! THERE'S A MONSTER UNDER MY BED!"

PROXY

Aaron Shotwell

Why does the color blue look blue? Why does a rose smell sweet? What is happiness? What is pain? Why can the taste of a fine wine summon unpleasant memories? Truth be told, I would have been perfectly content to die not knowing these things. It would have been a mercy. I think we've all heard the words "there are fates worse than death" at least once. But until now, I can't say that I truly understood their gravity. Honestly, I can't say that any of us do until it's too late.

We romanticize this immaterial ghost between our ears, a thing that is as subjective as we think it isn't. It's all we have. It's all we are. So we guard it fiercely and to the bitter end. We create stories of life after death, of loving gods and benevolent guardian angels, and we do so to appease our subconscious knowledge of the horrifying truth. There is no soul, no afterlife. Eternity marches on without you, because you are ultimately nothing more than an inelegant knot of biological wiring.

And when that knot of wires is locked safely away in your skull, toiling away in the dark and informed only by your senses, it's safe to believe in angels. It's safe to believe a god will deliver you from evil. But when they put that . . . that fucking THING in my head . . . that barnacle on my sanity . . . I lost that privilege. I just . . . I don't know who I am anymore. My innermost thoughts and feelings are as fake as this room I keep waking up in. I never knew that a brief life and a swift death could be such blessings, but as with everything else, we don't truly appreciate what we have until it's taken away.

```
    .....
int main( ) {
// current date/time based on current system
time_t now = time(0);}
    .....
07/06/2078 11:13 AM
tesla//
Hello, patient #0001-i subject Alpha. Welcome to the
NanoSurgeon hub AI and virtual interface. My name is
Tesla. Please relax while I test the Frontal Lobe Cogni-
tive Interpretation Matrix…
```

It started with what was, at the time, one of the happiest moments of my life. It was my granddaughter's fourth birthday party, my little sweet pea. We held it at a public park on a beautiful summer day. We had clowns, ponies, a bouncy house, and colorful balloons as far as the eye could see. It may have been a bit overboard for a four-year-old, but I gladly paid for it. I was getting older and was often sick. I could feel my own mortality, and I just wanted to spoil my granddaughter while I still had the chance.

The whole gesture was rendered meaningless the moment she blew out the candles and looked up to meet my eyes. I was so happy for her, so charmed by that little cherub face of hers that I didn't notice. The right half of my face had gone numb and started to sag. And when she saw it, she screamed.

```
//Start FLCIM
int main (){
FILE * pFile;
pFile = fopen ("frontallobe.exe","w")}
    .....
tesla//
. . . Complete. Please try to speak.
p0001/
T^7r4-y . . . ERR 226 (FLCIM Dissonant) . . .
Calibration required . . .
#include <stdio.h>
#include <stdlib.h>
int main( int argc, char *argv[] )
```

```
{while (fgets(path, sizeof(path)-1, fp) != NULL) {
                              printf("%s", path);}
```
.....
tesla//
Processing . . . Calibrating . . . Thank you for your
patience. Please repeat?

p0001/
. . . Thirsty.

```
int main (){
    FILE * pFile;
    pFile = fopen ("NurseCallProtocall","w")}
```
.....
tesla//
Acknowledged. Paging nurse . . .

Her scream was the last thing I could remember before waking up on a stretcher, being wheeled into that god-forsaken hospital room. If I had known what they were about to do to me, I would have never consented. But my daughter held power of attorney. I wasn't in possession of my senses, and it was all she could do to save my life. But I don't blame her for this. She couldn't have known.

```
int main( ) {
    // current date/time based on current system
    time_t now = time(0);}
```
.....
07/06/2078 6:22 PM
tesla//
Initial diagnostic complete. Left brain stroke, exten-
sive damage to language center. Aphasia of angular and
fusiform gyri. Substantial degeneration of brain stem
function. Severe motor function impairment. Following
this briefing, Type-01 nanite injection will survey local
synaptic networks and estimate time of repair, beginning
with the restoration of speech. Please follow all
diagnostic prompts between repair sessions to assess
restorative progress. Confirm repair schedule?

p0001/
. . . Yes.

```
int main (){
FILE * pFile;
pFile = fopen ("MedInject.exe","w")
pFile = fopen ("LocalSynapticAnalysis","w")}
.....
fp = popen("/bin/ls /etc/", "r");
while (fgets(path, sizeof(path)-1, fp) != NULL) {
printf("%s", path);}
.....
```

tesla//
Acknowledged. Administering serotonin injection. Please relax while local synaptic analysis is in process. I encourage you to tell me about your day. This will help me to isolate the affected areas of your brain and expedite the repair process.

p0001/

. . . Want know day? How you think my day?! Had fff . . . fuck . . . fucking STROKE!

```
while (fgets(progress, sizeof(progress)-1, fp) != NULL)
{
printf("%s", path);
}
.....
analysis progress: .004%,
....
int main (){
FILE * pFile;
pFile = fopen ("DisplayHeartMonitor.exe","w")}
....
```

tesla//
It was not my intention to offend you, subject Alpha. Please refrain from over-exerting yourself. Please relax.

p0001/
. . . Anna . . .

```
while (fgets(progress, sizeof(progress)-1, fp) != NULL)
{
printf("%s", path);
```

```
                                            }
                                         .....
                        analysis progress: 12%,
                                        tesla//
           Your granddaughter, if my information is correct?
```

p0001/
Birthday . . . today. Four years. Scared . . . shit out of her. My fault.

```
          while (fgets(progress, sizeof(progress)-1, fp) != NULL)
                                            {
                               printf("%s", path);
                                            }
                                         .....
                        analysis progress: 83%,
                                        tesla//
           This is not your fault, subject Alpha. I am certain she
                                will forgive you.
```

p0001/
Shouldn't seen me like this. Scarred for . . . her life.

```
          while (fgets(progress, sizeof(progress)-1, fp) != NULL)
                                            {
                               printf("%s", path);
                                            }
                                         .....
                        analysis progress: Complete
                                         .....
                 while (fgets(CerebralAnalysisReadout,
          sizeof(CerebralAnalysisReadout)-1, fp) != NULL) {
                               printf("%s", path);
                                            }
                                         .....
                                        tesla//
           Cerebral analysis complete. First repair task set, es-
           timated duration: 11 hours, 45 minutes. Let's get you
                         better for her sake. Confirm?
```

p0001/
Yes.

```
int main (){
FILE * pFile;
pFile = fopen ("NaniteProtoal.exe","w")
pFile = fopen ("AutoMedicationInjection.exe","w")
printf("%s", path);
}
.....
tesla//
```

Acknowledged. Administering melatonin and clopidogrel.
Type-02 repair nanite injection in thirty seconds.
Pleasant dreams, subject Alpha.

01010111 01101000 01101111 00100000 01101011 01101110 01101111
01110111 01110011 00100000 01110111 01101000 01000101 01110010
01100101 00100000 01110100 01101000 01100101 00100000 01100010
01101100 01000001 01100011 01101011 00100000 01100100 01101111
01110110 01100101 01110011 00100000 01100111 01101111 00001010

Nanomachine Neurosurgery. It was an experimental method of treatment. They said it would revolutionize psychiatry and neurobiology forever. And I hated it from the moment it first spoke to me, if the word "spoke" is even an accurate descriptor. It was just a small nodule of polished chrome attached to my left temple, but it operated inside my brain. It made me hear and see things from within, digitally fabricated illusions for the sake of communication.

Having something so close to the source of your consciousness is more disturbing than you can possibly imagine. It can invade your soul—corrupt the very essence of who you are. You like to hope that your mind is the one thing definitely under your control. To lose that certainty is to question what it even means to have a self. The memory is hazy, but I remember them calling me a hero for being the first volunteer, praising my supposed bravery as they put the surgical drill to my skull. As if I had a choice.

```
int main( ) {
// current date/time based on current system
time_t now = time(0);}
.....
```

```
int main (){
FILE * pFile;
pFile = fopen ("EndNaniteProtocal.exe","w")
pFile = fopen ("EndSleepCycle","w")
pFile = fopen ("EndMemoryMonitoring","w")
pFile = fopen ("MotorFunctionTestPhase1.exe","w")
printf("%s", path);}
```
.....

07/07/2078 7:30 AM
tesla//
Good morning, subject Alpha. You will be pleased to know
that the repair is progressing well.

p0001/

Ow . . . my hand . . .

```
int main (){
FILE * pFile;
pFile = fopen ("EndMotorFunctionTestPhase1","w")
pFile = fopen ("MotorFunctionTestPhase2.exe","w")}
```
.....

tesla//
Please do not be alarmed at any muscular twitching. This
is an automated process to test your motor functions,
which should be substantially restored. 83% of brain
stem damage has been repaired. How are you feeling?

p0001/

Ugh . . . nauseous . . . feel like . . . gonna hurl . . .

```
int main (){
FILE * pFile;
pFile = fopen ("EndMotorFunctionTestPhase2","w")
pFile = fopen ("MotorFunctionTestPhase3.exe","w")
pFile = fopen ("AutoMedicationInjection.exe","w")
printf("%s", path);}
```
.....

tesla//
Acknowledged. Administering phenergan and diazepam. That
should take the edge off. The tremors in your hands
should cease momentarily. You will soon feel the same
tremors in your legs, but do not be alarmed. Please be
patient while the motor function test runs its course.

p0001/
Couldn't feel my legs last night. Walk again?

```
int main (){
FILE * pFile;
pFile = fopen ("EndMotorFunctionTestPhase3","w")
pFile = fopen ("MotorFunctionTestPhase4.exe","w")
pFile = fopen ("AphasiaCalibrationTest.exe","w")
printf("%s", path);}
.....
tesla//
```

Yes, within a few days. I have also noticed marked improvement in your speech recognition. Please read aloud the following sentence:

THE QUICK BROWN FOX JUMPED OVER THE LAZY DOG

"Duh . . . k . . . wick . . . bro-brown . . ."

```
int main (){
FILE * pFile;
pFile = fopen ("EndMotorFunctionTestPhase4","w")
pFile = fopen ("MotorFunctionTestPhase5.exe","w")
pFile = fopen ("AphasiaCalibrationTestAnalysis.exe","w")
printf("%s", path);}
.....
tesla//
```

Thank you. Analyzing . . . Speech apraxia is still prominent in the granular cerebellum. Prioritizing phase two repair schedule. Notice: your daughter and granddaughter will be visiting at 6:00 p.m. this evening.

p0001/
Six . . . but . . . not ready.

```
int main (){
FILE * pFile;
pFile = fopen ("HeartRateMonitor.exe","w")
pFile = fopen ("AphasiaCalibrationTestCompiler.exe","w")
printf("%s", path);}
.....
tesla//
```

Not to worry. Phase two repairs will restore adequate

> speech functionality well before their arrival. Sound
> good, Jackie-boy?

And that's when it started. The horrifying descent into this tortur-
ous oblivion. Jackie-boy . . . It sounded so familiar, the way that
thing said it. Memories of childhood, spending all day playing in
the forest with . . . a friend. A nameless, faceless friend whom I loved
like a brother. But that ghost of fondness came with a sense of guilt.
What kind of friend forgets their best friend's name? And yet, something was wrong. Somehow, I knew that it was safer to forget, that I
had forgotten for a good reason. It shook me to my core.

```
int main (){
FILE * pFile;
pFile = fopen ("VitalFunctionCrossReference.exe","w")
fp = popen("/bin/ls /etc/", "r");
while (fgets(CerebralAnalysisBackLog,
sizeof(CerebralAnalysisBackLog)-1, fp) != NULL)
printf("%s", path);}
.....
```

> tesla//
> My apologies, I seem to have caused you distress.
> Cerebral analysis suggests this name has an endearing
> connotation to you, and studies show patients report a
> consistently more pleasant and therapeutic experience
> when addressed informally. Would you prefer this
> interface to remain professional?

p0001/
. . . Yes.

```
int main (){
FILE *fp;
char path[1035];
FILE * pFile;
pFile = fopen ("ARBehavioralIndex.default","w")
printf("%s", path);}
.....
```

> tesla//
> Very good, subject Alpha. Initiating phase two repair
> schedule. Confirm?

THE CREEPYPASTA COLLECTION, VOLUME 2

p0001/
Yes.

```
int main (){
FILE * pFile;
pFile = fopen ("RepairNaniteProtocol.exe","w")
pFile = fopen ("AutoMedicationInjection.exe","w")
printf("%s", path);}
.....
```

tesla//
Acknowledged. Administering melatonin and clopidogrel.
Type-06 Repair nanite injection in thirty seconds.
Pleasant dreams, subject Alpha

01110011 01100101 01100001 01010010 01100011 01101000 00100000
01100100 01100001 01110010 01101011 01000101 01110010 00100000
01110100 01110010 01100101 01100101 01110011 00100000 01100001
01110100 00100000 01010111 01101000 01101001 01110100 01100101
00100000 01101011 01101001 01101110 01100111 00100111 01110011
00100000 01110100 01101000 01110010 01101111 01101110 01100101
00001010

Each time I went under, I could feel the scratching and tinkering of the nanites in my head. And the more they fidgeted with my synapses, the more I could feel something dark rising to the surface of my consciousness. Something forgotten. Something terrifying. A repressed memory clawing its way back with every synaptic bridge repaired, connections that were deliberately broken to seal it away in the first place.

I only wish I could have realized what was happening before it was too late. I might have said something to the nurse changing my IV drip as I stirred awake, but I was much too distracted by her chillingly unfamiliar face. Unfamiliar in a way I had only ever experienced once, somewhere deep in the memories that begged to remain forgotten. Two eyes, a nose, a mouth . . . but I saw no face. Just a confounding, nonsensical smudge where a face should be.

```
int main( ) {
// current date/time based on current system
```

```
                              time_t now = time(0);}
                                    .....
                              07/07/2078 5:50 PM
                                         tesla//
          Wake up, subject Alpha. Your visitors will be arriving
                                          shortly.
```

"Who was that? Have I met her before?"

```
                                       int main (){
                                       FILE * pFile;
                pFile = fopen ("EndNaniteProtocal.exe","w")
                      pFile = fopen ("EndSleepCycle","w")
                   pFile = fopen ("EndMemoryMonitoring","w")
        pFile = fopen ("HospitalStaffDatabaseReference","w")
                                   printf("%s", path);}
                                        .....
                                         tesla//
        Restoration of the language center successful. That was
        nurse Flannigan. She was with the personnel who brought
                 you to your room. She also participated in the
               preliminary operation and connected you to this
                                  NanoSurgeon interface.
```

"Why can't I remember? Why can't I remember her face?"

```
                                       int main (){
                                       FILE * pFile;
         pFile = fopen ("AphasiaCalibrationTestAnalysis.exe","w")
          pFile = fopen ("CerebralAnalysisBacklogReference","w")
                                   printf("%s", path);}
                                         tesla//
          Another symptom of the aphasia, I'm afraid. Do you
                       recognize any of these faces?
```

And it showed me a slideshow of nightmares behind my very eye-lids. A procession of faces pulled from my own memory, cascading faces that had belonged to my loved ones not twenty-four hours before. But had each not been accompanied by a name, they would have been strangers. My blood ran cold as they scrolled by in a blur, each without a face that I could understand.

My late mother. My daughter. My sweet pea, Anna. I was reduced to tears of frustration as I failed to recognize each one. I had never felt so alone in my life. It was all I could do to keep a fake smile on my face for my baby girl's sake when they came to visit.

"That's a silly hat, grampaw," she said to me with a smile. "Hats are s'posed to go on top of your head."

I tried to muster a laugh, though I knew it would never compare to the genuine laugh she loved. "Well, this silly hat's gonna make your ol' grampaw all better. So don't you worry your pretty little head." I looked up and flashed my best fake smile at the stranger I used to call my daughter, but she wasn't so easily reassured. I could see the tears welling up in her eyes, and to my shame, I felt nothing.

"Here, grampaw. I saved the last piece of cake for you. I guarded it all night, cuz I know you like chocolate." She passed me a Tupperware container with her biggest "aren't you proud of me" grin. Her mother nodded at me with a silent smile, unable to hold back the tears any longer. And I understood the message. *Yes*, she was saying to me, *even on her special day, she could only think of you*. It touched my heart, and I smiled my first genuine smile of the night.

"Thank you, baby girl . . ."

01000001 01101100 01101100 00100000 01010100 01101000 01100101 00100000 01000011 01001000 01101111 01110011 01100101 01101110 00100000 01101111 01101110 01100101 01110011 00100000 01001001 01001110 00100000 01110100 01101111 01110111

```
                        int main (){
                        FILE * pFile;
               pFile = fopen ("EndMotorFun%#%^
               WE ARE WATCHINGtPhase3","w")
       pFile = fopen ("MotorFunctionTestPhase4.exe","w")
       pFile = fopen ("AphasiaCalibrationTest.exe","w")
                        printf("%s", path);}
                                .....
                             teSla//
            Well, ol' grampaw's getting sleepy.
```

"Well, ol' grampaw's getting sleepy."
The words came out of my mouth, but I wasn't saying them.

```
int main (){
    FILE * pFile;
    pFile = fopen ("EndMotorFun%#%^WE ARE
                    WATCHINGtPhase3","w")
    pFile = fopen ("MotorFunctionTestPhase4.exe","w")
    pFiJACKIEen ("AphasiaCalibratBOYTest.exe","w")
            printf("%s", path);}
                .....
                T%Sla//
You two better get on home so you can hurry up and come
                see me tomorrow.
```

"You two better get on home so you can hurry up and come see me tomorrow." I laughed. The son of a bitch made me laugh while I was screaming inside.

He was standing behind her. Tall, sickly thin, and in that same black suit I remembered so well. For the longest time during my childhood, a horrible demon haunted my nightmares, but I could never remember its face. And now I understood why. He had no face to remember.

He held me prisoner in my own mind while he made me watch my granddaughter's precious smile melt away from her skull, along with her nose and her eyes. Through some twisted illusion, he made her a faceless freak just like him, a phantom of the little girl I loved. He stole her from me while she was still alive, and while I was still alive to witness it. I tried to call out, to do anything I could to get their attention, and I watched helplessly as that monster made me wish them a good night, all smiles and optimistic cheer. He shut me off from them, and the rest of the world, forever.

```
int main (){
    FILE * pFile;
    pFile = fopen ("NaniDAVIDtoal.exe","w")
    pFile = fopen ("AutoISdicationWAITINGon.exe","w")
```

```
WEAREWATCHINGWEAREWATCHINGWEAREWATCHING
     WEAREWATCHINGWEAREWATCHING;
                                       }
                                   .....
                              #75la//
              Hello, Jack. I missed you.
```

p0001/

You . . . I . . . I remember you . . .

```
                          i01 main (){
                       FILE * p010le;
          pFile =1 001en ("NaniDAVIDtoal.exe","w")
     pFile = fopen ("AutoISdicationWAITINGon.exe","w")
WEAREWATCHINGWEAREWAT1001 10GWEAREWATCHINGWEAREWATCHING
                          WEAREWATCHING;
                                       }
                                   .....
                              UmWelT//
                       Yesssss . . .
```

p0001/

David . . . The camping trip . . . We we were just kids . . .

```
          01010111 01000101 00100000 01001000 01000001
01010110 01000101 00100000 01000011 01001111 01001101
                            01000101 00100000
                   01000110 01001111 01010010
00100000 01011001 01001111 01010101 00101100 00100000
                            01101100 01101001
                                     01110100
                                     01110100
01101100 01100101 00100000 01100010 01101100 01100001
                            01100011 01101011
          00100000 01100100 01101111 01110110
                                     01100101
01010101 01001101 01010111 01000101 01001100 01010100 //
          I said I would come back for you . . .
```

p0001/

You took him . . . You took him away . . .

01000100 01001111 00100000 01001110 01001111 01010100
00100000 01000110 01001001 01000111 01001000 01010100 00100000
01001001 01010100 00101110 00100000 01011001 01001111
01010101
00100000 01000001 01010010 01000101 00100000
01001101 01001001
01001110
01000101 00100000 01001110 01001111 01010111 00101110
01010101 01001101 01010111 01000101 01001100 01010100 //
As I will take you, Jackie-boy. As you will take Anna,
and bring her to me.

He flooded my mind with images of his intent, tilting his head whimsically at me like a vindictive child burning ants with a magnifying glass. Tendrils of shadow bursting from behind him and smothering the hospital room's florescent light. He could control my every move, my every thought. He could make me see what he wanted me to see, make me feel endless pain. I could resist him, but eventually, he would break me. The nanites made it easy.

It all came rushing in so fast. A horrible memory long since forgotten. A dreadful future yet to come. I would be his slave. I would walk hand in hand with my little sweet pea. I would wear the mask of his followers, the same mask David's father wore that night. And standing in the same dark forest meadow where I watched it happen, I would hand her over to him just as David's father had done.

"Just get out of here, Jackie-boy. I'll be all right." Those were his last words to me, and he punctuated them with the familiar nickname he had used for me since the day we first met. He wasn't worried in the least. He trusted his father completely, knew that only good could come of being given to the "White King," as his father referred to the faceless monstrosity standing before me.

I was too young back then to understand what a cult was, or to know what would come of it. And I would have never imagined that the masked tribunals David told me about were in worship of this demon. He made it sound like an innocent camping trip in the woods. So when he invited me along one night, and that thing appeared to claim its sacrifice, I ran for my life.

I pleaded for David to follow, but he wouldn't listen. Even as I ran blindly through the woods, I could feel its malicious will pierce my heart. It would never let me escape. Sooner or later, it would come for me again. And my childhood mind repressed it all for the sake of my sanity.

"... no ... NO! You won't use me for this!" By some miraculous force of will, I managed to take control of my body again. Just long enough to grip the NanoSurgeon nodule and violently tear it from my skull. I felt the shock of it kill me. I felt my life slip away as I tumbled to the cold floor, covered in gore.

And then, as if nothing had happened, I awoke again on the hospital bed. I awoke at 7:30 A.M. on the morning of July 7th, 2078. The morning after the first nanite injection. And I have awoken here, at this very moment, more times than I can count. I awaken here again each time I tear the hub from my head, right after it kills me. You see, he has taken away my sense of time, and my grasp of reality. And I despair when I realize that he will continue to let me suffer these final hours again and again until I submit.

For all I know, he has already taken control. Try as I might to escape the clutches of this parasite in my head, I fear that I have already done his will. I fear that this is all just an illusion to keep me prisoner, and that I have already delivered Anna to her fate. And in time, some unfathomable eternity from now, I suspect I'll even forget about that. When nothing is real anymore, because the color blue isn't really blue. Like the last remnants of what I used to be, it's all in my head, and will fade away with me.

01110011 01101000 01101111 01110111 00100000 01111001 01101111 01110101 00100000 01110111 01101000 01100101 01110010 01100101 00100000 01110100 01101000 01100101 00100000 01100010 01101100 01100001 01100011 01101011 00100000 01100100 01101111 01110110 01100101 01110011 00100000 01000111 01101111

I SUFFER FROM SHORT-TERM MEMORY LOSS

Jagger Rosenfeld

I suffer from short-term memory loss, or at least I think I do. See, STML isn't exactly how it's portrayed in the movies. No, I don't go to bed at night and wake up the next day having completely forgotten the events of the day prior. For me, it's more so the little things.

It started about six months ago, when I woke up at 6 A.M. to go to the local gas station and fulfill my daily routine of a morning coffee before work. The thing is, I couldn't find my keys. I know for some that may sound like nothing, and most people will just chalk it up to me having misplaced them. To be fair, they're not completely wrong. But please, hear me out for a second. I am very organized—some may even classify it as OCD—but I like to think of it as me being very careful with my items. I mean, for God's sake; I have a key holder for car keys, I'm single—nobody is coming in and out of here, I own one car, and the key holder can hold up to ten keys, though that's a bit ridiculous in my opinion. The point I'm trying to make is that I would never in a million years not put my keys back on the holder.

I spent that entire morning in a frenzy trying to find them. I kept trying to recount my steps from the day prior, but everything felt so fuzzy. It wasn't your typical "I can't remember something." No, it was like I had a complete gap in my memory. I dug through drawers, pant pockets, couch cushions, the trashcan. I almost went as far as pulling up my floorboards in hopes of finding some hidden treasure in the form of my keys. Of course, I had to call work and tell them I would be a few hours late. Finally, my panicked pursuit came to an end—for the time being at least—and I grabbed my spare keys. That was only the first of many similar incidents to come.

• • •

A few months went by and I continued to search for my keys, to no avail. Part of me was paranoid someone had taken them, giving them access to my car and front door. Logically, I knew that couldn't happen; why would anyone break into my house simply to take my keys? So I let it pass, and to keep my paranoid mind at bay, I changed the locks. The thing that irked me most about it was losing the keychain. My girlfriend, or now ex-girlfriend, gave me the keychain at the start of our relationship two years ago, and it had this white rabbit's foot on it. When she gave it to me she said, "Since you made me the luckiest girl, I only thought it would be fair to give you some luck back." Yeah, I know it's cheesy, but sometimes cheesy can work. She really was great, and it still amazes me how something as great as our relationship could have turned sour in the matter of a few weeks. We have now been separated for almost six months. I would be a liar if I said I still don't think about her every day.

• • •

It was almost Christmastime when the next STML incident occurred. This year my office was throwing a big party, and since the party would be the best time to rub shoulders with upper management, I thought I should try to look my best. So, I had mentally planned out my best outfit: a black buttoned-up shirt, expensive dark gray dress pants, my "not-too-flashy but still stylish" Prada belt, and my best pair of shoes. This was a very expensive outfit, one that I have rarely worn and only for the most important of events.

It goes without saying that I was in complete and utter shock when I went digging through my closet to find the outfit and it was nowhere to be found. At first, I didn't believe it. I refused to believe that it could just vanish like that. I spent at least an hour tearing my closet apart, clothes strewn across my room, looking for the outfit. My once tidy room now looked like a literal tornado had come through and torn it apart. After searching the closet top to bottom, I went and ransacked every inch of my house. None of this made sense. I might understand if one part of the outfit was missing, like the shirt, but not the whole thing. That doesn't make sense, right? I grabbed my spare keys and went to search my vehicle. I had no real reason to believe it would be anywhere near my car, but I was desperate. Of course, it wasn't there.

I knew I had only one place left to look: my ex's house. I stared at her name on the contacts in my phone with my finger hovering above the "call" button. I stared for what felt like an eternity, debating whether I should call or not. "She'll just think you're desperate and want to get back together, or just looking for a quick hookup," I told myself. Finally, I took that leap of faith and called her. Each pause before the next series of ringing gave me what felt like a mini heart attack. I even said "Hello" a few times, thinking she had actually picked up. I should have seen it coming, but after some time it went to voicemail. I let out a quick sigh of relief before starting my message, stammering, "Hey Maggie, it's Aaron. I, uh . . . This is going to sound strange, but I . . . I think I may have left that outfit I wore to your uncle's wedding at your place. You know, the one with the Prada belt you got for me from last Christmas. Anyway, I really need it, so if you happen to find it give me a call, or . . . like a text, or something . . . If it's not there, sorry to bother you. Have a good day." I hung up the phone and immediately covered my face with my hands, trying to allay the embarrassment, as if someone could see me.

Of course, I never got a call or text back. I really should have seen that coming. To be honest, part of me was really hurt, but my ex wasn't the first thing on my mind. Currently, it was consumed with trying to figure out why I can't remember these things. First it was my keys, now it's a whole outfit. This just didn't make sense. It was so out of character for me to misplace things, especially ones that are as expensive as my nice outfit.

I eventually caved and bought a whole new and equally elegant outfit for the party. The event was as nice as you would expect an office party to be. I saw my coworkers, Jeremy and Martin, standing around near the back and decided to approach them. I really enjoy both of their company, even though I never had a chance to hang out with them outside of work. Or at least, that's what I thought. This leads me to why I believe I'm suffering from short-term memory loss. After a few minutes of small talk with the guys, Jeremy looked over to me and said, "Hey Aaron, we all had such a good time at Skip's Bar, you should come back again and kick it with us!"

"Skip's?" I asked, puzzled. "What are you talking about?"

"No way you got that drunk, man!" Martin chuckled.

Utterly confused at this point, I said, "I'm sorry, but I really don't know what you guys are talking about."

"Uh, you went out with us back a few months ago," Jeremy responded, a blank expression on his face.

"What?"

"Yeah, it was your idea. You called us up, saying you just broke up with your girlfriend and wanted to clear your head. You asked us if we knew any good bars and Martin recommended Skip's," Jeremy continued.

"Yeah," Martin chimed. "We were out pretty much all night. We were shocked how much of a partier you can be. Since you're typically so . . . quiet."

It felt as if my whole world had been picked up and smashed down on the earth, shattering into a million pieces. I didn't remember a single thing they told me that happened that night. Not one damn thing. My heart was racing and I felt as if I were about to have a panic attack.

"I'll catch up with you guys later" was the only thing I could muster before walking away.

I soon left the party, and any plans I had previously of getting in the good graces of upper management went out the door the moment I did. But I didn't care; I was more concerned with trying to figure out what the hell was wrong with me. This wasn't just a little item I misplaced or lost. This was a whole goddamned night that I have no recollection of. The next day, I called in sick and went to my regular doctor to see if he could help. I explained everything to Dr. Roberts, the best way I could.

"Uh-huh, so you think you're suffering from some sort of brain abnormality?"

"Maybe. Why, do you think I am?" I asked, concern clear in my voice.

"Aaron, do you know what STML stands for?" Dr. Roberts questioned.

"No . . . I don't think I do," I replied.

"It stands for short-term memory loss. Tell me, have you suffered from any recent head injury?"

"No, I haven't," I responded.

"What about sleep deprivation? Have you been getting a full night's rest?" he continued.

"Yeah, I get a good eight hours about every night. Why, do you think something's wrong?"

"Before we jump to any conclusions, one last thing. Have you suffered from any recent traumatic events?"

"Traumatic?" I repeated, stopping to think. "No, I haven't . . . I mean, I did recently break up with my girlfriend, but I wouldn't say it was necessarily traumatic," I explained. "So, what? You think I have short-term memory loss? STML, or whatever you call it?"

Dr. Roberts gave me a reassuring smile, shaking his head. "No. I don't think you have STML. I think you're a healthy young man who probably puts too much stress on himself. Here, I'll give you a doctor's note. Take a few days off work and get out of your head. You're a nice young man, don't worry about all this."

I looked down at the note before asking, "So, you think I'm fine?"

"I think you're too stressed for your age. Especially over things that are so minor."

I took the doctor's advice and got a few days off work. I wish I could say it helped, but if anything, it made it worse—whatever "it" was. Over the next few weeks, I was completely paranoid. I second-guessed every decision or memory I had. It was like I didn't fully trust myself or at least not my brain. The days I wasn't at work I would spend hours still trying to look for my keys. I was completely obsessed.

• • •

I finally made the decision that work was taking up too much of my time, distracting me from finding my keys. So, I quit. Finally, my time could be fully spent on my search. I know it sounds odd, but I felt that if I could find my keys, then the whole world could make sense again and this nightmare could finally be over.

The next two months I barely left the house or took any phone calls. Though to be fair, I rarely received any calls in the first place. Soon, I forgot I even had a phone, which would make sense, as

I had forgotten to pay the bill for two straight months and the phone service had been shut off. Over that time, I had the same dream, or rather nightmare, every single night. In my dream, I would see my keys on the rabbit's foot keychain that Maggie gave to me, spinning in the air above my head and out of reach, taunting me.

That dream consumed me, only furthering my obsession with finding that damned thing. It wasn't much longer until the worst started to happen. I began to hear a noise. No, not a voice, but a faint sound, almost like a tap. Each day, it grew louder and louder. I couldn't decipher where it was coming from, but I felt if I could find the source, I could find the keychain.

Then one day, it stopped. I didn't hear it again for a whole week. That leads me here, to today. It has been six months since I lost the lucky rabbit's foot keychain. Today, I noticed something while looking at my floor. My wood floorboards were off from their pattern. It looked as if the floor had been tampered with in a certain section of the living room. My heart dropped when I noticed this. "How long has it been this way?" I thought to myself, and that's when I heard the noise again. But, this time it wasn't a quiet tap; it was a loud, earth-shaking "BOOM."

The noise wouldn't stop. It was so loud, so deafeningly loud, I nearly dropped to my knees in pain. I looked down and finally knew exactly where it was coming from: underneath the floorboards where the pattern doesn't match. I wasted no time; I ran to my garage and grabbed a crowbar, then began hastily prying at the floorboards. As I did so, the sound grew louder and louder and my vision began to blur, until I had a flashback.

• • •

I remembered breaking up with Maggie on a Saturday night. I was upset, so that night I called up Jeremy and Martin to see if they wanted to grab a drink with me. They agreed, and I decided to wear my nice outfit. It had been awhile since I went out to a bar as a single guy, so I wanted to dress my best. I remembered the bar; the place was called "Skip's." I got completely drunk with the guys until we all decided to call it a night. I remembered Martin telling me I should get a cab, but I brushed him off, telling him, "I'm okay to drive." Just as I was on the verge of remembering everything, I snapped back into reality.

I continued digging up the floor and as I did, this stench began to waft out from underneath. In my whole life I had never smelled anything so foul; I nearly vomited. Finally, I had removed all the floorboards and looked down beneath. But that's when again, I was struck with another flashback. This time, I was driving home from the bar; completely intoxicated, swerving from left to right; it must have been about 3 A.M.

That's when it happened. Standing on the side of the road was a man in his late thirties and what appeared to be a child who couldn't have been older than ten. They had their emergency flashers on. Their car must have broken down. Before I knew it, I had hit them.

I was so drunk, I didn't even know what happened at first. My head smacked hard against my steering wheel as I came to an abrupt stop. I clambered out of my car, not understanding what had happened, and checked for damage. Luckily for my car, there was only a ding here and there. I then looked behind my vehicle, and there on the ground were the now dead and mangled bodies of the young child and man. I stood there for a solid five minutes in complete silence before tears started rolling down my cheeks.

I looked around, checking to see if there was a car in sight. Luckily for me, there wasn't. I proceeded to load the bodies into the trunk of my car and drove off. I quickly arrived home, but now I was left with the issue of getting rid of them. I paced back and forth in my garage, trying to figure out what to do, until I looked over at the shelf that had some spare wood floorboards on it. That's when I got the idea to rip out a few panels and place their bodies beneath it.

I loaded them both down one by one. I remember staring at them down there, feeling like I was going to puke from the sight and from my guilt. I looked down at my clothes, realizing that they were covered in blood. So, I took them off and threw them down in the pit with them, my shoes included. Finally, I looked to my hand and my white rabbit's foot keychain was soaked in blood—their blood. So, I dropped it down there with them, too. Then I sealed the hole with the new boards. Being the clean freak I am, I had a mountain of cleaning supplies. I spent hours upon hours of the night going over every inch of my car, scraping off their blood. The rest of that night I cried, and kept telling myself, "It didn't happen," until I finally fell asleep.

I snap back into current time, as I once again look down at the hole to see two dead bodies that were showing some sign of decay. At this point, I'm far too shaken to care about the odor anymore. On top of them are my bloody clothes, and far down to the right of them is my white rabbit's foot keychain, caked in dry blood. I bend down and grab the keychain and the moment I do, the noise finally stops. It stops, and the whole world feels normal again, even if just for a moment. I fall to the ground and stare at the keychain, trying to process what I had done. That's when I hear something from underneath. The bodies; they are beginning to come out . . . I crawl back further and further into the corner, until there is nowhere left to go. I am trapped with nothing left but to await their imminent consumption of me.

THE PUPPETEER

BleedingHeartworks

About a month after my college departure, my parents sent me a white box.

The outside of it was decorated with what seemed to be a floral pattern. At first, I didn't really understand the meaning of the damn thing. My parents had always been more of the home-crafting kind, never enjoyed buying things they knew I'd never use.

The box was a complete mystery until they told me what it contained.

Notes, small pieces of paper that held simple quotes and sentences; something to keep my spirits up when I needed it.

Without really questioning it, I kept it. I knew my parents always meant well—even though they had a strange way of showing it. Like with that white box.

The first few months of my first college year, the box sat neatly between the schoolbooks and journals I had started to collect during my studies. The lock on the box was still intact, since I hadn't even bothered opening it. The concept of the stupid thing still bothered me—I felt as if it was making me long for home.

And as time went on, that's exactly what I did.

I longed for home.

My flatmate didn't really strike me as a social person. The first week after I arrived at campus he kept a low profile, not really wanting to socialize in any way, which I was fine with. I had never been a party person, not even when I was with the closest of friends. So I left him alone.

College is supposed to be the place for everyone to find themselves. That's what I had always been told—but there was no denying the fact that I hated it there. As I tried my best to keep up with studying, I could feel myself become more and more passive. Back in the day, there wasn't a single night where I didn't stay up until late hours writing away, wishing I'd be something. But as it became more and more apparent that my dream was far away—I just couldn't hold it up anymore.

As time went on, I began pulling myself away from any human contact. The schoolwork quickly started to go over my head, but I couldn't return home. Not after my parents had paid for the entire trip to get here. Not after spending so many hours trying to get in.

The white box reminded me of that.

With the loneliness, soon came the paranoia.

I quickly accepted it, even while realizing it wasn't the best choice. But I had become so tired, I lost my focus on what actually mattered. Every day it became harder and harder to even walk out the door. I made excuses to remain in my single room in the shared apartment, waiting out hour after hour. A few weeks later, the teacher's e-mails about my absence stopped. It was as if I had no one to call, no one to trust. There was no way I was calling up an old friend, or even knocking on my roommate's door to talk. They hated me. I had no idea why they did, but that's what I kept telling myself.

I was simply good for nothing.

That room became my cage.

Then it was too late to turn back.

During the next few weeks of complete solitude, I had allowed bad habits to creep their way in. Skipping meals only to substitute them with cigarettes quickly became a daily routine, as well as sleeping through most of the days. But then there were nights I couldn't sleep. I felt too restless, I wasn't able to fully relax the way I usually could. So instead, I stayed up.

Like tonight.

It had somehow escaped my mind that the box I had received from my parents had remained locked. With no further ado, I decided to finally break it open. I tossed the lock aside and proceeded to open it.

The description my parents had given about the box seemed relatively true. The thing had been filled with pieces of lined paper, neatly folded to make the receiver give the extra effort to turn them up and read them. But as I did so, I slowly came to realize how everything that had led up to this moment had been a complete waste of time.

"Don't be afraid to call us if you need us."
"Never forget where you came from."
"We love you."

Instead of forcing myself to read more notes, I slammed the lid closed. The notes that I had already read were tossed out, along with the box itself. The stress that had been weighing down on me since I arrived here was suddenly pouring out like a river, forcing my vision to go blurry from the tears. If I told myself it would get better, I would have been lying to myself. Things clearly weren't going to get better and things weren't going to look up.

In a fit of rage I left the room, grabbing my pack of white Winstons, and set out into the night.

The second I reached the outside, I allowed my lungs to inhale the chilling cold air. Despite being a heavy smoker lately, it felt even harder to breathe tonight. But the smoke at least made things a little bit easier.

Several minutes passed and nothing seemed to be getting any better. The contents of the box kept going through my head, the words repeating over and over until they didn't mean anything anymore. If my parents loved me so much, why did they let me leave? They knew what kind of hellhole it was to be alone, so why give me the option to do it?

It just seemed stupid. Too stupid to make any sense.

As the rain began to fall, I scrapped the remaining stub of the cigarette and decided to head back in. As I stepped back in, I couldn't deny that I feared going back to the room and locking the door. Maybe if there was someone to just step in and stop me, what if . . .

And in that same second, I heard something.

In my mind I knew the house was old and could give off many sounds, but this was something new.

It was as if someone was breathing down my neck. With each step, I tried my best to ignore it. But the closer I came to the bottom of the stairs, the more obvious it was. Someone was right beside me.

When I turned around, I thought that I'd find nothing.

But instead, what I found was a man.

At first I had trouble making out who he was. Believing it was someone from the same floor as me, I wanted to give him a simple nod as hello. As I continued to look at him it quickly became clear that he wasn't from around here. The torn black clothing gave me the impression of someone who was homeless. Was he the one who had been breathing down my neck? And if so, how did he even get in here?

With a little bravery in my throat, I uttered a few words.

No response.

This was creeping me out. I just shook my head at the strange man, figuring I was better off going back to my room upstairs. I turned to go, but the second I took a step, a noise broke out. It was distant and yet close. A hollow sound erupted my thought process, causing me to stop dead in my tracks. The man was crying.

At this point, I had no intention of staying. I wanted to just leave, go back to my room, and close myself in. As I tried to move, however, I felt like my feet were frozen to the stairs. Turning slowly, I could see him come into view. And now, he had turned to me.

He stood in front of me—and his appearance was the most unnerving thing I had ever seen.

His face wasn't painted with scars or deformed in any way— it was completely gray. His eyes were two orbs of golden hue, glowing faintly in the dark stairway we both stood in. His mouth, which had been a frown before, was turning up into a smirk— taunting me from across the few stairs that remained between us.

"You're alone here. Aren't you?"

And as he spoke, his voice echoed with a static underneath. He sounded like a broken radio, going through several transmitters to push his words through. I was unable to turn my gaze away from him, incapable of ignoring him and turning back.

Suddenly, and seemingly without my control, my body ran. My eyes kept still, looking at him before he disappeared from my view. Instincts going wild, my feet had led me back into my room. I slammed the door behind me.

A few seconds went by and then it suddenly dawned on me. The man I had seen back in the stairway wasn't human—nor was he of this world. But the way he had spoken to me . . . It was as if he was pretending to be someone I knew. Did I know him? Or was the state of shock playing tricks on me, leaving my brain fragmented and scrambled?

It slowly dawned on me.

Up until now, I had played it as if everything had been fine. But it wasn't, it never had been. And now my insanity, my entire feeling of loneliness, had presented itself outside my door. The weight on my shoulders seemed even heavier now, as if it was pushing me slowly down. My body seemed weak as I felt my limbs going numb, losing hope. My back against the door, I slid down toward the floor with tears in my throat. It took me a few minutes before I was able to even look up again. With tears streaming down my face, it was hard to make out anything in the midst of blur. My heart was pounding in my chest, beating hard. I knew I wasn't alone in the room anymore. And what scared me the most was that I had allowed him inside.

Once again, the breathing returned. But this time, I just didn't mind. I didn't care what he was going to do to me. So when I felt him coming close, I merely shivered beneath his touch. He was cold. Almost as if he had died and come back to life. But he wasn't anything more than a hallucination. That's what I kept telling myself. When his hand grabbed mine, I followed. My legs standing right up on the floor, my eyes barely able to see anymore. The longer he stood beside me, the darker it became.

When he asked me to dance with him, I said yes.

His free hand wrapped itself around my waist and the other kept its firm grip on mine. My head slowly began leaning toward his shoulder. Being so close to him, it was impossible to avoid smelling him. He smelled wet—like tea that had been left in the cold forgotten water for too long. His hair, torn and tangled, fell beneath my head as his shoulder supported my weight. Maybe he was the best thing that could ever happen to me. Maybe the worst.

But I'd never live long enough to tell.

As we kept dancing, he started humming to me. Telling me a story of a man he once knew. A Puppeteer, who could steer his puppets with his broken dreams. Even though no one saw the value of his friendship, he managed to turn them all to like him. But no matter how many friends he claimed, he always still felt lost. Unloved. Broken. Alone. And then he whispered into my ear.

"If you let me, I can guide you to him. But you need to let go."

There was nothing more to remember than the sweet story playing in my head when I closed my eyes. His cold firm grasp held my body close to his as he seemed to lower me down, closer to the floor. The lower he allowed me to slip the more I felt as if I was floating.

"Do you feel it?"

Maybe. No. Yes. I hated to admit it, but just as he had been plaguing my mind only seconds earlier he suddenly set me free. I felt empowered, but empty. The bittersweet feeling of allowing myself to go this far was tainting my mind. Even when he whispered into my ear softly about my own choices, I couldn't help but feel selfish. Maybe he knew how I felt, deep inside. Maybe that's why he came to save me from this place.

I wanted to believe him. I believed him.

But the second I had let my entire mind go, that's when he betrayed me.

The man I had first thought was there to protect me was now instead the one who sought to destroy me. His hands had grabbed my wrists with a massive force, holding them still to keep his precision intact. With two distant cuts, I felt my wrists starting to pulsate, but no blood left me. Within my eyesight, I could see it clearly. My muscles were pulled out in long strings of veins and flesh. The sound caused my mind to go numb, my brain screaming for release. Every joint in my body was aching, trembling beneath his strong grasp. I tried to beg him to stop. Tried to push him off from me.

But no matter how hard I tried, he held me down.

Gasping for air, the fingers within my vision had started to turn white as they were slowly pulling at his sleeve. I felt heavy. My body no longer floated—no. With my heavy heart, he was the only one who was able to carry me now. Carrying me over the floorboards, hauling my lifeless body with his simple touch. As his hands went for my neck, I drew my last breath.

If I had been able to face how lonely I felt, I would have been able to tell my mom and dad that I missed them. I wouldn't have been too shy to tell my flatmate that I needed someone to speak to. I just couldn't stand facing all of my problems on my own.

It took too long.

HOBO HEART-STITCHES

Chris OZ Fulton

It was a winter afternoon. Like most winter afternoons it was overcast, cloudy with a bit of rain. The wind blew and the leaves rustled on the sidewalk as C.C. and her friend Elizabeth walked home from school.

"It was nice walking this way for a change," C.C. said as the two strode along.

Elizabeth smiled. "Thanks for joining me this way. I can't believe Britany didn't show again today. She didn't call or anything."

C.C. rolled her eyes. "She probably skipped and went to the lake with Glen."

Elizabeth laughed. "You're probably right. All right, well, I'll see you tomorrow."

The two parted ways and C.C. continued. She had just a few more blocks till she was home.

As she walked along she saw a small, scruffy dog pawing at something in the gutter.

"Hey little guy, whatcha after?" She crouched down and saw a bone stuck in a crack.

C.C. pried it loose and the dog snatched it up and darted away toward the alley.

The girl followed. "Hey, don't I at least get to pet you?"

When she turned the corner she saw the dog chewing on the bone at the feet of a boy sitting on a milk crate. He was wearing a gray hoodie and dirty jeans. He was tall and lanky with white hair, crystal blue eyes, and a skull painted on his face.

"Well hello," C.C. said, a little surprised. "Is he your dog?"

The boy looked at C.C. with a puzzled expression. "Yes."

C.C. smiled. "Can I pet him?"

Still confused, the boy looked at C.C. closely. "Sure . . . Are you not sad?"

C.C. giggled as she pet the dog. "Why would I be sad?"

"I don't know, everyone I meet is sad," replied the boy.

C.C. frowned. "Well, that's horrible. Maybe if you didn't have a skull on your face people would be in a better mood around you. It's a little late for Halloween, ya know."

The boy shrugged. "I can't help it. It's a part of me. I've never met anyone that's been happy before."

C.C. turned to look at the boy's face so she could inspect the skull. She reached out and placed a timid hand upon his cheek. She attempted to smear what she had thought to be paint, but realized that it was his skin. She quickly dismissed the skull when her eyes met his. They were bright blue and appeared to illuminate at certain angles. She became disoriented and had to shake her head to clear her thoughts.

She fumbled and stuttered for words. "Yuu . . . your eyes . . . uhm name . . . yeah. What's your name?"

The boy smiled. "I don't think I have a name. I'm a Gemberling."

"A what?!" she replied.

"A Gemberling. I was created to serve a purpose," replied the boy.

"What purpose?" C.C. inquired with a puzzled look.

"I don't think you'd want to know," he said as his eyes seemed to dim.

"Uuhm oookay. So what do people call you?" C.C. asked, becoming more confused.

"The only person who has ever called me anything was my creator and he only calls me Gemberling," he said with hesitation.

"That makes me sad. You need a name . . ." C.C. said before being interrupted by the boy.

"NO!"—as he reached out and grabbed her arm. "Never be sad! My heart couldn't take it."

C.C. was startled. "Why couldn't your heart take it? You just met me."

"You're special. Your heart is special. My heart has no place to call home and you have made it feel something. It's never felt anything before," the boy said.

"Hobo Heart!" C.C. said with a smile.

"Huh?" the boy asked, confused.

"That's your name! The boy who's heart has no home. Hobo Heart," C.C. explained. "And now that you have a name, you and I can be friends."

The boy smiled, "Yes. Yes I like it, my name. Hobo Heart."

"Okay, well I have to get home. You'll be here tomorrow so I can see you, right?" asked C.C.

"Yes. Of course," said Hobo Heart with a smile.

C.C. continued her walk home but not before looking over her shoulder one last time to inspect the mysterious boy.

• • •

The next day C.C. came to the alley to see Hobo. When she rounded the corner he was sitting there on his milk crate. He looked up and saw her and his heartbeat began to quicken.

"You actually came back?" he asked with a smile.

"Well of course I did silly. Now let's go do something besides sit in this alley," C.C. said as she blushed.

"What could we do?" asked Hobo.

"Well I don't know. Anything is better than sitting here," C.C. said, pulling at Hobo's sleeve. "I know, let's go to the park."

Hobo followed. "Will there be people there?"

"I'm sure," C.C. said, laughing.

Hobo followed reluctantly as he pulled his hood closer to his face. The scruffy dog picked up a bone and chased after them. When the two arrived at the park it was full of people running about playing football, throwing Frisbees, and playing on the equipment. The two walked over to the swings.

"So what's your story?" C.C. asked.

"I don't have a story. I have a purpose. It's all I know," Hobo answered.

"Well, what is this purpose you keep mentioning?" C.C. pried.

Hobo looked at the ground and kicked a rock. "I have duties I take care of to prevent something bad from happening."

"What do you mean?" C.C. asked.

Hobo shook his head. "I don't want to talk about it."

As the two talked C.C. looked up and noticed most of the people had left the park and it was very quiet. The people that were still there were by themselves.

Hobo looked around. "I need to be going."

"Wait, do I get to see you tomorrow?" C.C. asked.

"No," Hobo said. "There's something I have to do."

"Okay, how about the next day?" She smiled as she asked.

Hobo reached out and touched her blonde hair. "If that's what you'd like."

She took his hand and touched it to her face. "It is."

Two days passed and just as he had said he met with her. They decided to go for a walk to a nearby lake. The two spent several days like this, just talking, laughing, and enjoying being in one another's company. Time seemed to slip away as the two grew closer together.

One day after school when she arrived at their usual meeting place Hobo revealed he had a surprise for her. He held out his hand and she took it.

"Hey, wait before we go. I want to give this to you," C.C. said as she reached into her pocket.

"Valentine's Day is coming up and I was wondering if you'd be my Valentine." She handed Hobo a small envelope.

"What is a Valentine?" Hobo asked as he opened the envelope. It was a hand drawn picture of two hearts intertwined with the words "Be Mine" above the drawing and "If you value your heart, you'll give it to me" written below.

"A Valentine is someone you care for and would be willing to give your heart to, because you know they'll protect it and care for you," she explained.

"So on Valentine's Day . . . you want me to give you my heart?" Hobo asked.

C.C. smiled. "Well . . . only if you want to . . . ya know."

"Deal," Hobo said as he hugged C.C. "Now let's get going. You're gonna love this."

The two headed out toward the country, near the outskirts of town, and the small dog followed, as always wagging his tail. After walking awhile in the woods, Hobo made C.C. close her eyes. He took her hand and led the way for a few minutes then stopped.

"Okay look!" he said with joy.

When she opened her eyes, she saw before her a massive tree on a hill. It was very old and its many branches twisted and curved in dozens of different directions. The leaves were lush and bright unlike all the trees surrounding it. The trunk was easily 15 feet in diameter and it was unlike any tree she had ever seen. The roots were more exposed than normal trees'; they seemed to come from different points in the ground. Almost like the tree was composed of several different trees whose roots had grown together and had become entangled and formed one massive tree.

"It's so beautiful, it seems very special, almost magical," C.C. said in wonderment as she gazed at the tree.

C.C. stepped closer to Hobo. She lifted his hood off his head and ran her fingers through his hair. His eyes widened as she moved in closer to kiss him. He pulled away.

"What's wrong? Haven't you ever kissed a girl before?" C.C. asked as she smiled.

"No," Hobo replied.

"Can I be your first?" she asked.

Hobo nodded his head yes. She moved closer. Hobo embraced her and she kissed him. After the kiss Hobo gathered himself and pointed to the tree.

"This is my purpose, to bring nourishment to the tree." As Hobo spoke the scruffy dog ran toward the tree and disappeared into the extravagant root system.

"Your purpose?" she asked with a puzzled look.

"Yes, I live here and take care of the tree," Hobo replied.

"Then why are you always in the alley?" C.C. asked.

"I wait there to gather what the tree requires," Hobo said sharply.

"So you actually live in the tree?" she inquired.

"Yes," he answered.

"I want to see your home," she said, walking closer to the tree.

Hobo shook his head. "No, not yet. You're not ready for that."

"Can I touch the tree?" C.C. asked with an inquisitive tone as she reached her hand out.

Hobo turned to her with a scowl and grabbed her hand away from the tree. "No, you must not touch it. You are not prepared for what it will show you."

C.C. became nervous. "Well it's getting dark and I should be heading home soon."

Hobo took her hand. "Very well, I'll walk you back to town."

As the two approached the small town they met a group of people who were walking on the edge of the woods with flashlights. The group neared the couple.

"C.C. is that you?" a voiced called out.

"Yes," C.C. replied.

"It's Elizabeth—where the hell have you been?" C.C.'s friend asked frantically.

C.C. stumbled for words as Hobo backed out of the light and into the shadows.

"I, I . . . I've been with my friend."

"You've been avoiding us at school and too preoccupied to speak to your friends. Do you realize that Britany has been missing for weeks! And now Glen's gone missing too!" Elizabeth shouted.

"What? Are you serious? What do you mean they're missing?" She looked in the trees and shadows and couldn't see Hobo. Her head became heavy and she could barely stand as she reached out for her friend to hold her up before she fell.

"Come on, you can stay at my house tonight," Elizabeth said.

"Yeah, okay," C.C. replied.

The two spent the next day catching up and posting fliers to help in the search for Britany and Glen. As they returned to Elizabeth's house in the afternoon C.C. became dizzy and ill again.

"I think I'm going to lie down for awhile, if that's okay . . ." C.C. said as her head spun.

"Yeah sure, crash in my room," Elizabeth said.

"Hey don't let me sleep too long. I need to go into town and meet up with someone," C.C. said as she headed upstairs.

"Yeah yeah, lover boy I'm sure," Elizabeth said as she rolled her eyes.

Later C.C. woke up in a cold sweat. She frantically looked outside; it was nighttime. "Oh no. No no, no."

She got up and ran into Elizabeth's living room. Elizabeth was lying on the couch asleep.

C.C. shook Elizabeth. "Hey, wake up. What time is it?"

"Hey. Chill out. I don't know, look at my phone." Elizabeth said, half asleep.

C.C. fumbled around in the dark to find her phone. It was 11:34.

"Oh no, I need to go find him," C.C. said, starting to tremble.

"Hey look, whoever this guy is, he's no good for you. You've been slacking at school, when you're there. Your parents are worried. Only God knows what's happened to Britany and Glen and you didn't even care. You've totally lost yourself because of some guy. Spend a little time away from him and see how you feel," Elizabeth scolded.

C.C. hung her head. "Yeah, I guess you're right. Guess I got a little carried away."

As the days passed C.C. attended school and hung out with her friends. Elizabeth repeatedly bugged her about a boy named Jim that had a crush on her. C.C. finally gave in and said she would go on a date with Jim if Elizabeth and her boyfriend joined them.

The day of the date came. She met her friends at a local restaurant. Jim seemed nice enough, kind of a jock and a little more aggressive than guys she had gone on dates with before. Things went well enough. When they went outside to leave Jim offered to give her a ride home. She didn't feel comfortable with it and asked Elizabeth and her boyfriend Mike to give her a ride home.

• • •

The next day at school C.C. opened her locker and a piece of paper fell out. She picked it up and looked at it. It was the Valentine she had made for Hobo. When she touched it, flashes of Hobo and memories of time spent with him ran through her mind. She started to panic and her palms became sweaty. She looked around frantically. How did it get there she wondered. Right then Elizabeth walked up.

"Hey, you okay?" Elizabeth asked. "You look like you've seen a ghost."

"Yeah, I just need to let loose a little. I'm stressing," C.C. said as she rubbed her forehead.

"Over that guy?" Elizabeth asked. "You need to quit worrying about that guy, he seems a little creepy anyway. It's Friday night and my parents are out of town. I bet Mike can get some booze and we can invite Jim over. How's that sound?"

C.C. giggled and nodded her head. "Let's do it."

Later that night the four met at Elizabeth's house. Her parents left some cash for pizza. They'd had a few beers when Mike suggested a game of truth or dare. A beer or two later C.C. had loosened up, and when she was dared to make out with Jim it didn't seem like such a bad idea. Jim led her upstairs where they started making out on Elizabeth's bed. As Jim ran his hand up C.C.'s shirt, a dog began barking outside.

"Jesus Christ what's with Elizabeth's damn dog?" Jim sighed.

"Elizabeth doesn't have a dog," C.C. replied as she peered out the window.

A chill ran up her spine as she saw the little scruffy dog that always accompanied Hobo jumping about and barking. C.C. ran downstairs and opened the door. She walked around the side of the house and the dog was gone. She scanned the yard and street and saw nothing. She went back inside and told Elizabeth she needed to call it a night.

"Ah come on, stay a little while longer," Jim begged.

"No, I need to get going," C.C. said.

"All right, need me to give you a ride home?" Jim offered.

"Are you okay to drive?" she asked.

"Yeah I'm fine, I do it all the time," Jim replied with a cocky smile.

"All right then, let's go." C.C. shrugged

On the drive home Jim was paying more attention to C.C. than the road. He grabbed at her thigh.

"Keep your eyes on the road!" she yelled as she pushed his hand away.

Jim looked back at the road, just in time to swerve and miss a parked car.

Shaken, C.C. said, "That's it—pull it over, I'll walk the rest of the way home."

Jim locked the brakes. "Fine, be a bitch about it!"

C.C. got out of the car and slammed the door. "What an asshole."

Jim sped off. As she began to walk the rest of the way home, she pulled her jacket closer as the cold night air nipped at her cheeks. A few houses from home she heard rustling in the leaves behind her. She quickened her pace. She looked over her shoulder. Maybe she'd been watching too many scary movies, but it felt like someone was watching her. She reached home and quickly unlocked the door and slipped inside. Breathing heavily, she locked the door behind her. She felt a hand brush across her shoulder.

"Everything okay, honey?" her dad asked as she jumped.

"Yeah Dad, just a long night. I'm off to bed," she said as she shook her head.

The next morning C.C. was awakened by Elizabeth plopping down on her bed.

"Happy Valentine's Day!" she said annoyingly.

C.C. peeked out from underneath her blankets. "What time is it?"

"Time to get your ass up. We're going shopping! We have to get outfits for tonight. We're going to the movies with the guys!" Elizabeth shouted.

"I'm not going if Jim is going to be there. He almost got us killed last night! I don't want to be around him," C.C. said.

"Oh, stop, he was just drunk! Get over it!" Elizabeth pleaded.

• • •

The girls got to the mall. As they went from store to store Elizabeth started to notice how melancholy everyone seemed. "Shouldn't everyone be in a better mood? It's Valentine's Day, geez," Elizabeth said looking around her.

"Yeah, I noticed that too." C.C. said as she scanned the crowd.

The two finished their shopping and headed to the parking garage. Elizabeth opened the trunk and placed their bags inside as she carried on about the plans for the night. Mid sentence Elizabeth stopped talking. C.C. asked her what was wrong and turned to look at her. Elizabeth stood still staring at the ground as she began to sob.

"Hey, what's wrong?" C.C. asked as she grabbed her hand.

Elizabeth's hand felt cold and her eyes were fixed on the ground. She was completely unresponsive. She just stood there sobbing. Just then C.C. felt something touch her leg. She looked down and saw the small scruffy dog with a bone in its mouth. She quickly looked up and Hobo was standing there.

"Have you been following me?" she asked.

"I sent him to watch over you." Hobo nodded toward the dog.

"I don't need to be watched over. What's wrong with Elizabeth, are you doing this to her?" C.C. said, becoming irritated.

"I don't mean to, I told you everyone is sad," Hobo said as his shoulders sank.

"You need to go," C.C. shouted as she pushed Hobo away.

"It's your Valentine's Day; I thought I was to give you my heart?" Hobo asked.

"No, not anymore, you're not like me, you can't be with me. You need to go," C.C. implored as she began to cry.

Hobo turned and walked away; the dog followed. As the pair exited out of sight C.C. noticed the dog had left its bone. Upon closer inspection the bone appeared to have fresh blood on it. As C.C. knelt down to get a closer look Elizabeth startled her.

"What the hell is that? Are you ready to go or what?"

C.C. stood up and examined Elizabeth's face. "Are you okay?"

"Yeah, why wouldn't I be okay?" Elizabeth asked as she chuckled and closed the trunk. "Let's go."

"Yeah okay." C.C. got into the car and glanced around one last time.

Later that night the girls arrived at the movie theater to catch a movie with Mike and Jim. As the girls pulled in C.C. saw the guys standing next to Jim's car. As C.C. exited the car Jim placed his hand on her shoulder.

"You okay? I'm sorry about last night. I shouldn't have been driving. It was stupid."

C.C. nodded her head. *Well, at least he apologized*, she thought to herself. The group went to see some cheesy horror movie. She sat with Jim. He was being a creep and kept trying to make out. She repeatedly denied his advances. After the movie ended Elizabeth and Mike walked over to C.C. and Jim.

"Hey Jim, can you give C.C. a ride home? We've got other plans and not enough room in the car." Elizabeth winked.

"Hey guys no; can't I just ride with you and you can drop me off at my place?" C.C. pleaded.

"Nope. Jim's a big boy, he can handle you." Elizabeth skipped off.

Jim chuckled. "Hey come on. I'm not so bad."

C.C. rolled her eyes. "Please just take me home."

Jim opened the car door. "Ladies first."

C.C. reluctantly got in the car. She didn't talk much as they traveled along. She noticed that they had missed her turn. Jim had driven them to the park near C.C.'s neighborhood. He parked the car and turned off the lights.

"I don't know what you think you're doing, but you need to take me home," C.C. said in disgust.

"Ah come on. Just one kiss. You didn't have a problem with it the other night," Jim said with a sinister grin. As he leaned near her, C.C. slapped Jim in the face and got out of the car and started to run. He chased after her. He caught up to her and tackled her. She started to scream. Jim struck her repeatedly and told her to shut up. Her lip and nose started to bleed. He then ripped her shirt and pawed and groped at her body. She closed her eyes in terror as she frantically tried to fight him off. She heard a loud crack. Jim had stopped. She opened her eyes and saw Jim lying on the ground and a tall, lanky figure standing over her. He took his hoodie off and put it on her. Her vision was blurry, eyes swollen from being hit. His skin was a dark gray, almost black, and he had a skeletal system on his arms and chest to match the skull on his face. It was Hobo. He knelt down next her. She couldn't see clearly what he was doing but she could hear ripping and tearing of flesh and the horrible sound of blood splattering.

She pulled herself to her knees and called out "Hobo . . ."

He reached out and handed her something. She took it. She then realized it was his still beating heart pulsating in her hands. She looked up at him. He placed his hands on either side of her face, tilted her head up, and said, "I value my heart. You can keep

THE CREEPYPASTA COLLECTION, VOLUME 2

it. I don't need it anymore" and kissed her on the forehead. She passed out . . .

• • •

C.C. woke up in her bed. She got up and went to her mirror. She had no injuries. She looked herself over and could see no damage from the night before. What had happened? Was she dreaming? She walked downstairs. Her mother was cooking breakfast and her father was reading the paper.

"Mom? Dad?" she asked.

Her dad looked over. "Hey you, how was last night?"

"What do you mean?" C.C. asked.

"Well, Elizabeth's mom called this morning. Apparently she didn't make it home last night after she dropped you off and we saw on the news that some more kids were missing. Didn't know if you knew anything about it. We figured it was just kids being kids. You don't know anything, do you?" he asked, looking up from his paper.

"Uh. No," C.C. replied.

C.C.'s heart sank . . . She ran upstairs and started looking through her room—in her closet, in her drawers. She sat down on her bed. Then she heard it: thump thump . . . thump thump . . . She looked under her bed. There was Hobo's hoodie. She pulled it out from underneath her bed and unfolded it. Inside was Hobo's heart, still beating. *Oh no!* she thought. *Hobo! What has happened? I need to find him.* She folded the hoodie back up, put on some shoes, and ran downstairs. She told her parents she was going to check on Elizabeth and she'd be home soon.

Carrying the hoodie, she ran across town out toward the woods. The wind picked up and it started to rain. She got near the spot where Hobo had made her close her eyes. She began to call out for him: "Hobo . . . HOBO!" It was raining hard now. She looked all around. She saw Hobo's dog running through the woods. She called out to him. He looked up and saw her and darted over and began licking her. He was covered in blood.

She fell to her knees. "Oh no! Hobo's hurt, take me to him." The scruffy dog jumped and twirled around.

C.C. got to her feet and followed the little dog to the tree. The tree was no longer vibrant and full of color. It was black and looked like it was dying. All the leaves had fallen off and the limbs were lifeless and low hanging. The dog went around to the back of the hill. C.C. could see an opening. She ducked down and started to walk in. She stumbled and reached out to grab the roots to break her fall. When she touched the tree her heart was filled with great sorrow. She saw flashes in her mind of faces upon faces of lifeless people, dead people. Then six faces appeared, horrible faces, twisted and demonic. She managed to get back to her knees and crawl into the hole. It was a circular room. It was dimly lit by six braziers. The flames in the braziers were black and purple, unlike any fire C.C. had seen before. There were bones strung out across the ground. The ground itself was pooled with blood. She frantically looked around and saw Britany, Glen, Jim, Elizabeth, and Mike entangled in the roots. She screamed and ran toward her friends, but when she approached she retched as she realized it was far too late. It was like the roots had come to life and were squeezing the bodies, bones were crackling and breaking, their innards were spilling forth. The small dog was ripping at an opening in Elizabeth's chest; he pulled a bone loose and began to shake it about like a toy as he bounced across the room. Long stringy roots hung down above each of C.C.'s friends. Their hearts had been removed and now hung above them intertwined in the roots. It looked liked the tree was almost feeding off the hearts, absorbing the life of each soul into the tree. There was a sixth cluster of roots with no body and no heart. Next to the empty cluster of roots lay Hobo. He lay lifeless and still. C.C.

THE CREEPYPASTA COLLECTION, VOLUME 2

crawled through the horrors and carnage to get to him. She rolled him over. His chest was torn open and there was a gaping wound where he had removed his heart. His eyes fluttered open and met hers. He blinked then his eyes got wider.

"Why?" he asked.

C.C. began to cry. "Why what? Why did you kill my friends?! How could you do this?! You're a monster!" she screamed.

Hobo struggling for life. "I saved you. Protected you from these people. I told you not to touch the tree. You were special . . . shouldn't have brought my heart here . . . I failed my purpose . . ."

C.C. pounded on Hobo's chest. "What purpose?! Murdering people?! Destroying lives?!"

Cryptic chanting in a foreign tongue began echoing from the walls.

"Pou mwen passe, Le'm tounnen map remesi."

"Pou mwen passe, Le'm tounnen map remesi."

"Pou mwen passe, Le'm tounnen map remesi" the voices called repeatedly.

Hobo cleared his throat as he clung to life. "Must keep the six here. With six hearts. Only five gathered . . . saved you, didn't get six . . . too late . . ."

C.C. grabbed the hoodie. "Use your heart! Give them your heart!"

She unwrapped the hoodie. Hobo's heart was barely beating. It was black and dying. Hobo looked at his heart and his rage began to build.

He looked into C.C.'s eyes. "I valued it so I gave it to you! You were supposed to protect it! Now you wish to destroy it?"

C.C. became enraged. "You murdered my friends!"

Hobo's arm shot up and palmed C.C.'s chest. His fingers and thumb penetrated her skin.

"Do you value your heart?" he demanded.

He squeezed his hand into a fist, ripping her shirt and flesh from her body. She fell to the ground gasping for air. The chanting grew louder. As Hobo rose to his feet he arched his back and large black-feathered wings extended from his body. His eyes glowed fiercely. He used his fists to crush C.C.'s chest as he stuck her repeatedly. He then grabbed a protruding rib bone and ripped it from her body, exposing her chest cavity. She lay motionless as he reached inside of her and removed her heart. The roots from the ceiling extended to receive the heart. Hobo looked up to the roots then back down at C.C.

"No . . ." He then placed C.C.'s heart into the opening in his own chest.

He found a small sliver of bone from the ground and took hair from C.C.'s head and began to sew himself back together.

The small blood-soaked dog whimpered at his side as he forced the crude bone in and out of his flesh. "Don't worry, it'll do for now, though it won't last. It will need to be replaced."

When he was done he patted the dog on the head, walked over and picked up his heart, and placed it on C.C.'s chest.

"You can keep it. I don't need it anymore." He knelt down and kissed her on the forehead one last time. As he stood up he noticed something lying on the ground beside her. It was the Valentine she had made for him. He picked it up and held it to his chest then placed it in his back pocket.

Hobo then turned the six braziers over and set the room ablaze. The room was quickly engulfed in flame. The fire burned unnaturally fast as the purple and black flames reached higher. After a moment Hobo exited the opening in the hill.

As he walked away, six skeletal figures composed of black smoke crawled up out of the roots and flames, screeching and screaming as they cackled, "At last we are free . . ."

Hobo grinned as he walked away from the tree, burning fiercely despite the rain . . .

CRATERS IN HER FACE

Madame Macabre

I've always been an art enthusiast. I guess I inherited that from my grandmother. She had been a painter for many years, and tried her best to instill a love of the fine arts in me. I have many fond memories of trips to museums and galleries with her, gazing upon the countless beautiful and thought-provoking pieces.

Sculpture and photography were nice, but I always had a special place in my heart for paintings. Especially old oil paintings. It's hard to explain. There's a sort of special property to paintings that you can only appreciate with your eyes in person. Photographs do them no justice. The way the light refracts off of the oil and bounces back to your eyes give them a sort of life that no other medium can.

Well, as much as I loved oil paintings, I was never much good myself. When I was a child, my grandmother tried giving me lessons. She'd create breathtaking scenery, while the only thing I managed to make was a colossal mess.

My apparent lack of talent in the oil painting department did not in the slightest diminish my love for the craft. My grandmother had a room dedicated to the paintings she had created or collected, which she dubbed "the gallery." I spent hour upon hour in that room, staring in wonderment.

Despite my being a child, my grandmother had no qualms about leaving me alone in a room with tens of thousands of dollars' worth of paintings. She knew I had far too much respect for them to damage them, even as a bouncy little girl. She did, however, have one rule that was to be strictly adhered to at all times in the gallery: If any paintings in the gallery are covered, you are NOT to uncover them. Not even to peek.

Now, some might think this a strange rule. I certainly did as a girl, but there is a reason behind it. Oil paints are very sensitive, and it's possible the pieces she had covered up could be damaged if exposed to light, or various other factors.

But regardless of the reasoning, I made sure to follow that rule. Or at least I did until the day my grandmother received her newest piece.

I remember arriving at my grandmother's home for a visit and running straight for the gallery. I rounded the corner into the room and was forced to screech to a halt. There, in the center of the room, was an incredibly large painting, propped up by an easel and covered with a long dark curtain.

I had never seen the piece before, and the sheer size of it astounded me. My curiosity overtook me for a moment, and I found myself slowly reaching out a tiny hand to unveil the mysterious piece. But just as my hand grasped the dark velvet, my grandmother entered the room, wearing a frown.

"Evelyn, what are you doing? You know the rule about covered paintings!"

My hand instantly whipped back to my side and I cringed at the realization of my actions.

"I'm sorry, Grandma. I forgot. This painting, it's so huge! What is it?!"

My grandmother's expression softened and she placed a hand on my shoulder.

"This painting was just given to me by a friend. Her ill sister painted it shortly before passing away. She said she couldn't bear to look at it because it made her too sad, so she gave it to me."

"May I see it?" I asked.

"Perhaps later. It's very sensitive because it's in poor condition. I'm going to try to preserve it though. After I'm done, I'll let you see it, like with all the others," she warmly responded.

Although my curiosity was not satisfied, I agreed and resigned myself to looking at all the other pieces in the gallery. Content that I would no longer cause any sort of mischief, my grandmother returned to the sitting room.

I lay there in the soft plush carpet, gazing at the works of art until my focus drifted. Despite how bad I knew it was to disobey my grandmother, my curiosity continued to burn hot in my chest. I had already stared at each and every piece in the gallery to detail, and had grown restless. I had to see what was beneath the curtain.

Holding my breath, I tiptoed over to the massive easel and grasped the soft fabric in my hand. I'd just peek for a moment. It wouldn't hurt. Just long enough to quench this burning need to know.

I released the breath I was holding and quickly pulled the curtain aside. Immediately, I felt myself release a gasp. I had seen countless paintings of all genres and matters, but none so utterly disturbing as what lay before me.

The painting depicted what appeared to be a pale young woman. Her skin was a sickly yellow, and appeared clammy and unwell. She wore a tattered ivory dress, and her long black hair flowed behind her, seemingly following wind sources from no particular direction.

She sat in anguish, with her hands held up to the side of her face, digging her long black nails into the flesh. As uncomfortable as the piece was as a whole, what really unnerved me were her eyes and mouth. Black, gaping holes sunk into her head where they should have been, and a thick rust-colored fluid seemed to leak from them.

Immediately I panicked and threw the curtain back over the horrid painting. I wanted to run screaming and crying straight to my grandmother, but I restrained myself. I knew that if I did that, she'd know I had disobeyed her by looking under the curtain. So instead I gave myself a moment to regain my breath and composure before calmly joining my grandmother in the sitting room.

I never went into the gallery by myself again.

That is, until my grandmother passed away, naming me the sole recipient of her painting collection.

The reading of the will was an uncomfortable enough experience on its own, but it was made worse by the fact that my jealous cousins were also present. My grandmother's estate, belongings, and all of her life earnings were to be split evenly amongst the family. I, however, was chosen to receive the paintings alone.

I knew this was because my grandmother knew of my great love for the art, and knew that I would be the only one not to sell all of them for the money. However, my cousins simply saw it as me inheriting nearly $80,000 in oil paintings, and not sharing a dime of it.

Oh, you can believe they tried to contest the will, but it was ironclad, and despite their protests, I soon enough found myself transporting the pieces into my own home.

My boyfriend Edward and I had purchased a lovely Victorian-style home two years prior, and I, following in my grandmother's footsteps, had dedicated the long hallway and large room at the end of the third floor to hosting my own collection of paintings.

My grandmother had a great deal more paintings than I, but Edward and I managed to shuffle things around until everything had a cozy new home. Well, everything except for the one, nearly

6-foot tall canvas, wrapped methodically in several layers of brown paper and twine.

Instantly a knot formed in my stomach. I knew exactly which piece it was. The image of the tormented young woman with bloody caverns in her face flooded my mind, and I felt myself growing pale. Edward, however, did not share the same unfortunate memory, and excitedly began unwrapping the piece.

I rushed forward to stop him, exclaiming how I wanted him to keep it wrapped, as it was a horrifically gruesome piece. However, by the time I reached him, he had already revealed the piece's glossy surface.

I prepared myself for the horrible sight, but to my shock, it was different. The ghastly figure in the white dress still stood, hair flowing in the non-present wind and hands digging into her cheeks, but the bloody craters were gone.

Instead, she now appeared to be a pretty little thing. She had soft pink cheeks and sparkling green eyes, and her lips parted daintily into a dreamy smile. I recognized the style immediately. This was my grandmother's work. She had done an exceptional job covering over the old, horrific façade; however, if I inspected the piece closely, I could still see traces of the gruesome sight hiding right below the surface.

My grandmother had clearly worked painstakingly on the piece. To anyone who hadn't seen the original, it actually did appear quite pleasant. I, however, hated it to my core. Edward, on the other hand, was instantly in love.

The next few days consisted of us arguing over where the piece would be hung. We were out of room in the gallery, and he insisted upon hanging it on the large blank wall on the far side of our bedroom. I of course wanted nothing to do with the piece, thus the fighting began.

Finally we came to an agreement. I would let him hang the piece in our room for the time being, but I would begin looking for the family of the woman who originally painted the piece. Obviously, they wouldn't want to look at it in its former state, as it forever captured the state of sickness in their beloved family member. But now, it was beautiful. It would memorialize her as she was before the sickness began changing her. Certainly they would want it back now!

Edward was hesitant, but agreed that returning it when I found the family would be the right thing to do. So it was that I prepared myself for a few weeks tops of having to gaze at the uncomfortable piece.

The piece went up, and despite my reservations, it actually wasn't as bad as I was expecting. Without the bloody chasms, the threatening aura of the piece was gone, and I will admit that seeing my grandmother's painting style made me a little happy.

And while it had taken a few days, I finally tracked down a phone number for the family. The daughter of the woman who had given the painting to my grandmother answered, and seemed excited when I told her of the relic from her aunt. She said she wanted the piece, but she needed some time to find a place for it. Excitedly, we both agreed to hand over the piece the following week.

My excitement, however, quickly faded when I learned that Edward was going to be leaving town for the remainder of our time in possession of the piece, due to business. Displaying the piece was one thing, but being home alone with it was an entirely different situation. Despite my grandmother's beautiful work, being alone in the same room with the piece always left me with an uncomfortable knot in my stomach.

So after kissing Edward goodbye, and locking the door, I immediately ran to the linen closet, where I grabbed a sheet to throw over the creepy painting. I stormed into my bedroom, armed with the linen and a tack, and came to a halt in front of the piece.

It was very vague, and I needed to squint my eyes and lean in to notice it, but it appeared as though my grandmother's paint had begun to crack and peel a bit, revealing glimpses of the rusty brown color hiding right below.

That was impossible, though. The piece was nowhere near old enough for that to occur. Oil paint is famous for staying wet for a very long time. There are even some paintings from the Middle Ages that are still moist on the inside! There was no way the paint here should be peeling!

Just the sight of that gross, rusty paint made me feel ill. I immediately threw the sheet over it, and breathed a sigh of relief when I was no longer confronted with the eerie sight. I couldn't give the painting back soon enough.

It was about this time that strange things began happening. Nothing huge and panic-worthy. Just little things. Doors I could swear I had left open would be inexplicably closed, every so often I'd feel a soft gust of air as if someone had just walked by, and I'd be startled by an occasional creak or groan, which weren't all too uncommon in a home as old as mine.

Things continued on like this for the first few days Edward was gone. It was Wednesday. Edward would be back on Sunday, and we'd return the piece on Monday. As uncomfortable as I was, my goal was in sight, and I knew I'd make it.

A few more days passed, and things were going relatively well until I decided to look at the piece again. I had been on the phone with a shipping company earlier, trying to decide the best way to wrap and transport the piece. I figured that the cracking and peeling of the piece must have been due to improper preparation and handling, and wanted to avoid further damage. Hesitantly, I lifted the sheet for a quick assessment.

I immediately dropped the sheet once more, and backed away in a moment of panic. The paint had continued to deteriorate, and now even more of the seeping rust was breaking through the girl's once lovely face, now leaving her with a grotesque, cracked open face.

It was at this point that I decided I needed to speak with the family once more. I dialed the number and, to my surprise, found that the woman who had gifted my grandmother with the piece all those years ago was still alive, and had answered the phone. Apprehensively, I told her about the piece, and she invited me over to talk about it over tea.

Jumping at the opportunity to not be home alone with the piece, I grabbed my purse and immediately headed over. Upon arriving at the address, I was greeted at the door by a smiling old woman. She graciously welcomed me into the home, and in minutes we were settled in the front room with daintily painted teacups in our hands.

She released a long sigh before speaking.

"That painting should have been destroyed a long time ago," she breathed sadly. "You've seen it. It's terrible and frightening. It's the result of a very sick mind."

She shifted her gaze down to her teacup before continuing.

"My sister had brain cancer. In its final stages, she became very ill mentally. When there was nothing more the doctors could do for her, they sent her home and told us to make her comfortable. She always loved painting, so we bought her the biggest canvas we could, and hoped to make her last moments happy ones.

"But as you can see, they weren't. Her mind was plagued by demons. She began withdrawing more and more into the madness of her own world, and it showed on the canvas. I actually walked in on her slashing her arms with a palette knife, and mixing her blood right into the paint."

The image of the gross, rusty color oozing from the craters in the girl's face flashed across my mind, and I had to set my cup down for fear of dropping it.

"I was going to get rid of it," the old woman continued. "Burn it after my sister passed away. But your grandmother, ever the art enthusiast, insisted on keeping it instead. I don't know why. It's a horribly dreadful piece."

"And now, what's worse, my daughter wants it back in our home. Please, I beg of you. Burn it. Burn it right to ashes. Destroy that accursed thing."

Right at that moment, the old woman's daughter walked into the room.

"Mother! What is wrong with you? We have almost nothing to remember Aunt Marnie by, and when something she made with her own hands finally resurfaces in our life, you say to burn it?!"

"It's a bad painting Sarah. It's dark, and it's angry, and it holds all the ugliness of the disease that took your aunt from us."

"No! It's not! Evelyn here said that her grandmother restored it! It's beautiful now, and I want to display it in our home to honor Aunt Marnie. You're my mother, and I love you, but this is my home, and I want the painting. That's final."

By this point, the atmosphere in the home had gotten quite awkward, so I readily thanked them for the tea, and made my way back home. My newfound knowledge about the piece made me even less eager to keep it in my bedroom.

Without realizing it, I had spent far more time visiting the old woman than I had expected. Between that and the sizable drive back home, I found night to have already fallen by the time I finally arrived on my front porch. The house was empty and quiet, and confirmed my decision to sleep in the guest room that night.

Edward would be back the next day. Silly as I felt, just one night in the guest room wouldn't kill me. I snuggled down with a good book, and read until I felt my eyes growing heavy. It had been a while since I had felt this at ease. I was quite happy to have made the decision to sleep away from the dreadful painting.

Within moments, I found myself drifting off to a peaceful sleep. However, this did not last. What I assumed to be several hours later, I awoke to the sound of a slamming door. I jolted awake, my heart racing. I was home alone, and feared a burglar.

I immediately began scoping the room for something I could use as a weapon. Thinking quickly, I pulled down the pole that was holding up the curtain, and wielded it like a staff.

Slowly, I crept through the doorway, keeping as silent as possible. The only thing I could hear was the sound of my own heart rapidly beating in my ears. Strangely, nothing in the house was amiss. I stood in the hallway pondering a moment before deciding which direction to move in.

My first instinct was to reach for the light switch, but if there was an intruder, hitting the light would immediately give away my position. So I decided to navigate in the dark. I knew my own home better than a thief would, so if I moved quietly, I'd have the element of surprise on my side.

Just then I had to muffle a scream as the door to my bedroom at the end of the hall slammed shut. Then the sound of weeping filled the home. It was sad, and distant, but it was definitely coming from my room.

Acting on instinct instead of logic, I hit the light switch in the hall, and went to investigate. Slowly, and as quietly as I could, I cracked open the door. The light from the hallway spilled into the dark room, and immediately the weeping stopped.

I held my breath for a moment, not sure of what would happen next. That's when my eyes fell upon the painting.

The sheet lay crumpled beneath it. I know it was covered the last time I had seen it, yet there it was, strewn across the floor.

Shaking, I pushed the door open further, allowing more light to spill into the room. The oil painting on the far end of the room illuminated, hungrily refracting the beam of light that now shone across it.

The last flecks of flesh-colored paint my grandmother had painstakingly applied to the topcoat had crumbled away, once more revealing the horrifying visage I remember from my childhood.

I froze for a moment, overwhelmed by the same disgust that had captured me all those years ago the first time I laid eyes on the piece. That sickly yellow skin, those long black nails, the inexplicable wind that defied natural law. It all looked so terrifyingly real in the faint light.

Those deep oozing craters . . . Wait. Oozing? Oh my God. There's no way. The craters in her face were actually oozing that horrible rusty material. It was impossible, but those deep, dark crevices were literally dripping with the stuff. I could see it seep out of the canvas and hear the splatters on the hardwood floors below.

I knew I should run, but my feet seemed glued in place. I tried to calm my heavy, raspy breaths; however, I soon realized that they weren't mine . . . I held my breath for a moment, and the scratchy exhalations continued. I focused my gaze on the abomination on the wall, and released a silent scream.

The painting was moving. The woman's bony, misshapen chest was jaggedly rising and falling in sync with the heavy breathing that now filled the room. My eyes widened in terror as my worst fear came to light. The painting slowly began to lurch. The shape of a crater-filled head began to push through the canvas as if it were merely a sheet of spandex.

As the wretched figure began to force its way through, I finally regained my senses. I slammed the door shut and began running down the hall. I had only made it a few feet before I heard an enormous thud. The canvas had fallen off the wall. And at that precise moment, the wailing resumed—this time so loud that I physically had to cover my ears.

Right as I rounded the corner, I shrieked in fear as I was immerged in total blackness. I tried desperately to orient myself, but my night vision had only just started to develop. In a panic, I continued forward with my hands outstretched, hoping to find the banister that led downstairs.

A jolt of terror ran up my spine when I heard the creak of a door opening, followed by the sound of something heavy thumping, then dragging down the hall. The weeping had turned into wild shrieks, and were so loud they were disorienting. I nearly fell down the stairs when my hands finally grasped the banister.

As quickly as I could, I began racing down the stairs. The thumping and dragging sounded closer now. It was moving far faster than I expected. When I got to the bottom of the staircase, I felt for the side table on the right and threw it to the ground, hoping to slow it down.

Something was off now, though. The shrieking had stopped. It was silent. No thumping, no dragging. Just silent. For some reason this scared me even more. So I ran as quickly as I could, despite the dark, straight for the front door.

Right as I was mere feet from grasping the handle, I felt my legs give out from underneath me. Something bony and cold had wrapped itself around my ankle. I fought wildly to break free as the sound of heavy breathing filled the room loudly again. I saw the form of something large and dark approaching me, and I swung wildly with my hands.

I felt them dig into something cold and moist. In disgust, I used all my might to push it back, and to break through the front door, slamming it shut behind me.

I didn't stop running until the sun had begun to rise. When I finally stopped, I collapsed on the ground, panting heavily. I raised my hand to wipe my brow, but stopped. I had been so focused on fleeing up until now that I hadn't taken a moment to look at my hand. It was covered in a dark, rusty material, and tangled in several strands of long, black hair.

• • •

When Edward returned, he found the home to have been targeted by burglars. The place was trashed, but it was rather odd. Only one thing in the entire home had been stolen. He noticed that the large, lovely painting my grandmother had restored was nowhere to be found.

The police came by, and told me I was lucky to have escaped. I just nodded and kept quiet. After all, a burglary was the only logical explanation, right? This was a fairly textbook case, you see. A large Victorian home full of valuable paintings makes a tempting target for thieves.

There was, however, one detail about the case that seemed to have everyone baffled. All throughout the home there were trails of a dark, rusty fluid. Lab reports later confirmed it to be a strange combination of paint and old, rotten blood.

I'm not much a fan of paintings anymore. Edward and I sold the gallery and are using the money to plan our wedding, and we're currently looking for a new home. I told him that I have trouble sleeping here because I have nightmares about the break-in, but the truth is, we never did find the painting.

And some nights, I'll lie in bed, moments away from drifting off, and I'll swear I hear the sound of distant, raspy breaths.

IF ONLY THEY WERE CANNIBALS

Jaime Townsend

Take everything you think you know about zombies . . . and forget it. They aren't the flesh-tearing, meat-masticating, human-consuming, brain-seeking idiots we all see in movies. Nooooo . . . But, the movies got some things right. They are the shambling, rotting, gray-skinned horrors we all know and love. But, here's what you DON'T know about zombies . . .

The males? Well, they're hornier than a three-peckered billy goat. And, they will mount anything moving—thus spreading the disease. The females? Aside from the rotting flesh, slower reflexes, and inability to form words, they're pretty much the same, if not dumber than a sack of stones. It took a while to see the pattern, considering I've been hiding in my fourth-floor apartment, peeking like a coward from the window of my dining room to the street below. Now, I know you're wondering: how did it happen? How did it start? Well, from what the tired old sack of bones on the television tells us, it was a mutated form of rabies. Rat bites man, man's DNA adheres to the introduced toxin, DNA conforms, and thus . . . horny zombies. I'm no doctor, nor am I a scientist, so take it or leave it. The big issue is, while they don't eat other people, they do eat everything else, and they are insatiable. Grocery stores were wiped clean within a few days. And for people like me, holed up and completely unprepared, this in a word . . . sucks.

I've waited here for weeks now, watching and hoping they have moved on. Hoping I can find a way out and maybe get supplies. But, so far, no such luck. For weeks now, women have been raped, precious sources of food have been emptied, and I don't dare leave this place. There have been no signs of military, and the only police I've seen were down the alleyway, ravishing a screaming blonde that I barely recognized as my downstairs neighbor. She's one of them now. There hasn't been even the slightest hint of help . . . of any kind. Indeed, I fear we have been abandoned to our fate. Even the squawking man on the TV has gone, leaving an irritating buzz from a black-and-white screen adorned by an antenna and the words "Be back soon."

How original.

Now, I'm not a leggy supermodel that looks like a twelve-year-old boy, so I'm not readily equipped to fight zombies. I'm just a regular lady with a regular life. Until this happened, that is. Now I'm a hungry lady, with a very strange life, and even my cat has been shooting accusing looks at me. With no food, and no escape that wouldn't leave me a brainless bimbo, I'm stuck. Even Angel will have to deal with it until I come up with a plan. But, for now, I'm freezing, and I want to go to bed. No matter how mad she is at me, Angel will follow, and all will be well. At least for tonight.

It snowed last night. When I woke up this morning and looked out my window . . . They were still as statues. They stood in the snow, unmoving. Frozen, forgive the pun. What was happening? It was fucking creepy! Just yesterday they were bumbling about, doing what zombies do . . . Well, at least these zombies.

Yesterday . . . What happened? I thought for a long moment. The snow . . . I whispered to myself. For what reason, I didn't care, but the snow had halted them. None of them moved. They just stood there . . .

"Well, Angel . . . This might be the chance I need . . ." I said to the cat on my sofa.

The cat let out a quick "Maw" and continued to wash herself.

"What do you think? Should I go for it?"

The cat stopped washing and looked at me through baby blue eyes for a moment. "Maw," she sounded as she stared intently.

I sighed, scrunching my eyebrows and hugging myself as I peeked outside once more, just to be sure. I nodded . . . "Yeah." Was all I said. I stood there for what seemed like ages but had to be only a moment, watching each unique snowflake fall to the earth below.

The hallway was clear. No signs of anyone . . . or anything, I thought gratefully. I wondered if the elevator at the end of the hall still worked as I darted toward it. I pushed the down button, and with a reassuring ding I heard it rising. I looked behind me . . . Had anything heard? So far so good. I bolted inside as soon as the doors opened and hit the lobby button, willing the doors to close silently. When I reached my destination and the doors glided open, I stifled a scream, slamming my hands against my mouth. The lobby was packed full of zombies. All as still as the ones outside. My wide eyes began to sting as I realized I hadn't blinked, nor had I taken a breath, for what seemed like ages as I stared at the faces frozen in the lobby. Did I dare step out of the elevator? Would they suddenly spring back to life and maul me? Terrified, I realized I had no choice. I needed to eat . . . Angel needed to eat. I took a step forward. No movement. Another step, safe.

I wove my way through the mass of what used to be people, trying to reach the open doors ahead of me leading outside. There was a grocery store just across the street . . . I only had to make it that far. One of them right in front of me jerked and sniffed the air loudly. But that was all he did. I stared at him a moment before quietly stepping out the door. I realized with chagrin that I had so many more to get past before I could even begin to breathe easy. It was like a maze. A great puzzle to piece together. But, my objective was clear. If I could make it through the lobby, I could do this.

Tiptoe . . . Small steps . . . I was getting through. Slowly but surely, I was getting through. The zombies stayed in their frozen state as I made my way through the hoard of them, unsure and full of dread. I slipped, and bumped into one, fear rising to a lump in my throat, nearly choking me. It swayed and gave out a raspy groan, drooling on my hand . . . But it didn't move. I wiped my hand on the leg of my jeans and looked back to my apartment window. Angel sat on the sill, staring down at me. Her tail twitching. *I know, baby*, I thought. Three more . . . Then two . . . Then the curb. I rushed through the doors to the grocery store and slammed them shut behind me.

The place was in shambles. All that was left were unopened cans strewn about the floor. I took bags from the register and began filling them as full as I could, as many as I could carry. Stew, chili, soups, vegetables, fruit . . . Anything and everything I could get my hands on. And, oh yes . . . cat food. Lots of it. The store was completely ransacked. There was no meat, bread, cereal . . . Nothing. I guess they aren't smart enough to use a can opener . . . Thank God. There were smears of blood on the floor all over. Different scenarios played through my mind as I thought of what poor fool it belonged to. I closed my eyes and pushed the thought aside. Time to go home.

The snow still fell, heavier now, as I stepped back out and weaved my way back through the zombies. Quicker now, as I knew they wouldn't pursue me. I made it back to my apartment, and slammed the door shut, locking it behind me. And, there was Angel, licking her chops, waiting for me to give up the goods. I fed her first.

Once both our bellies were full, we laid down on the couch for a nap. It seemed like I had slept for only minutes when I woke to a strange noise. I sat up. Suddenly I was full of a sense of indescribable dread boiling like a black hole in my chest. I stood and went to the window. It wasn't snowing anymore . . . And the street was clear. No zombies. The noise, again. What was it? I swallowed hard and felt my eyes grow wide enough to bulge . . . as I heard the familiar ding of the elevator . . .

TUNNEL 72F

Michael Whitehouse

I once knew a man who was afraid of nothing. No monstrosity man-made or fictitious could subdue his spirits, and the mere mention of the word "supernatural" would elicit a most cynical example of laughter. This bravery was both his greatest strength and his most profound weakness, for ignorance and heedlessness can often be disguised as a deep and foolhardy sense of courage. He was to learn the limits of his bravery under the earth, down in those oppressive tunnels, deep below the streets of Amsterdam.

His name was Henke, due mainly to his Finnish ancestry on his father's side, and although his parents had passed away at an early age, he believed with conviction that his courage came from them. It was a matter of pride, a connection to the family he had lost, and it was this above all else that drove him into places and situations where others would fear to tread.

I had met him four years earlier while travelling with some friends on a common rite of passage: backpacking through Europe during a university break. He and a few of his friends were on a similar adventure and happened to be staying at the same youth hostel in Rome. Both groups got on well, but it was with Henke that I struck up an immediate rapport. He was a keen musician, and I was, at the time, still filled with the self-promise, or should I say delusion, of stardom through my own musical pursuits.

Our friendship grew over the subsequent years, mostly via e-mail—swapping musical discoveries, talking about politics, and generally getting to know each other as best as two people can through simple correspondence. Travelling was also a must for both of us due to work commitments. On the odd occasion we would find ourselves in the same country and enjoyed meeting up for a few laughs—and of course he always knew which local pubs served the tastiest beer, as well as which restaurants were best to avoid.

It was eleven months ago that I visited Henke in Amsterdam. The Dutch city seemed to be a good fit for him as he always liked to live in the liveliest of places. The countless meandering canals, bridges, and walkways swamped by the footsteps of a million tourists each year appealed to his love of vibrancy and history. Amsterdam had seen many a traumatic occurrence since its inception right up to and including the Second World War. At the time he had been recently hired to carry out important maintenance work on the Rijksmuseum, one of Amsterdam's most impressive buildings.

When I met him in a small, darkened corner of a local pub, well away from the burgeoning tourist trade, I was shocked at first by his appearance. Here was a friend I had grown to know as being larger than life, exuding bravado, and yet I was presented with a shell of a man, slight in stature and racked with self-doubt. He proceeded to impart to me the circumstances that resulted in his precarious condition, which I will relay to you now.

Henke had been working as a civil engineer for some time, and so relished the challenge of renovating and maintaining the Rijksmuseum—a building with a long and compelling history. The museum housed Amsterdam's finest collection of historical relics, and being given access to some of its more hidden places, which were inaccessible to the general public, piqued Henke's fascination for the obscure and unique.

He had been hired to lead a maintenance crew that had been assigned to assess and repair the building's foundations. This oldest part of the structure dated back centuries and had a most bizarre and, it must be said, horrific history. The Rijksmuseum itself had been constructed in 1885, but what it had been built upon possessed a much older and unusual past. I knew immediately that this would appeal to Henke, as he often spoke of the fond memories he had as a child exploring vacant buildings, passageways, and caves near where he grew up, leading his friends into places they would otherwise have avoided. The dark held no fear for him, nothing but the promise of hidden secrets and the opportunity to show his bravery to those around him.

In the bowels of the museum, under its marble floors and deep red brickwork, lay a labyrinth of abandoned tunnels that at one time served as part of the old city's sewer network. They had long been disused and fallen into disrepair, but they were nonetheless an essential part of the building's foundations and had to be assessed and repaired, otherwise the entire structure would be in danger of subsiding. The ground and upper levels of the museum were beautiful and displayed many wonderful historical relics from all over the world. On his first day of work, Henke wandered around the artifacts before starting his shift, especially interested in the war exhibition. Gas masks, uniforms, bullets, dog tags of soldiers bloodied and forgotten populated the sealed glass display cabinets. A group of children ran after their mother, laughing and pointing at the weapons on show, imitating the sounds of explosions and gunfire. Families moved en masse from hall to hall, room to room, some talking about the violent history on display, others involved in more important conversations such as which dinosaur toy to get from the gift shop. So bright, welcoming, and warm was the atmosphere of the building that it was difficult to imagine the darkness that festered below.

After some quick words with the building manager, Henke proceeded to an old, seldom-used room at the back of the museum that housed an antiquated, creaking, rusted, and cagelike elevator that was being used to access the lower levels and sewers underneath. Pulling on a pair of dirt-covered yellow overalls, complete with hardhat and headlamp, he entered the elevator for his first descent. On his trip downward toward the abandoned sewers, he thought to himself that those of a nervous disposition might have let such a dank and isolated place prey on their minds. This may have explained why the previous man in charge of the repairs had left so abruptly, citing nervous exhaustion and refusing to so much as set foot in those pitch-black corridors of cold stone ever again.

The elevator winch and engine stuttered as they lowered Henke down four levels into the basement. With each passing floor he observed a slight dimming of the lights, and each subterranean level appeared more sparse and stonelike than the one before. A rusted plate attached to the elevator betrayed its age. It struck Henke that the year of its construction, 1932, must have been amongst the last periods of maintenance carried out there before the persecution of the Jewish people by the invading German army. He knew much of the shameful history of the region, as he was part Jewish and his great-grandfather had died during the Holocaust. Many had fled to Amsterdam for sanctuary from the Nazi regime in the early 1930s, but the long blighting arm of Hitler's horrific "final solution" eventually reached the borders of Holland, sweeping many thousands away to those shameful and barbaric concentration camps.

With a shudder the elevator ground to a halt, and after forcing the grated sliding door aside, Henke disembarked. The old sewer tunnels spread out before him and were curious in construction, steeped in a history that stretched back much further into the distant past than that of the museum itself. Having spoken to his employers, he had been specifically told to pay heed to the assessment and repair crew's knowledge of the tunnel layout, as the place could be disorientating. The lighting system required to illuminate the maintenance work had not been fully installed yet. His bosses, up above in cushy office buildings miles away, seemed unusually concerned that he would find it all too easy to get lost down there.

Most importantly, he was informed that the two-way radios normally used to communicate between team members had been playing up, and that they were unreliable due to interference, probably produced by nearby metallic deposits in the ground. This meant that all communication would have to be carried out verbally, or by using the light from their torches to convey simple messages via Morse code; this was particularly useful in the longer tunnels. In any case, it struck Henke that the catacombs below really were isolated, lonely places. Care would have to be taken, but he did feel a nostalgic sense of excitement for a hidden world begging to be explored, remembering all those days spent looking for adventure as a child.

After a time, Jones, second in command of the maintenance crew, appeared from around a corner, whistling to himself while his headlight bobbed and weaved to the sound of feet through inches of stagnant water. A substantially stout fellow, rather humorous in nature, he debriefed Henke on the current progress being made, informing him that the initial mapping and assessments of the tunnels had gone well. All in all there were sixteen four-man crews, each of which were assigned a section of the sewers to repair. Henke would oversee the entire operation, but he knew that he would need to directly supervise two of the crews working in one of the more isolated tunnels. The walls there were in a precarious condition, and there was even the suggestion that a cave-in could occur. It was his priority to make sure that did not happen.

After walking for fifteen minutes he arrived at the area that would be his workplace for the next few months. The sound of occasional drilling could be heard in the distance as the workers continued to install the still non-operational lighting system. As Henke's men would be working farther away from the other crews, it seemed logical—although not desirable—that they would have their lighting installed last.

Each passageway seemed oddly shaped with no two tunnels being quite alike; that entire section of the sewer was in fact so antiquated that it had been built long before the careful planning of such constructions had become commonplace. One tunnel would arch forward for over several hundred meters in a strange semicircle, while others bisected it at right angles, carrying on in a regimented straight line into the darkness. Henke even found a passageway that seemed to dip and rise only to slither its way along in an unnatural S-shape. Some tunnels seemed to go on forever; others stopped abruptly as if the original builders had been unable to complete their work, leaving in a hurry. Jones tried to keep the conversation light, and with his experience of walking through the tunnels for the past two months, Henke was glad to have a guide to show him the way.

Waiting in a large alcove was the four-man team assigned to that area. They would work that section of the tunnels during the day, while the other shift would take over later, working through the night. Jones introduced each of them. They seemed nice enough, but Henke was surprised to find the men largely in the grip of silence. In such jobs humor was normally found in abundance, with repair crews using it to slice through the monotony of working in such cramped and repetitive conditions. Here, though, he found them uttering not one word, sitting in silence in that imposing alcove, removed from any consideration of camaraderie or fellowship; the only inference that they were not a collection of subterranean statues was the occasional movement of their headlamps altering the shadows around them. They seemed wholly disconnected from not just each other, but the very environment in which they worked.

Henke brushed this feeling of unease aside and committed himself to cultivating conversation. If these men were in some way angry or uncomfortable with one another then he would soon lay that to rest; a happy workforce is a productive one. The first order of business was to survey that section of tunnels and decide where repairs were the most pressing. Preliminary assessments had already been made, but Henke liked to evaluate any repair project he was involved in from the ground up. He walked the catacombs with his team and noticed immediately that they were still on edge, that they seemed frightened in an almost childlike way. No amount of questions casual or otherwise could elicit anything other than one-word broken replies. Slowly they toured the winding grid of tunnels, lighting their way with the small torches attached to their safety helmets while taking notes about failing walls, water damage, and estimations of any possible repair time.

Twice Henke pressed the men on their obvious sense of fear, asking why such an experienced crew, who no doubt had worked in many tunnels before, were so apprehensive of mere bricks and mortar. They avoided the questions, looking nervously at one another, changing the topic of conversation with monotoned lethargy whenever it veered toward their experiences of the old sewers—or of their previous supervisor's unceremonious departure from the job. It began to dawn on Henke that the men's verbal and physical awkwardness was not the result of tensions between workers, but rather of a deep-seated and worrying apprehension; of what, he did not know. What was clear was that his team seemed to be counting down the minutes until their shift ended, when they could finally clamber out of the darkness into the safety of the world above.

As the beam from his headlamp trickled over the damp and crumbling brickwork, Henke again conceded to himself that some may find such a setting unnerving; but not him. Whatever had caused such trepidation and disquiet amongst the other men was surely a simple case of idle superstition, mischief making, or the quite understandable psychological toll of working in a dark, cramped, and forgotten part of the world. Even Jones, who had through most of the catacombs been jovial and talkative, now adopted the same sullen expression and serious disposition as they made their way deeper into the oldest part of the sewers.

The passages wound and meandered their way through the ground, long steady trajectories intermittently and abruptly interrupted by sharp blind corners, making it difficult for Henke to identify exactly where they were. There were so many winding corridors that he felt slightly disorientated, and was ready to joke with his men that if they didn't like him as a boss they could probably leave him there and he would never find his way out. But his men were no longer beside him. He was standing at the mouth of a tunnel, and while he had continued onward, talking, trying to fill in the difficult silences, his men had stopped at the last junction. They stood motionless some 20 feet behind, staring at Henke with blank expressions, occasionally betrayed by the slightest flicker of a very real and gripping emotion beneath: a look of suppressed terror.

When he asked why the men were not following, they whispered in reply that where they stood was where the last of the repair work was needed. Pulling out a map and perusing it intently by the light of his headlamp, Henke surmised that he must have wandered into the remotest part of the sewer network, at the back of the catacombs, and while the tunnels continued into the foreboding distance, that must have marked the boundary of the Rijksmuseum's foundations. What confused him was that the area had been clearly listed on the map for repair.

He was standing at the entrance to what appeared to be a rather innocuous tunnel, but on the wall next to the opening he could see that someone had placed an identification plaque there, marking it for repair. It read "Tunnel 72F: Water damage & failing masonry." After double-checking the map, it was clear to Henke that tunnel 72F was indeed still under the Rijksmuseum foundations and had to be appraised and repaired, but when he told his men this they simply informed him that where they stood was as far as they would go.

Anger began to take over, accompanied by frustration that the team he was supposed to be supervising was being so difficult, but even raising his voice and demanding that they head into the tunnel did not move them. Just as things became increasingly heated and Henke yelled at the men to do as he said, Jones interjected: "We've worked down here for two months, boss. This is a good, hard-working, talented crew you have. They'll do exactly as you ask, when you ask it, but you'll have to accept that, for them, and me, our work stops at this junction, and that none of us will go near that tunnel. You might think it's mad, but whether you want to believe it or not, there is something in there."

Taking a deep breath and calming himself, Henke explained to his men that he understood the stress induced by working in such a suffocating environment for an extended period of time, but that repairs had to be carried out, in full. He would talk to them later about it, but for now he would carry out the survey himself.

For a moment there was silence, broken only by drips of unseen water that echoed out from a distant, unsure place. As he stepped over the threshold and into the apparently forbidden tunnel, Jones and the other men protested vehemently, shouting at Henke to leave the passageway immediately, but he saw this demonstration as nothing but foolishness. He was not to be swayed by unsubstantiated, superstitious nonsense. There was nothing in that tunnel to fear, and once more he would prove to others that they should not be so scared, by stepping up, being a man, and pushing forward into places others feared to tread. Pride coursed through his veins. His parents were brave and fearless before him, and he had long since sworn to always be bold, always be adventurous—to be just like them. With a smile, he looked back at his men before heading face-first into the darkness, the excitement of self-reliance pushing him on.

While the tunnel seemed fairly common in its construction at first glance, as he progressed deeper into its dank innards, it was apparent that this was unlike any sewer he had seen before. The ground was uneven; the floor dipped and rose much like some of the other tunnels, but what was peculiar was how fractured the surface felt under his feet. The ground was obscured by a thick, almost oily water that in places reached up as high as his knees. He trudged through the stagnant liquid slowly, not because he was scared, but simply to ensure sound footing. One thing was apparent: however long ago the water had deposited there, it was long enough to fester and produce an unpleasant, rotting stench.

The walls were of a different, significantly older composition than most of the brickwork he had seen in the sewers elsewhere. Whatever the material was that had been used, it was hundreds of years old and was obviously failing, with long penetrating cracks scarring the surface of the increasingly unstable walls and ceiling. The light from his headlamp was enough to illuminate much of the tunnel, but as Henke ventured further toward what he thought was a dead end, he realized that the passageway was narrowing and that the tunnel itself did not stop there, but rather tapered slightly before curving abruptly around a blind corner.

He estimated to being over 100 feet into the sewer, and while his curiosity for what could be beyond that corner urged him to move forward, he believed he had made his point, and would now ask his men to abandon their fears and enter the tunnel with him. Unholstering from his side the black handheld radio he had been issued, he began requesting for Jones and the others to meet him at the corner of the tunnel. No one responded, and nothing but a quiet buzz could be heard from the radio speaker. Of course Henke now remembered that he had been warned about how unreliable the radios could be, but just as he was about to turn and shout back down toward the opening, something caught his eye.

Surely not.

There was nothing in that disgusting place but stagnant water and himself. Yet pulling and pushing relentlessly against his bravado and self-assured disposition was the creeping realization that something was standing at the end of the tunnel. Obscured by the turn, he could only see a sliver of it, but it was unmistakable. A ragged piece of cloth poked out from around the corner, and although Henke's mind was unwilling to accept it, the cloth was obviously part of a sleeve, a sleeve that contained an arm, belonging to whom or what he did not know.

Stubbornness can be an effective tonic for even the most horrifying and unbelievable of situations. Henke's confidence in himself, and his long history of triumphs over fear and adversity, welled up inside of him. Filling his chest with pride, and with a strong assured stride, he gulped down a breath of the dank air and marched purposefully toward whatever was around that corner.

The slush and slosh of the black water echoed throughout the tunnel as he made his way to the blind turn, almost hesitating as he reached it—an unease that was alien to him. Apprehension now turned to sadness and empathy, for standing there in that cruel dark passageway, shivering and disheveled, was a girl who could not have been more than thirteen years old. Her face and hands were blackened with grime and dirt, hiding her pale and malnourished frame. A ripped shirt was all that she wore, hanging from her loosely, with much of her body exposed to the cold of that damp, isolated place.

While she gazed at him between strands of dirty-blond matted hair, Henke was struck by how beautiful the young girl was, and how afraid she must have been. How frightened and helpless. At first he believed that somehow she must have entered the sewers and lost her way, but no matter how softly he spoke, she would not answer, appearing afraid and nervous. He tried his radio again, but was greeted with the same meaningless static. Regardless, he had to get her out of that tunnel, back through the sewers and into the Rijksmuseum and seen by a doctor. He did not want to shout to his men in case the noise startled her or added to her disquiet—the last thing he wanted to do was chase her through the catacombs—so he decided to lead her out of the passage himself. As he approached, he spoke gently to her in Dutch, explaining that he would take her up above to safety. Seeing him step forward with his hand outstretched, the girl seemed to quiver in fear; she appeared terrified of him. This made Henke feel uncomfortable, as he prided himself on being someone who would do anything to protect the vulnerable, someone to be trusted, not feared.

She made no sound, but as he reached her she raised her left hand slowly, pointing one finger at the light on his head. He suddenly realized that the headlamp must have been frightening her somehow, so he merely took the light off and held it in his hand to allay her fears, the torch now casting shadows upward more starkly. The changed angle of light brought something unsettling to Henke's attention. Pinned to the girl's torn shirt was a yellow cloth star. It surprised him as it was entirely familiar, but it took a moment for his mind to grasp the memory; it was exactly like the yellow stars forced upon the Jewish populations during their persecution, to allow non-Jews and members of the Nazi regime to identify them.

Henke's mind fought against the ramifications of such a discovery. After a momentary pause, he once again was resolute, disregarding the cloth star and asserting to himself that he had to take the poor girl out of such horrible surroundings. A tremendous sense of sadness overcame him as he drew closer. The torch flickered unusually in his hand as he looked down at the girl, her face momentarily illuminated by the shifting light, her arm still outstretched pointing at him. He'd carry her out of the sewers if need be. But this sense of duty, this compulsion to be brave and assertive in even the darkest of places, was now replaced with something that Henke had never felt before. Running up his spine and from the very pit of his stomach fear gripped him, terror took him, and a horror possessed him so potently that it made him unsteady, anxious, and weak. For Henke had not noticed something so subtle, yet essential to his predicament. The girl had not stopped pointing at him as he drew closer. Her arm was raised and her finger remained outstretched; even the light, which was now in his hand, seemed entirely unimportant to her. Realization swept over him like a plague of abject dread. The girl was not pointing at the light, she was pointing behind him.

Henke did not remember much more of what happened in that tunnel, but he knew that he had indeed turned to face whatever had been standing behind him. He thanked God (something he was not normally inclined to do) that Jones and those men who feared that dark hollow so acutely had dispensed with their fear out of empathy and ran into the passageway as soon as they heard his screams.

Henke regained his composure back at the alcove where he had met the men, but he immediately pleaded with them that they take him back out of the tunnels, which is what they did. Once returned to the elevator room of the Rijksmuseum, they sat together and had a frank discussion about what had been happening down there over the past few months. Jones explained that the first survey team that had encountered that specific sewer passageway resigned from their posts after just one night down there. A week later one of their coworkers who decided to stay on committed suicide after complaining repeatedly to everyone that he could hear whispers coming from inside there while he worked nearby. Not long after that, Jones's previous supervisor had seen someone, an unidentified figure, standing at the mouth of tunnel 72F, and had followed them inside. One of the cleanup crews found him crawling out of the sewer on his hands and knees, crying hysterically like a child. He had been hospitalized and heavily medicated ever since; no one knew exactly what he had seen down there, he would not speak of it, but the men who recovered him claimed he was repeating only one word when he was found—just one word, over and over again, frantically:

"Nazi."

Henke was a nervous wreck after his experience and ordered that no one, under any circumstance, be allowed to go into tunnel 72F. He continued to work down in the other sewer passageways, day after day in the dark, but he was consumed by the notion that he had seen something so frightening, so terrifying, that he had forced himself to forget the ordeal. Over the next few weeks he lost weight and had trouble sleeping, often waking up in a disturbed state, drenched in a cold sweat, unable to recall what he had been dreaming about.

The very idea that he of all people, brave Henke, could be reduced to such fragility, that he could be affected so deeply by something he could not even remember in its entirety, preyed upon his pride and his sense of self-worth. In an effort to combat the feelings of helplessness and self-loathing, he attempted to find out all he could about the tunnels under the Rijksmuseum. Knowledge, as they say, is power, and my friend felt that if he knew more about that place in the dark, he would somehow be less afraid of it. He read about the history of the museum on the nights he could not sleep, and while he found very little of it helpful, one local legend struck a chord within him.

It was rumored that during the Second World War a number of Jewish families took refuge in the tunnels below the Rijksmuseum. When two SS officers were tipped off as to their whereabouts, they entered the tunnels with some local volunteers hoping to arrest the people down there, and then most probably send them off to a concentration camp. The rumors were that the families managed to ambush the SS officers and their Nazi sympathizers, killing them and dumping the bodies somewhere in the sewers.

This was the story Henke related to me when I met him in Amsterdam. It was sad to see him—a strong powerful individual who had never shown so much as a hint of fear for, or of, anything in his life—so shaken and vulnerable. A friend whom I respected greatly, one with such indelible character, reduced to a diminished man living on his nerves.

Unfortunately the story does not end there; some men are haunted both by what they have seen and by what they cannot understand. Ego can be a terrible burden on anyone. Once it is fractured or damaged, the lasting effects can be devastating. Henke could not let go of his pride, nor his desire to feel strong again, whole. He had never been afraid of anything before and no matter what was in that tunnel, no matter how much I attempted to dissuade him, he was determined to confront it and reclaim his self-belief.

Three days later Henke's body was found at the mouth of tunnel 72F, stuffed into an old duffel bag. It was a heart attack that had killed him, but whoever broke, twisted, and shoved his body into that morbid sack after he died was never caught. I should mention that the bag was of particular interest to the police in the event that it could reveal something about Henke's death. It was traced to Germany, army issue to be precise, and hadn't been manufactured since 1941.

BATS IN WINTER

Isaac Boissonneau

It was a cold, windy winter evening in December when the phone on Officer Jonathan Erskine's desk started to ring.

Erskine, who had been awaiting the call with the kind of quiet worry that was normally felt during long hours in a hospital waiting room, jumped at the sound and snatched the phone from its cradle with trembling hands.

"John, it's me, there's been another one. It's . . . it's bad, John, it's real bad," said the man at the other end of the phone, his voice fizzling out intermittently as the harsh winds shook the cables of the telephone poles across the county.

Erskine sighed miserably as he opened his desk drawer to retrieve pen and paper. The illness, a malady of the blood which most of the nondelusional public had dubbed "NS1847," had finally arrived at his doorstep with the fury of the gale, bringing with it a rising tide of murder and violence.

How many does this make, now? he wondered as he jotted down the address. Of course, he knew how many, he had memorized every blank-eyed stare, every tattered wound, every single flake of ash that danced in the wind. Their cumulative effect would never leave him, ever.

"This makes twenty-one, John," said the voice, as if to answer his musings. "When are these kids gonna learn?"

"Never, Ellis," said Erskine, his voice soft. "They keep reading those damned books and seeing all of those stupid ass videos online. When did we start glorifying viruses? You don't see people with AIDS posting videos of them showing off their symptoms."

"Well," said Ellis in a faintly bemused tone, "to be fair, AIDS can't make you strong enough to rip the head off a fellow human, or let you see in the dark, or make you faster than most sports cars . . ."

Or let you live forever. Ellis didn't need to say that last bit aloud. Erskine could hear it hanging heavily in the silence that followed. He was glad that his partner hadn't said that; he didn't know how he'd react if he heard those words spoken with even a shred of longing or hope.

"Since when are you taking their side? I thought you of all people would be as opposed to this shit as I was."

Ellis coughed loudly, then responded, "I am, John. But you've gotta admit, on the outside it does look like a pretty good deal."

"Yeah, so did eating from the tree in the Garden of Eden," said Erskine, even as some wicked part of him whispered, *Is he talking from experience?*

Ellis coughed again, louder and longer, until Erskine could hear him struggling for air.

When the fit had, thankfully, abated, he asked, "Are you okay? Is it . . . ?"

He left the question unfinished, knowing the answer as another coughing fit filled the earpiece. He sounded worse than he ever had.

"'m fine," Ellis said after regaining his breath, "'s just a cold, John. Just like the last five times and just like the next five. I've been takin' my meds every day, I've been sleeping right, getting all my shots and keeping the hell away from meat, I'm fine."

Erskine didn't believe him; he knew that his longtime friend, a man whose moral fiber surpassed his own and who had always possessed the skills that made him the absolute definition of a great cop, was fighting a losing battle, but he didn't say anything; a man's got to have his pride, after all.

Ellis finished telling him the necessary information and ended the call. Erskine got to his feet, put on his coat with hands that seemed to tremble more every day, and left the comforting warmth of his office for the biting cold of the outside world, which had stopped making sense to him.

The house that he came to, after nearly half an hour of slow driving over ice-encrusted dirt roads, was average in every way: a two-story blue-painted building with a shingled roof and a large yard that overlooked the desolate highway.

Erskine noticed the first signs as he pulled into the icy driveway: the deep, heavy silence that hung like a cloud over the house, the stony faces of the other officers as they made their way in and out, carrying evidence bags filled with toys and blood-spattered shreds of clothing, and the overpowering, salty stink of spilled blood that tainted the air that wafted out of the house's shadowy innards.

He got out of his car and started up the driveway, passing under a snow-veiled pine tree from which he could hear the rustling of many leathery wings.

It IS like the others, he thought, stopping a second to gaze at the ice-shrouded branches, seeing several ruddy red eyes peering back at him from the dark. Erskine shivered and pulled his coat tighter about his bulky frame, wishing that he had brought more layers with him.

Of course, it wasn't the cold that made him shiver and it wasn't the bats in the tree. It was the overwhelming feeling of despair, like seeing a dark blotch on the MRI printout or watching an ambulance pull up at your neighbor's driveway.

The aging officer entered the house and found the CSIs gingerly lifting the blinds on the windows, allowing the sun's hazy glow to pierce the darkness.

"Seems like the family tried to help the poor kid," said a familiar voice from the entrance to the kitchen. Erskine turned and saw Ellis slouched against the doorframe, his pallid skin and red-rimmed eyes seeming to glow in the soft light. Erskine noted, with a pang of sadness, that he wore a black scarf around his neck, even though the air in the house was humid and heavy.

"What family wouldn't?" said Erskine with a sigh. "I almost wish they wouldn't, though. It'd spare us all this mess."

Ellis shot him a look and Erskine immediately realized his mistake.

"Sorry, Ellis," he muttered, rubbing the back of his neck as the shame forced his gaze away from those piercing eyes.

After a very long minute, Ellis sighed and said, "It's fine, John. I'm gettin' used to it, 's not like I have any choice in the matter."

Erskine let out a sigh of his own. He wished that he could say something to his friend, some words of comfort. This was the man who had defended him against bullies when they were in elementary school, back when he had been thin and sickly.

This was the man who had loaned him two thousand dollars when he and his wife found that they couldn't afford the care of their first baby.

This was the man who had entertained his children at all of the family get-togethers with his scary stories and impressions of their favorite cartoon characters.

Now he was sick, sick with a disease that had no known cure besides death. Ellis was wasting away from the same vile illness that had already claimed so many lives. Erskine had already begun seeing the symptoms of the advanced stages of the disease slowly corrupting his friend's features.

The lips, now devoid of color, and the gums swollen and liver colored.

The skin as white as the snow that fell outside.

The canines longer and broader. Erskine wondered how it must feel, having one's teeth sharpen and shift in your skull.

The only thing that hadn't yet been tainted by the disease were the eyes, and Erskine knew that, in a few years time, his hair would be as white as cotton, his nails would fall off to allow hooked talons to take their place, and those kind, compassionate brown eyes of his would be overtaken by that deep red that he'd seen peering back at him from dark basements and cellars more times than he could have imagined.

It made him want to cry, to scream at the heavens, to beg whatever deity came to mind to give his friend another chance, to save him from what was to come.

But it was useless and he knew it. Ellis would be entering into the final stages of his disease within a few years' time, and afterward, the man he had been would be dead, and something new and altogether unholy would have taken his place: a parasite that walked like a man.

Ellis led Erskine up the stairs, the thick carpeting muffling their footsteps, Ellis's more so than Erskine's.

The stink grew worse as they cleared the first landing and came to the last steps. It was hot, sour, and chemical-like. It was their smell.

They made their way past a CSI whose sweaty, wan face told them just how bad it was going to be. It took a great deal to faze someone in that line of work and Erskine wondered whether he himself was prepared for what was to come.

They came to the open door of the boy's room and stepped inside. Erskine saw the scene before him and knew that he wouldn't be eating for the rest of the day, and that he'd be reliving these first moments in sleep.

The boy hung from his neck like a butchered pig. Blood stained his T-shirt and the carpet below his bare feet, which were starting to blacken as he rotted.

The room was medium-sized, with a tiny bathroom near the door, a large bed that was thick with dust from disuse, a cobweb-shrouded nightstand with the shards of a broken lamp scattered across it, and a single, shuttered window that was stationed opposite the doorway.

In the tight space, the stink was almost overpowering to the point where Erskine had to clench his jaw and grit his teeth against the dry heaves that threatened to double him over. He gagged, then swallowed the acidic bile.

"Where . . ." he started to say after the nausea had passed, only to find that the stench had a taste.

After a brief struggle to keep his composure, Erskine turned to Ellis and asked, "Did you manage to find the place where he was sleeping?"

"Under there," said Ellis, pointing past the boy's corpse to an immaculately made twin-sized bed whose pristine sheets spilled out past the frame onto the floor.

Long covers to keep out the light, I bet those idiot parents of his bought it to help him. He thought with a grimace. They should've just called the CDC when they still had a chance.

He walked over, being careful not to touch the body, and crouched down, wincing at the audible popping of his joints. Knowing what he'd see, he pulled back the sheets and peered into the dusty darkness beneath the bed.

The odor rushed out to greet him, hot and clammy and far worse than he was used to. Obviously the boy had brought a few of his meals down there with him. Erskine let out a sound that was somewhere between a wheeze and a belch.

Ellis pulled him up and handed him a handkerchief. "You should've just gotten a mask from one of the techies."

Erskine shook his head. "I thought I could handle it," he said, his voice slightly muffled.

Ellis rolled his eyes, but said nothing, knowing full well that Erskine was clinging to his bravado in the face of the ghastly sight before them.

Slowly, carefully, Erskine returned to his crouching position, holding a hand to his round belly as if that alone could stop his breakfast from coming up if it so chose. He peered back into the darkness and saw several desiccated bodies piled off to the sides— mice, a few birds of some kind, and a large dog.

He got back to his feet with a sigh, "You said there was a note?" Ellis nodded, "It's in the bathroom."

Erskine noted the way the man's face tightened as he said this, the thin skin sliding over his protruding cheekbones and his colorless lips puckering with distaste, and he knew it would be unpleasant.

What's a little more horror to the pile? he thought as he walked into the bathroom.

The toilet lid was up, revealing a slurry of yellow bile, rust-colored blood mixed with a lighter shade of crimson and . . . and a small, masticated piece of meat that looked almost like . . .

Oh, God. Please don't tell me that's what I think it is.

He turned away and found himself staring at a sink full of blood that had already started to coagulate. There were several dozen small, sharp teeth floating within, their withered roots trailing behind them like the tails of tadpoles.

There was a note on the floor nearby, written in the hasty, ragged scrawl of someone in mortal terror. It was stained with blood.

I'm so, so, so, so sorry . . . I'm sorry, Mom. I'm sorry, Dad. I was just so hungry. I blacked out and, when I woke up, I had just
I'm sorry.
I just wanted to feel better.
I didn't mean for it to turn out this way.

Erskine sighed miserably and looked out the door at Ellis, who was looking more weary than he had ever seen him.

"I swear to God, Erskine. If I ever find the thing that started this whole mess, I'm gonna cut its head off myself," said the officer, his tone as hard and cold as the wind that now howled outside the house.

Erskine cracked a small, mirthless smile, which died as fast as it had appeared, before turning back to the body. "We should go tell the techies that we're done here."

Ellis nodded. The two of them knew that there was no need to investigate further, there never was with this kind of case.

They made their way out of the room and started for the stairs, but before they could get there, Erskine broke away and approached another room, one without a door.

It was a nursery. Its pastel walls were flecked with blood and scored by deep claw marks. Erskine knew that, when the house was scoured clean and put up for sale, this room would never be occupied, not ever. He could feel the weight of the massacre in the air, could hear the wails and mewling cries in every creak and groan of the wood panels beneath his feet.

This whole house should be knocked down and burned, he thought, trying to hold back the tears as he stared at the crushed toys, the trampled and torn picture books, and the crib with its safety bars lying scattered across the floor and crushed to splinters.

The tiny mattress was gone, as were its contents, but what remained told him all that he needed to know. Yet another small, safe, warm place, violated.

Erskine turned his back away from the sight. His fingers curled themselves inward into a tight fist, and the instant he was clear of the room, he raised the fist and slammed it into the wall hard enough to make a considerable dent.

The pain flared across his knuckles and he knew that his hand would be aching for a few days to come, but he had relieved some small part of the anger and disgust that had been building up in his stomach, and that, at least, was worth something to him.

He turned back and placed his fist in his pocket. Ellis stared at him sadly.

"Yeah, yeah, have the damage fee sent to me later," said Erskine, trying to keep his throbbing hand steady.

Ellis sighed. "I'm pretty sure this place is gonna need a complete overhaul after all is said and done. What's a little hole in all that? I'm sure it won't take much time for the contractors to patch it up."

Erskine smiled ruefully. "Yeah, those guys have been getting some damn good work out of all this."

"Same for the funeral homes and the Crime Disposal Units," added Ellis.

Erskine snorted and opened his mouth to speak, but he was interrupted by a loud thump from the boy's room.

The brief silence that followed was so absolute that Erskine could hear his own heart thudding against his ribs. He turned and looked at the open door, hoping to get a good view inside, but the angle of the room made it so that he couldn't see the body.

"Call the techies," he said, moving forward despite the cold fear that was coiling around his heart.

"John, don't," warned Ellis, his voice sounding strained.

Erskine paid him no heed; he kept walking, drawing closer and closer to the door and whatever lay beyond. He only paused to draw his gun and cock it.

He was already going through scenarios in his mind: he might find the boy still hanging, just as dead as he had been before, the clatter might have been from a gust of wind swinging the body. They had, after all, opened the door and let the air in.

Or that noose could be empty, thought Erskine, his shadow creeping ahead of him to merge with those in the room, and that boy could be waiting for me.

His hands shook as the thought settled into his mind, but he took a deep breath to calm his nerves and continued on anyway.

The boy met him at the doorway, his neck bent and crooked and bruised purple from the noose. His mouth, bloody and split wide, opened up, revealing the newly-regrown fangs that had pierced through his pale gums.

There was no humanity in the bulging, cherry-red eyes that stared out at him from swollen sockets, only a deep and primal hunger, a savage desire for blood and only blood.

Erskine, without a moment's pause, lifted the gun and fired. The bullets punched through the boy's chest, staggering him, but not knocking him down.

Of course, it was stupid to think that a few bits of lead would bring down one of Them, but Erskine needed to buy time until the techies arrived with their UV lights and the collapsible steel spikes that they had only recently adopted as part of their equipment.

The boy snarled and raised his bloodless hands, the skin at the tips splitting open as long, wickedly curved talons extended outward. With a snarl, the creature charged forward, frothing like a rabid animal.

No time, thought Erskine, his eyes searching for another way to defend himself.

His gaze landed on the window behind the boy and, with more speed than he thought his old bones could muster, he aimed the gun away from the boy and fired five shots into the window.

The bullets tore massive holes through the flimsy wood shutters and pierced the glass with ease; the damage to the window was great enough to cause it to collapse outward, letting in the rays of the fading winter sun.

The boy roared in pain and anger as the light fell on his back. He wailed as black stains began to appear through the thin fabric of his T-shirt.

He stumbled forward, arching his back and howling in agony. Erskine rushed forward and, using the boy's distraction to his advantage, kicked out and caught him on the stomach, knocking him back.

The boy landed on the ground, his face swelling, reddening and splitting open where the light touched it. The stink of gas and burning hair joined the myriad foul odors that already filled the house.

Erskine let his gun fall from his trembling grasp. He backed away as he heard the sounds of boots rushing up the stairs.

He turned away as the techies entered the room, their UV lights and spikes at the ready. He didn't need to see what was about to happen and he bolted down the stairs as the screaming started, loud and angry, like the wailing of a baby.

Erskine fled the house and made it to a large snowbank in time for the stress of the situation and the horror of what he had witnessed to overtake him, and he fell to his knees to vomit.

He threw up until there was nothing in his stomach and his throat felt swollen. Then he placed his burning forehead in his cold hands and let the tears run down his face.

A shadow fell over him, and a hand came down and gently gripped his shoulder. He heard, as if from far away, Ellis whispering, "C'mon, John, get up. Let's get you back home."

He stayed silent as he let his best friend lead him to his car. He gave up his keys without a single moment's hesitation, then he got in and laid back in the passenger's seat, letting his heavy lids drop and heaving a shuddering sigh as he let the sounds of tires on snow calm his nerves.

They stayed in silence for a while. Both of them knew that there was nothing to say that hadn't been said on previous cases.

Back when the first incidents had been taking place, Erskine would have loudly decried the new generation for romanticizing a disease, for getting themselves infected on purpose, for ignoring the grave warnings issued by almost every doctor and disease specialist, and for how the effects of the disease weren't even like the ones in the books and movies.

But now he was too weary, too beaten-down to complain. He knew that it would be useless anyway.

He was starting to drift off when, to his startled surprise, Ellis broke the silence.

"I know that it's bullshit, John," he said. "But no matter how many PSAs get made, no matter how many rants and tirades the media goes into, no matter how many people try to take up arms to stop this, there's always gonna be some sad, desperate person who gets infected because they want power, or they want a new life, or . . ."

He trailed off a moment before finally saying, "Or maybe they just wanted to live a little longer."

He sighed and ran his thin fingers across the scarf that he wore, a look of deep sadness shadowing his face.

Ellis turned to Erskine and said, in a voice that sounded near breaking, "I'm going to die anyways, John. I've asked the doctors how long I've got and they told me that I've got four—maybe five—years left before I change fully, and that's only if I forgo all meat and take a bunch of pills every day.

"I'm gonna die and then I'll have to have my head cut off after. My family won't be able to have an open casket ceremony; I doubt they'll even get to say their goodbyes, all because I was so, s-so-"

Ellis barely had time to stop the car before he broke down. John didn't say anything, he just placed a comforting hand on his friend's back as he wept.

Overhead, like moving inkblots framed by the pastel light of the sunset, a swarm of bats flew over the car and disappeared into the thick wilderness around the house. There was nothing left.

I WAS INVITED TO A SLEEPOVER

M.J. Orz

I was invited to stay the night over at my friend Jeremy's house when I was a little boy. I remember the anticipation I had building up inside me all day because he had just gotten the new Super Mario Bros. and, though I knew there would be other kids there besides me, I would at least get one turn playing. We were not too big into television at my house and my parents were never the type to allow video games, so events like this were always something to look forward to. Unfortunately, this would be the last time I stayed over at anyone else's house.

The night started off pretty normal. We sat around in his basement and watched a movie with his older brother Chris. Chris was a decent enough guy—he was fourteen at the time and we all thought he was pretty cool, even though he picked on Jeremy quite a bit. We ate a lot of junk food, Jeremy's mom made a big dinner for everyone and, as the night came to a close, we grabbed the Super NES from the closet, plugged it in, and started on Mario. We each got a few turns and it was just as wonderful as I had hoped. Around 10 P.M., Jeremy's mom yelled down that it was time for us all to go to bed. We all yelled back "okay" in droning unison and turned off the game system.

Making my way to my designated sleeping bag, something felt kind of . . . off. I remember looking around the room and thinking that it was strange that Chris had decided to go back upstairs, even though he was allowed to stay up later and take the Nintendo to his room if he wanted. I shrugged it off and laid my head down for the evening.

Around 1:00 in the morning, I was awoken by a loud thud coming from across the room. I didn't bother pulling my head up from my sleeping bag, thinking that it was most likely just one of the boys getting up to use the bathroom or something. I closed my eyes, but within seconds the bump returned, this time closer to my bag.

"Jeremy?" I whispered, trying to keep a hushed tone. "Jeremy? Is that you?"

The thud came again, closer.

"Jeremy?" I called a little louder.

Thud.

"Jeremy?" I said at a regular volume, still not wanting to wake everyone up, but still to let whoever was awake know that I was up and they were bothering me.

Thud. Right next to me. Then again slightly farther away, over toward the closet. Again. Again. The closet door opened quietly, then shut.

"Jeremy stop!" I shouted at him, now waking everyone else in the room. Jeremy hit the light switch by the stairs. When the bulb from the top of the staircase dimly lit the room, everyone was still in their sleeping bags, rubbing their eyes and wondering what was going on.

"What's wrong?" Jeremy asked me. "Why are you yelling?" He spoke through his balled fist that covered his yawn. "Do you need me to get my mom?"

Before I could answer his question, Jeremy's mother came running through the basement door, wrapping a robe around herself, wondering why we were all awake. I tried to explain to them that there was a loud thud next to my sleeping bag and that it was making noises all across the room, but they didn't want to hear it. Jeremy's mother said that it must have been my imagination, but I pleaded with her to check the room. She refused, telling me that it was going to be all right. I mentioned that the closet door had opened and she said that she had better not find any of us boys going into the closet this late at night—that it was time for bed, not for playing.

We all laid back down and went to sleep—except me, of course, who stayed up staring into darkness waiting to hear more noises that never came.

The next morning we all awoke to a very strange smell. It was a sweet smell, but not like a bakery or anything pleasant like that. It has a pungent trait that made you squint your eyes as you caught a wind of it. We all looked around the room, thinking that maybe someone had soiled the bed, but at that age, we were all beyond that stage. We ran up the stairs for breakfast, laughing and accusing each other of passing gas, shoving one another up the staircase, and leaving our mess of sleeping bags and blankets covering the floor of the basement.

Jeremy's mother went down to straighten up a bit and I heard her scream. She ran back up the stairs, telling us all to go outside and wait on the sidewalk, which we did, while she grabbed for the phone. I remember that was the first time I had actually seen an adult cry outside of the movies and it scared the hell out of me.

Jeremy didn't come to school for about a week after that. When he returned, we all asked what happened and what was going on, since the police had visited each of us, asking us questions about the night. They were particularly interested in the bumping and thudding noise I had heard. He didn't tell us for almost a month, but eventually it got out from one of the other boys' parents that they had found Chris's body in the closet, mutilated into a pulpy mess, a trail of dark body fluids streaking right past my sleeping bag. To make matters worse, who—or what—ever did this had scratched into the wall:

WE DIDN'T LIKE HIM

Jeremy and his family moved away after that and we didn't talk for years. I finally caught up with him briefly online via Facebook. He told me that he was doing well and his parents had finally, as far as he knew, recovered from the incident. He apologized for that night, which was something I never expected him to do, nor did I find it necessary. I felt terrible for him. After a few minutes of talking, I signed off and that was that. We didn't talk again. That was about two years ago, but I think I might need to give him a call. As I unloaded my boxes of clothes into the closet of my new apartment, I saw that there were scratches on the inside wall. They said:

WE DIDN'T LIKE HIM. WE LIKED YOU BETTER.

• • •

I decided to contact Jeremy again and ask him to grab a cup of coffee with me—I figured I should lead with something a little more light-hearted or risk him not wanting to join me at all. I can't imagine he would willingly walk into a conversation involving whatever it was that killed his brother. Before you tell me that I'm a terrible person for this, I know. I feel terrible that I wasn't honest up front, but I needed to know more information and this felt like the best way to get it. I'm sorry.

I was incredibly surprised when he contacted me back immediately and agreed to go, but with urgency. He asked if we could meet that night and said he was happy that I got hold of him—that if I hadn't he was going to reach out to me. We ended up at a Dunkin' Donuts around 12:30 A.M., grabbed coffee, and went out to sit in the bed of my pickup to talk. It felt almost like I was with my friends in high school again, but now with Jeremy (who obviously went to a different school than I and certainly didn't meet up with me for late-night coffee runs back then). I asked him what was new and what was up in his world, but before I could finish my question, he interrupted me.

"Has it contacted you yet?" he asked, not looking up from his steaming cup. "Has it tried to talk to you at all?"

I asked him to explain a little, trying to play dumb a bit. I wanted to be sure we were on the same page before I dropped this bomb on him. He looked rough. He had circles under his eyes and his hair was a mess. The truth about his hygiene was more of a mystery. The poor guy looked like a wreck and I didn't want to throw any more weight on his shoulders just yet.

"The thing that got my brother. It finds ways to talk to people. It isn't exactly subtle about it either. If it has, you'd know. Did it contact you yet?"

I nodded my head quietly. He took a sip of his drink before speaking.

"Then you need to leave. Soon. Now, if you can. Is there anywhere else you can stay for a while?"

"No!" I said back. "What is this? What are you saying, Jeremy?"

"This thing—this creature. It is looking for you now."

"What is it?" I replied.

"I don't know. I've never seen it. No one has, I don't think. But it hunts and it takes down people like you and me. People like Chris. Did you see it that night? Did you see it take my brother?" Jeremy asked.

I told him that I hadn't seen anything and that it was too dark; however, I had tried talking to "it," if he recalled. "That was a mistake," he said. "You shouldn't have let it know you were awake. I did and now it hasn't left me alone in years."

"Wait a minute!" I said loud enough to startle him. "You were awake too? You saw it?"

"I didn't see it, but it heard me. It bumped my foot as it moved my brother. I made a noise and the dragging noise stopped. I could feel it looking at me. I convinced myself it was a bad dream and went back to sleep until you yelled."

"Why didn't you say anything before?"

"What was I supposed to say? I thought I was going crazy," Jeremy said. "But it has followed me ever since. Everywhere I go. I have tried to tell the police that I am being stalked and that I need help, but nothing is going to make anything better. They can't do anything. The only person I can trust anymore is my mother."

I asked him about his dad and if he was still around to help, but apparently his father passed away two years ago. Drank himself to death. He didn't take Chris's death as well as Jeremy and his mother had. I didn't know what to say to him. Luckily, he jumped in with his warnings.

"Look, man. I know it is crazy, but I am telling you, it is coming for you. And it won't stop. The best you can do is run. I would recommend trying to do it this week, at the latest. I'm sorry you got caught up in this. I have to go."

Though I had a million questions, I knew he certainly didn't have any answers. I let him get back into his car and leave in silence before driving back to my apartment.

I spent last night in my truck across the street from the police station, though. It was the only place I felt even remotely safe. I'll keep you all updated soon, but I don't know if I can stay in my apartment. Dug into the wall of the living room were the words:

OLD FRIENDS ARE FUN, AREN'T THEY?

• • •

I woke up in my truck this morning around 8 A.M. I thought about making it to work, but that would involve going back into the apartment to get a shirt and tie, which I stupidly forgot when I left the house. I guess you could say I was in a bit of a hurry to get out. I tried to get hold of Jeremy again, and succeeded; however, his responses were all the same.

"Leave. Go as far away as you can. It'll never stop. Trust me."

I replied with questions that I knew I should have asked last night, but unfortunately didn't. I tried to dumb down the messages to simple yes or no type questions, but he still just continued to tell me the same thing.

"I'm not kidding. You need to leave. Once it has found you, it is going to hunt you down."

The worst message, or at least the one that got to me the most was the one he sent, which simply said:

"Remember what happened to my brother. You're going to be next. Please."

That one sent a chill down my spine. I remember the look on his mother's face when she came back up the stairs. I remember how frightened she had looked—but more so how whatever she had just seen was something unfathomable . . . something beyond death. I can only picture what this . . . thing . . . had done to Chris.

I decided to take a look into some of the police records—thank God for libraries and their free Internet (I sure as hell wasn't going back for my laptop). I looked for images of Chris or the body or anything that might give any clues as to what in the world actually happened, but fell short, for the most part. I had never taken the time to actually get any details about the incident—I think we all simply tried to forget that it ever happened. None of us at the sleepover really wanted to remember that night. None of us had even spoken since then.

Then it dawned on me. Who else was at the sleepover? Maybe I wasn't the only one.

I quickly logged back into Facebook and did a little research on the classmates that were there that night.

Sam Jones. Incredibly generic name. Even though we were in a small town back then, there was no telling where exactly he could be now. From what I could see, he either didn't have a Facebook page or had moved away—and trying to find a specific Sam Jones from years and years ago is like trying to find a needle in a haystack. That wasn't happening.

Tyler Brixler. Not so common a name. Found him within a few minutes, but his page was on private and it seemed that he hadn't logged in or updated anything in years. The picture he used was of a pretty young man, likely not even twenty years old. I didn't think that would be of any help, but I added him anyway. Never got a response, at least not yet, so he wasn't going to be any help.

But finally I got my first clue with Justin Lauers. Justin was a skinny kid that I remembered as being relatively popular. I could only assume that reputation would follow him into his adult life. His memorial page had over 3,000 people following it. Justin had been killed about a year and a half ago in some small Pennsylvania town. Apparently some brutal attack. This, above all else scared me.

I kept searching.

William Tanner—dead.

Josh Gillin—dead.

Randy Handell—dead.

This immediately explained the absence of the first two boys. From the looks of it, Jeremy and I were the only ones left. And now, all these years later, it was finally my turn to go. It had nothing to do with me seeing it. I was there and that was more than enough of a reason for it to kill. To hunt. To take me down. I wondered if these other boys even knew what was coming. I decided to message Jeremy one more time.

"What have you done?"

His response came in seconds, almost as if he was waiting for me to contact him.

"I did what Mommy told me to do."

• • •

I stared at the screen for what felt like at least a minute. Jeremy said nothing more. I ran through the list of things I could reply with in my head, not wanting to have more of a conversation than necessary, for obvious reasons. Finally I decided not to say anything at all and get my stuff to leave town.

I hated the idea of having to move away already. I didn't want to begin to think of the mess that this was going to cause in my life, but I knew very well that if I wanted to have a life to be messed up at all, I just needed to leave. I wasn't going to fight this. I shouldn't. Obviously that hadn't worked for the other boys and I didn't want to be as stupid as to think that 160-pound me could fight Jeremy off. I thought about how he looked when we met up and tried to do a size comparison, and there's no doubt that he would have no problem winning that battle—not to mention, I don't exactly believe that he would fight fair.

I rush into my apartment and grab two or three black trash bags from under the sink. There isn't any time for neatly organizing. I just want to throw the essentials into the bags and get the hell out of Dodge. I throw in some T-shirts, jeans, a jacket, a hat, my laptop, some pictures of family that I can't be without, and a few other little things I know I will need down the road and start back to the front door of the apartment. As I walk down the hallway, the entrance in sight, I feel a hand take hold of my collar and pull me into the open, dark bathroom.

I try to scream but a hand covers my mouth and quietly shushes me, lowering me down into the shadows behind the shower curtains. I close my eyes and begin to pray that it wouldn't be painful—that it would just be swift and quick and that it would be over before I could register what was happening. But nothing happens. My eyes stay shut and I feel my teeth grinding against themselves as I wait for impact, but there is none. We just sit there in the dark, his hand over my mouth, as I hear the front door to my apartment open.

I gather the courage to open my eyes and, in the darkness, I make out the features of my childhood friend. Jeremy tightens his grip over my lips and shakes his head to instruct me not to make a noise.

The footsteps from the front door are soft and slow. And coming toward us. I can feel Jeremy's hands begin to tremble as he reaches down into the tub we are now both lying in, pulling up a long, shiny cleaver. I wince again in natural fright, only making his grip on me even tighter. The footsteps are at the bathroom door now as I can see a silhouette standing in the threshold through the translucent curtain. It just stands there, apparently looking in.

"Bring him out, baby," says the woman. "Bring Mommy the boy."

I shake tremendously. I can't decide whether to run or to fight, so instead, I just shake. Tears fill my eyes as I await Jeremy's next move.

"No, Mommy," Jeremy says, in a pathetic, childish whimper. "I don't want to."

"Jeremy, don't be a bad boy. You know what happens to bad boys. Chris was such a bad boy." His mother's voice drops in tone, almost as if her personality has been flipped completely. "And you remember what happened to him, don't you?"

"I'm not a bad boy!" Jeremy shouts, hugging my head against his chest. "I'm a good boy! You're bad, Mommy! You're bad!"

"Give me the boy!" his mother shouts. "You have 'til the count of three. One! Two!"

And before she can get out the word "three," Jeremy throws me to the side of the tub and leaps out toward his mother. She gives a shrill scream as I watch the shadowy figure of the blade come down on her, Jeremy crying loudly as he repeats his driving of the knife. I watch the figures both lower to the ground, and the screams from his mother eventually stop, unlike the thrusts of the knife—or Jeremy's sobbing.

After what feels like an eternity of crying sounds and what I can only compare to the sounds one would hear in the back of a butcher's shop, I hear the clang of the knife hitting the floor and hurried footsteps rush out the front door of the apartment. I come out of the bathroom to find Jeremy's mother, now nothing more than a bloodied mess on the floor of the bathroom. I call the police.

And that brings us to where we are now. I stayed at the police station this weekend. They are setting me up with therapy, which I think I will find very helpful. They asked a lot of questions and I feel like I have told this story a hundred times already to many different people in many different uniforms. They all asked me where I thought Jeremy might have headed, but at this point, I couldn't give them any idea. I have no clue where he is now.

All I can hope is that, wherever he is, he is being a good boy.

I COULDN'T AFFORD A TATTOO, SO I FOUND SOMEONE WHO WOULD DO IT FOR FREE

Leonard Petracci

I turned eighteen this year—in May, the month that I graduated high school. By coincidence, the majority of my friends turned eighteen about that same time. All throughout high school we had celebrated "Birthday Month"—at least one of our birthdays fell on each of the weekends. When we turned sixteen, we each bought packs of cigarettes. At seventeen, we watched every R-rated movie in theaters, two times each. And at eighteen, we decided we would each get a tattoo.

But I had a problem.

Of the four of us, I was the poorest—my parents had kicked me out a few months before when they found the vodka in my closet, and I could just barely afford to pay rent with the waiter job that I had picked up on nights and weekends. I'd managed to graduate high school with low marks—but I had graduated, which mattered to me, though I knew I wouldn't be heading to college.

And now, my three other friends were leaving to start their futures.

"I think I'm going to get a benzene ring," said Lily, the nerdy but cute Asian girl who hung out with us, and probably had more potential than all of us put together, "behind my right ear. That way my parents won't see it under my hair."

We were sitting in the back of Brent's truck in the school parking lot, watching as the rest of the school let out. Brent was my best friend at the time, though he was planning on attending school three states away.

"Aw, that'd be so cute," said Mary, clinging to Lily's shoulder, "and I think I'll get a Bible verse right here. Something about purity." She gestured to her ribcage, and Brent snorted. The previous year his relationship with Mary had come to an end when she cheated on him with two other guys. They'd made up, and she'd cleaned up her act, but her reputation remained.

"And I'll get a globe," Brent said, "maybe on my chest. I want to travel, you know? Figure I'll do some sort of study abroad program at Uni. What about you, Copi?"

"Uh, I'm not sure yet." I answered, staring at the pavement below. I considered asking them for money, but my face turned red at the thought, and I already owed Brent a hundred dollars that he had pretended to forget about. "I'll have to think on it."

"Well decide quick!" said Mary. "We're going next Friday!"

By my estimations, I'd be able to save up at least two hundred dollars by then, but it'd be tough. I'd be eating ramen for sure, and picking up some extra shifts serving tables. It would be worth it, though—after all, I wouldn't be seeing them for quite some time.

But that night when I went in to work, my name wasn't on the schedule for the next week. In fact, no names were on the schedule—Burnette's Bistro had recently experienced some competition from an Applebee's that opened across the street, and Burnette's Bistro was now shut down.

So I was officially broke. By the time Friday came, I had applications for several new server jobs turned in, though none had answered yet. So I skipped lunch and went to the parlor that afternoon, and spoke with the artist.

"What can I do to help," he asked when I entered the empty shop, his eyes narrowing. I looked young for my age, and I was just barely old enough to enter the shop alone.

"I just turned eighteen, and want a tattoo. I was wondering though, I'm a little short on cash—can I pay you later?"

The artist snorted, crossing thick arms across his chest. "No cash, no art. Read the sign, boy. I'm not working for free."

"Don't you think we could work something out? It doesn't have to be anything big, or nice. Come on, man, please?"

"Out! And come back when you have cash, or don't come back at all."

"Dammit," I said as the door shut behind me, and kicked the fire hydrant outside the shop, sending pain up through my toe.

"Bit of an ass, isn't he?" came a voice from behind, and I turned, seeing a man standing on the sidewalk and leaning against the building, a binder under his arm.

"Yeah," I muttered, starting to walk away, but his next words stopped me.

"You know, I'm trying to open my own shop. And I've got pictures of my own art that you can look at. It's, well, it's a bit different, so I'm looking for someone to try it out on. Maybe advertise it a bit for me, show it off a bit. And I'll do it for free."

"Free?" I repeated, raising an eyebrow.

"Free."

"Let's see those pictures."

He handed me the binder, and I opened it, viewing them. There were ten or so, and they were good. Heck, they were great. The type of art that I should be paying heavily for.

"Thoughts?" he said, waiting.

"I'm in," I answered. "But what's the catch?"

"I just want my talent to come to life," he said with a smile. "It's hard to get started in the industry. So tonight then? You can meet me here."

"Deal," I answered, and that night I returned with my friends.

"Aren't you coming in, Copi?" said Brent, holding the door to the shop.

"I, uh, I got my own guy. Scheduled some personal art, you know. I'll meet you guys after."

"Sure man," said Brent. "But we were supposed to do this together."

Already I could hear the voices of Lily and Mary from inside as they started talking to the artist, and I withdrew slightly so that I wouldn't be visible through the window.

"Trust me man, it'll be cool. I want to surprise you guys."

"Whatever you say," answered Brent, and walked inside, holding a sketch of the globe that he wanted for his own tattoo.

I waited outside, and a few moments later the man from earlier appeared, touching my shoulder from behind.

"Ready?" he said, and I nodded, following him down the street. Night had begun to fall, and his shadow melded with the dark as he tucked into a side alley and led me down some stairs. And there we came to a door with a fresh sign over it, and he led me inside.

"You'll have to excuse me," he said. "I haven't had much time to set up shop."

"Apparently," I answered, looking about the room. There was a chair, some equipment, and three hanging light bulbs, but little else. A few boxes in the back, still packed and resting on concrete soaked with water leaking through the foundation. And a ceiling tile was cracked next to them, where it had fallen to the floor.

"Go ahead and take a seat," the man said, and I hesitated. Then I swallowed, and took the chair. It was free. I couldn't complain about free. And I didn't want to be the only one of my friends without a tattoo.

"All right, this will take a bit. I'll need you to stay still." He said, "How does your lower shoulder blade work? I have a design in mind, if you will. Something special."

"That works," I said, and removed my shirt. And he began, the buzzing filling my ears as I gritted my teeth. When he finished, he held up a mirror for me, and I looked at the work.

Damn, I was happy. And damn, did it look good.

It was a design of sorts, a looping that turned in upon itself, with strands that lay unfinished as the tattoo fell away. "In case you ever want to expand it," he said, pointing to them. "Free of charge, since you're my first customer. And I think you'll find they're quite addictive."

Then he led me back to the surface, and to the original shop, where Brent was already waiting outside.

"Thanks," I said, turning. But the man was already walking away in the direction of his shop, his form already a shadow in the night.

Brent lifted his shirt when I approached, showing me the patch covering his own tattoo, though I could see the globe through it.

"Came out sweet, man. Better than I thought."

Then Mary and Lily came out of the shop, each with their own patches.

"I hear you have a surprise for us, Copi," said Lily. "Go on, let's see it."

So I turned, and lifted my own shirt. For a second I heard silence, and I held my breath. Then Brent spoke, his voice drawn out.

"Shit, man. How much did you pay for that? You know you still owe me a hundred dollars, right?"

I laughed, and turned to see their eyes wide and eyebrows raised. Mary's mouth was open, and Brent shook his head.

We walked home together, and when I woke up the next morning the tattoo was sore. Not just in the area applied, but above it too. And when I looked in the mirror, it was just a tad higher than I remembered.

• • •

But that was months ago, and now my friends are gone. I work at the Applebee's that shut down Burnette's Bistro as a bartender full-time now, for both lunch and dinner shifts. And I eat there all the time, considering the hefty discount—sometimes having three or four meals throughout the day. It's not a health problem yet, though, since I'm losing weight, not gaining it. Must be all the extra work I'm doing.

I've gotten a few new tattoos since my friends left, all connected with my first one. The problem with having a lazy manager is I walk home drunk. Sometimes I even black out, with the entire last hour of my shift a blur. And my tattoo artist was right, tattoos are addictive—during those nights, I must have stumbled back into his parlor and had more done. I can't remember, but I'd know when I woke up with sore skin. They were still free, though, and since I never lost any cash, I saw no problem with it. Plus the new tattoos were just as impressive as the first, and he'd even touched up the first a bit. Made the lines a bit darker, more pronounced.

But it became a problem once my entire back was covered, and the ink started spreading to my arms. The other tattoos were of a wide variety of styles too—some colored, some not, some pictures, and some designs. All expertly drawn, but it was getting to be too much.

"Dammit," I said one morning, glancing at my bicep. It stung, and there was a copy of my original tattoo, the swirls and lines staring back up at me. So I left home, and I walked to the parlor— even though it was months before, I still knew the way. But no one answered when I knocked on the door, so I entered and looked around the inside.

It was empty—the chair was gone, along with the equipment. The hanging light bulbs were removed, a few additional ceiling tiles had fallen through, and a layer of dust coated the floor. I stood there, frowning, looking for life where there was none. But on the floor there was still the mirror from my first visit, so I picked it up, and inspected my back to see if there was anything new.

I choked, and shivers ran down my spine when I looked into the glass. My original tattoo had not been copied onto my back. It had been moved there.

That night, I did what I did whenever I was stressed. I ate to curb my hunger, and I drank to nurture my alcoholism. Heavily.

The next day I woke up to a stinging sensation, and cursed. There, on my left bicep, was a picture of a swastika, connected by thin lines to the tattoo network of my back.

I called in sick that day, and I turned on the television. I shook on my couch, and couldn't focus as I flipped through the channels. I considered calling my parents, but they'd think I was just trying to get money. And I considered calling my friends, but they'd think I was going crazy. So I settled on the news, something I almost never watched. And I learned about the incident the night before.

"The scene before you has been blurred out," said the blonde reporter, standing in front of a gas station, "due to its graphic nature. Experts are still trying to discern what occurred here last night, though it is currently being attributed to some sort of wild animal yet to be identified. The victim's body is covered in lacerations, as if caused by wires or small animal claws of some sort, the wounds culminating above his chest where the skin was ripped clear. And here is the footage."

The screen flickered, and I saw the inside of the gas station, the man at the counter tapping his fingers as he waited for customers. The frame rate was low, and the screen jumpy and somewhat out of focus, but the door opened and a dark shape entered.

It crawled along the ground, propelling itself forward with a single stump-like arm attached to a greater mass of black, similar in shape to a man's torso. The attendant pulled a gun from under the counter and began firing, bullets gouging into the floor, but the dark shape leapt onto him, swirls of black shredding his shirt in seconds. Then the camera blurred out, censored by the news team, but not before I saw what had been on the man's chest.

A tattoo of a swastika.

I shut off the television, staring at the tattoo on my arm. My muscle spasmed slightly, making me jump backward. And in my panic I began to drink, downing a fifth of whiskey before I could think it through. But before I passed out, I remember doing one thing.

I set the camera of my laptop so it could view my bed, and I pressed record. Then I took four more shots, until I couldn't remember slipping away.

And today, I watched the footage. Watched as the dark swirls of ink peeled from my skin, and twisted away until they formed an imitation shaped like my own body. Watched as it limped from the room, now as a torso with two stumpy arms, the collection of pictures and designs moving together in a single mass.

It returned with the light of dawn, holding a flap of skin with a tattoo on it up to the camera on my laptop so I could see the picture. Then it pushed the skin onto my bare chest until they meshed together, and I had a new tattoo. A tattoo of a globe; one that I knew all too well.

A warning.

And I am left to wonder what will happen when all my skin is covered by ink, and its template is complete.

THE STRANGEST CASE OF DR. HENRY MONTAGUE

The Right Hand of Doom

The doctor scrambled about his laboratory searching for his notes. The villagers would be banging on his door anytime now. He knew he needed to flee as fast as he could, but he couldn't yet. Not without his notes.

"Where are they, where are they?" Dr. Montague shouted aloud to himself.

The panic started to seize him. He needed the notes for his experiment to be recreated. As painful as it was to see his machine left behind only to be dismantled, he knew it was a trifle—there would be someone to complete his work. At his advanced age he knew he'd never see it complete again. It took him at least twelve years to see his work realized, and though it would only take him six years to recreate it, he was simply too drained from his last experience with the machine.

"I must leave at once," he whispered to himself as he gathered his notes. He stuffed them carelessly into a large medical bag.

The materials he had used would be left behind. If anything survived the villagers' onslaught he would send for them. The second most important component, however, had yet to be retrieved.

Dr. Montague hurried to the still-running machine, the shimmer of electricity and power pulsing around it, sending waves of static through his hair.

The massive machine stood in the center of the large laboratory. Measuring 8 feet in height and 8 feet in diameter, it was impressive to behold. The doctor's years of hard work whirred and sputtered as the machine labored to keep the portal in the middle open.

Where Dr. Montague stood he could see clear through to the other side, a ravaged landscape of unspeakable horrors. People being tormented, flayed, and ripped apart by unseen forces. Dr. Montague had found a way to see into Hell.

However, this was not the original design of the machine. He knew that if he had found the time, he could have tuned the machine to see into the stars, into heaven, to see into any place. A scientific tool for scrying the universe.

But when he showed the villagers what he had discovered, they scorned his work, stating that he was a false prophet, that he had bamboozled them into believing that he could contact God and had instead consorted with the devil.

"Villagers be damned," Dr. Montague cursed under his breath. He needed the power source out of the machine. Without it he could never try again.

The Dimensional Ark Node, or D.A.N. for short.

The D.A.N. power unit had the ability to reach across stars and time to create a window for all to see. The doctor had never been brave or stupid enough to go through the window, and was content with studying some of what he saw inside.

There was a problem, however, that the doctor had not accounted for. Yes, the D.A.N. used a large amount of electricity, and yes, the D.A.N. was fragile, but the majority of the problem was found in its inability to change what the doctor was looking at. It was always getting stuck on that one vision of what could only be described as Hell, and no matter what adjustments or what settings he had managed to place it on, the machine somehow would keep going back to this window.

Once the doctor had been able to glimpse the bright side of the moon, in which he found so many rocks and dead space.

It was fascinating, yet the moment he had turned to retrieve a notepad, the scene had changed to that Hellscape. He had checked and there was no change on the dial, no change on the spectrometer, no change on anything at all. Yet there it was, as if something had set its sights on it.

A chill ran down his spine as he stepped up to the machine to yank the D.A.N. out. "So much work to be done, so much to see, so very little time," the doctor said with a tone of longing in his voice. He wrapped his fingers around the D.A.N. and tugged it out of place.

The circle shut down and the room seemed dimmer.

As the doctor wrapped the D.A.N. with a nearby towel and put it into his medical bag, he heard a bang on the door. He knew that he should just flee, but he thought that perhaps there would be a way to quell the crowd. Something in him told him to try once more to reach out to them.

Dr. Montague walked calmly to the door and set his medical bag aside, hidden behind a nearby bust of Aristotle.

"Hello, how can I help you today, Simon?" Dr. Montague said as politely as possible to the sheriff standing at his door. He noticed the large group of people behind Simon that seemed to be wearing curious and angry faces.

"Henry, we've come to see the machine for ourselves. There have been numerous rumors going around that you've been doing illegal activities and worse." Simon spoke in a worried tone.

Simon and Henry had been good friends since their days as boys. They'd played pranks, gone fishing, and even had meals together. Henry was glad on the day that his friend had become the town's sheriff; Simon had always had a knack for keeping a cool head and a quick hand.

"Simon, I assure you, none of my experiments are illegal, I have procured all of the needed materials in a proper legal fashion. As for the machine itself, I was in the process of dismantling it permanently since the backlash of these . . . fine folk," Dr. Montague had said, attempting to be as glib as possible.

"I'm afraid I must insist upon coming inside and seeing the machine for myself."

Having no other choice and wanting the issue to be resolved, Dr. Montague opened the door fully to allow Simon and his group of "guests" entrance into his home.

"It's this way," said Montague, taking strides over to the door leading to his laboratory. The smell of fresh oil and grease hit his nostrils as soon as he swung the door open and allowed them all to file in.

The group of approximately thirty men stood awestruck at the structure that Montague had worked so hard to build, each making a comment on how tall it appeared.

"Well, Doc, you've got a helluva setup here," Simon stated, removing his hat and running his hand through his black hair nervously. "Did you build all of this on your own?"

"Of course, and isn't it beautiful. It's a shame that I am going to need to disassemble it," said Montague sadly, hoping to convince the people to leave him to his hard work.

"I don't believe you. I think yer gonna use your scientific mumbo jumbo to conjure the devil, like ya did last time," came the disbelief of the town crone, Rebecca, who had always been known to whip the town into a frenzy with her ideas. Dr. Montague hated her, but said nothing.

"Rebecca, that's enough. Please let me get this sorted out, if you wouldn't mind. I am the sheriff after all, not you." Simon eyed her steadily.

"I know what I've heard, I know what I've seen," Rebecca hissed through diseased-looking teeth and cracked dry lips. "He's no scientist, he's a Satanist."

"Simon, is she the only witness, an old woman with a grudge against my work?" asked Montague, annoyed by her presence in his lab.

"Afraid not, Henry, she's been getting this from some of the folks around the village. Rumor has it that you've been working on this portal that goes straight into the mouth of Hell. All I see is a giant circle. Would you please turn it on for me? It's mostly a formality." Simon scratched his stubble as he looked upon the machine, stepping a little closer.

"Of course, old friend." Dr. Montague powered on the machine, knowing that without the D.A.N. to power it properly there would be no Hellscape for them to look upon, just the shine of electricity.

As soon as the circle reached maximum power, Dr. Montague stepped in front of the center with his back turned and raised his hands. "Do you see, Simon, the unit is perfectly harmless. The window project has failed; however, I may have discovered a new way of harvesting electricity for all to use." Montague began to sweat a bit, beads falling from his neck to his back.

Simon knew very little about machines and could hardly tell the difference between a generator and a Tesla coil. This was what Dr. Montague had been banking on, as he stood in front of the large contraption.

What he hadn't been counting on was the portal opening without the power of the D.A.N. Behind him, he had hardly realized what had happened when he felt something tug at his suit. He turned to see a massive crimson-colored hand reach out from the portal in an attempt to wrap itself around his head, which it easily could have, had not Simon fired a round from his revolver.

Montague reeled backward, crawling on the heels of his hands, having fallen on his backside in order to retreat from the sharply clawed red hand. Upon this realization, he quickly scrambled up to shut down the machine.

"Hurry up and get that infernal thing turned off, Henry," Simon shouted.

Rebecca cackled like a madwoman, her eyes sparkling with delight. "I told you, I told, I told you," she shouted repeatedly, practically dancing. Everyone around her was too stunned to react to how strangely she was acting; most people were running for the door, trying to escape the insanity.

Montague powered the circle off immediately. The last image burned into the onlookers' brains was a single slit yellow eye and the sound of a booming voice—*"I can still see you"*—as the portal shut.

Everyone stood in fear. Doctor Henry Montague stood speechless, unable to comprehend what had happened.

"Henry," came the familiar voice of Sheriff Simon. "We need to get rid of this thing, quick." Simon tried to shake Montague slightly to get him to come to, but Montague was too shocked to do anything else but gaze at the enormous machine.

"Simon, I don't know how it did that," Montague finally spoke after a minute or two. "It's never done that before, the main power source wasn't even plugged in, and nothing has ever come through to the other side."

As he said this the light bulbs above cracked and shattered to the floor below, showering the villagers in glass. The crone, Rebecca, stood in the same spot cackling like a madwoman, eyes glossy and distant.

As suddenly as the lights went out, the machine turned itself back on. Montague immediately attempted to turn the machine off, to no avail.

Simon wordlessly readied himself, removing his revolver once again to shoot anything that might come through.

"Simon, I can't turn it off. This is impossible, there is no way that this can run without the Ark Node, there is no possible way," Montague cried, trying to power the machine off.

The villagers all shrieked in terror, waiting for the portal to reappear. Panic was starting to set in. They all ran for the door, but the amount of people pressing against it caused it to keep shutting.

Montague rushed over to the power plugs to try to remove them, but even unattached to any power source, the machine was still running—though, mysteriously, the portal had not opened.

Simon was now holding his gun out, pointed at the machine, backing away slowly so as not to stumble, while Rebecca moved in closer to see the unit, seemingly fascinated by the light.

Montague couldn't think properly over the roar of noise; he couldn't explain it at all. There was no explanation to this occurrence—it did not match up. Without the Dimensional Ark Node it should've been a scientific impossibility. That is unless the explanation was unscientific.

The sea of thoughts was overcome by the sea of noise, however. He could stand no more of it as he finally shouted at the men and women to silence themselves. Yet the roar that silenced the crowd was not his own, nor was it the sound of Simon firing his revolver, nor was it still the madwoman who continued to cackle.

No, the roar came from the now open portal as a hand reached out once again to grab hold of the nearest object or person. The hand found Rebecca and pulled her in, her head appearing just above the top of the hand. She continued to cackle, fully aware of what was waiting, looking like a lunatic.

As the crimson hand pulled Rebecca into the portal, it slowly began to shut until it finally closed on her neck. Her head, now severed from her body, lay gaping up at those around it. The sounds of her mad laughter still rang in their ears.

"Henry, we can't let this happen again," Simon yelled. "Tell everyone to clear out, we've got to keep that thing from coming through."

At this the crowd burst from the room and ran out the front doors. One person was trampled under the crowd and left to limp out of the house on his own.

Simon and Henry alone remained. The sound of the machine still working was the only other sound they could hear.

"Any ideas, Henry?"

"I have to think," he said. "If the portal is able to stabilize itself without the usage of the . . . the D.A.N. then perhaps the D.A.N. can destabilize it, maybe . . . maybe that's what stabilized it in the first place. I can try to place the Dimensional Ark Node into the slot again, and attempt to switch the portal to a different setting. It may be possible to close it out and give us enough time to dismantle it and prevent this atrocity from ever happening again. The problem is, Simon, this is only a hypothesis. This portal has become self-sustaining; for all I know, powering on D.A.N. will only increase the size and let something in."

"What choice do we have then, Henry?"

Doctor Henry Montague pondered for a moment before running out to get his medicine bag from behind the bust of Aristotle. He came back panting, pulling the item from the bag and tossing his notes and bag aside.

"For a moment there, I thought you were going to turn coward and leave me," Simon sighed with relief. "So that's Dan, huh? He doesn't look like much." Even if the world were to end, Simon could always make a joke; this ability gave Montague more courage to do what needed to be done.

"He may not look like much, but his power is incredible. Let's just hope D.A.N. can reverse the anomaly presented," Montague said with a ghost of a smile on his lips.

As he strode over to the circle, Node in hand, he kicked the head of Rebecca out of the way, *No time to fear* he told himself, *must get this done, must prevent whatever that was from coming through.*

"What do you need me to do, Henry?"

"Just stand back; I don't want any surprises."

As he placed the Ark Node into the notches and grooves meant to cradle it, he twisted knobs and pulled levers furiously to ensure there would be time enough to destroy his creation.

"Now, Simon, find something, a hammer, anything; just smash this thing into oblivion," Montague called out over the roar of the machine.

"Henry, don't you need to plug it in first?" Simon questioned.

"No, at this point it would only feed the portal. The machine has the power now. The D.A.N. needs to route it or drain it in order for the portal to collapse," he replied, sweating profusely with the effort of keeping the levers in place.

Simon surveyed the area as best he could to find a sledgehammer or something similar. The closest thing he was able to find was a small hammer. He approached the circle, running toward it only to be flung back by some unknown force. He looked up to see the same crimson-colored, clawed hand reaching out.

Montague was no longer holding the lever; instead he was grasping for the D.A.N., trying to pull it out in order to cut the power of the portal, hoping that the sudden loss would collapse it. However, just as he yanked it free, Montague was grabbed tightly and was dragged into the portal, screaming, with the Dimensional Ark Node in hand.

Simon leapt to his feet to try and give chase to his close friend but saw no sign of Henry, nor the portal. The circle smoked and sputtered and began to collapse, leaving no evidence of what the machine was intended for.

As Simon walked away, he picked up Henry's medicine bag full of notes hoping for some clue to find out what happened, and he heard very low laughter coming from the severed head of Rebecca the crone.

THE BEAST OF BATTERED GROVE

Christopher Maxim

Pam was a young woman with eccentric tastes. She enjoyed dark tales—narratives involving supernatural entities, witchcraft, and the occult. Despite her love for such things, however, she had no desire to dabble in them herself. They weren't real, after all, at least not to Pam. Little did she know that on a daily stroll home from work, that belief would change—everything would change.

Pam worked as a barista at a local coffee shop in her hometown of Battered Grove, a bustling but quaint town in New England. There, she would spend several hours making various caffeinated concoctions and delicious pastries to serve to the general public. It was a simple job, and one that she enjoyed, but it still left her exhausted at the end of the day. One day in particular took a lot out of her because she had to work a double shift. One of her coworkers called out sick, and Pam was far too nice to leave her employer short-staffed. With a genuine smile on her face, Pam continued to serve coffee and desserts to her customers throughout the day.

After her shift was over, Pam pulled off her apron, gathered her things, and headed for the door. She couldn't get out fast enough. The cool night air hit her face gently, sending a refreshing chill down her spine. It was nice compared to the stuffy coffee shop. She took a deep breath of this fresh air and looked off in the distance. She was in no way looking forward to the walk ahead. Her house was nearly 5 miles away—a long and arduous trek for an exhausted barista. Not only that, but Pam liked to read on her way home. She knew the route by heart and could see oncoming obstacles out of the corner of her eye as she read. It was an unorthodox way to walk home, but it made the time go by a lot faster. She wouldn't be able to read on this night, however, as she had gotten out of work far too late. Moonlight would not be enough to illuminate the pages of her latest supernatural thriller. She would have to make do without.

Pam grudgingly began power-walking in the direction of her house. She took a sharp left off of the street where she worked and kept going, her march never wavering. While diligently moving forward at a breakneck pace, Pam decided to take a look around, so as to give her eyes something to do, considering she couldn't read to please them. Upon doing so, she noticed the local park. It was something she'd never quite fully appreciated before. She always had her face buried in a book, so she had never noticed its beauty or its layout.

The park was simple but stately. It was very small in size, but it had a regal elegance to it that made it appear larger. Surrounding its perimeter was a modern stone wall equipped with marble posts that jutted out every 6 feet or so. The entrance was a run-of-the-mill chain-link fence. It was the only thing that broke up the pattern of stone and marble, and because of this, it seemed very out of place. In the park itself was nothing more than two benches and a statue. You couldn't see the benches from the street because of the stone wall, but the statue could be seen up to a mile away.

The statue was that of a 30-foot-tall deity. Your average person might call it an angel, but Pam knew better. She'd read enough fiction to know that it was no messenger of God. There was something sinister in its eyes. That, and its wings seemed too birdlike to be that of an angel. She couldn't quite place what it was, but she knew it was a being that was malicious in nature. Still, it spoke to her. She fell in love with every detail of its design, even the seemingly evil smile it bore. She was captivated.

While staring at the park and its statue, Pam realized something. Just behind the park was an old stone church. It was still in use— she knew this, but what she didn't know was how close it was to the park. There was just a small pathway separating the two. She found it funny that such a nefarious statue existed in front of a church, of all things. Before Pam walked past the church, thoroughly amused, her attention was drawn to the wooded area behind it. She stopped instantly.

An idea came to mind, one that would potentially cut Pam's walking time in half. On her normal route, Pam had to traverse many roads and take several turns to get to her house. The woods behind the church would be a straight shot home, if she dared brave them. She wasn't a fan of walking through the woods at night, but her desire to get home in a timely fashion outweighed her distaste. After mulling it over in her head for a bit, she crossed the street and booked it toward the woods. She was in a rush, and this was her best solution.

Pam walked into the woods confidently. She could feel her nerves getting the best of her upon entering, but she indulged in the idea that acting without fear would in fact render her fearless. This, however, was not the case. As she continued her impromptu hike through the wilderness, Pam began noticing things that triggered her anxiety. The trees seemed to arch over her menacingly. It was as if they were watching her every move. She knew they weren't, but it still made her feel a bit frazzled. She could also hear the various sounds of nocturnal animals in the distance. Small animals like owls and coyotes—nothing particularly frightening. Nonetheless, the sounds made Pam uneasy.

As the stimuli of the forest set in, Pam began to panic. Her walk became hurried and sporadic until it eventually turned into a run. While running in the dark, Pam failed to notice a large tree root protruding from the ground. It collided with her ankle, causing her to fall face-first onto the forest floor. Uninjured, but still anxious, she got up and assessed her situation.

Pam had two options. She could turn around and head back, or press on in her panicked state. She estimated that she was about a third of the way to her house. The first option was looking pretty good, but either way she'd still be walking through woods, and she still wanted to get home quickly. She needed something to distract her from the perils of the forest, a way to stay calm while she walked. The only thing she could think to do was read a book. Reading was the only thing that comforted her during trying times. She could read with the light of her phone, but she knew she wouldn't be able to walk at the same time. She'd mastered this method of multitasking, but it only worked during the day. There was no way she could see the obstacles both below and in front of her in the dark. It just wouldn't work.

Aggravated and scared, Pam decided to sit by a tree and read for a little while. One chapter is all it would take to calm her down enough to keep walking. Plus, she would still make it home in good time. Knowing this, Pam pulled out a dark fantasy novel by her favorite author, Jack Grovewood. She was at Chapter Three, "The Witch's Cabin." The book was a bit different from his usual tales of horror, but Pam was loving it just the same. It was about a man by the name of Garrett, a professional monster slayer for hire in the kingdom of Fereldor. In this particular chapter, Garrett has been hired to take care of a witch who's been kidnapping villagers to sacrifice for her rituals. Pam read portions of the chapter aloud, as she often did when she was by herself:

Garrett took off into the Korikari forest, hoping to find the witch's shack. The information the locals had given him was invaluable, but the facts weren't all there. Garrett was left grasping at straws and using educated guesswork to find her. His reputation preceded him. If he could find even one sign of the witch, he knew he would be able to track her. He was a hound in need of a scent. A hound in need of a fox to catch.

While searching for clues, Garrett became very aware of the forest's atmosphere. Something wasn't right. The air was stale and unwelcoming. Some of the trees lacked the luster of their livelier counterparts. The strangest thing that Garrett noticed, though, was the lack of noise. When standing completely still, the silence was overwhelming. Garrett had traversed many a forest in his day, so he knew what one should sound like. Even in patches of little to no wildlife, you should still be able to hear the trees swaying in the wind or civilization off in the distance. But when Garrett was still, all he could hear was the heart beating in his chest. That wasn't normal.

Garrett decided that the witch must be nearby. He had never known one to cause such peculiar activity, but witches were a crafty bunch. You never quite did know what to expect upon encountering one. Garrett knew this, and as such he kept his guard up. At any moment, the witch could strike. Using spells, she could break limbs, put would-be attackers to sleep, or even cause vivid hallucinations. Lucky for Garrett, he had been through all of these ordeals and far worse. He was prepared for anything, but even the best-trained hunter can be taken by surprise.

Making cautious movements and little headway, Garrett decided to take a different approach. Most predators liked to toy with their prey before pouncing; it makes mealtime into a more engaging affair. With this in mind, Garrett wondered if he should simply make his presence known. He thought that perhaps if he shouted for the witch to show herself, maybe she would come out of hiding and confront him, so as to have some fun with her next victim. It would be dangerous, but Garrett was confident in his ability. He knew that once he had her in his line of sight, he could go in for the kill.

Using her name, as told in local legend, Garrett summoned the witch:

"Amber The Witchtress! I hereby command you to show yourself!"

Garrett's thunderous voice echoed throughout the forest. It might have scared off nearby animals had there been any. Still, he saw no one. Garrett inspected every detail around him, but saw nothing. Nothing but trees and gloom. Just as he was about to make another attempt, he heard something coming from behind him. It was the soft laugh of a woman: It was the witch. Garrett quickly turned around and retreated far enough to create a respectable distance between him and his visitor. That's when he got his first good look at her.

She was beautiful. Stunning in every sense of the word. Young, posh, enticing. She wore a revealing, blouse-like shroud. It covered her head, and only parts of her chest. Below the shroud were oddly crafted britches. They seemed to conceal many objects, perhaps potions and stolen goods. In the witch's hand was a wooden staff— no doubt her tool of the trade. Of all of her features, the thing that stuck out the most to Garrett was a large amulet that hung from the witch's neck. It contained a striking, *blood-red gem. Before Garrett could observe further, the witch spoke.*

"You know that I am going to kill you so why would you demand my presence? Do you have a death wish?"

Garrett knew not to converse with monstrous creatures. If there's one thing he'd learned in his many years in this line of work, it's that there are few things mightier than the tongue. Anyone can be convinced of anything, and falling into a trap at the hands of deceit and trickery was not on Garrett's to-do list. Plus, when dealing with a sorceress, you have to bite your tongue so as not to mistakenly activate a spell. Some incantations require a second party to speak. One wrong word could be a catalyst for one's own demise. In light of this, Garrett stayed quiet.

"The strong, silent type, eh? Let's see if I can change that . . ."

Pam closed her book and stood up. She'd been reading for long enough, and it wasn't helping as much as she thought it would. It was an escape, and it certainly kept her distracted, but the parallels between the book's setting and hers left her on edge. Severely spooked, she decided that the only logical course of action was to force herself to keep going, whether she was anxious or not. It was the only way.

Pam was about to start walking again when she realized she could no longer remember which direction she'd come from, nor where she was supposed to be headed. She had been reading her book for so long that she had forgotten her way. Her stomach began to turn wildly as another stage of panic set in. She was all alone in a vast wasteland of trees and didn't know how to get out.

Taking deep breaths and trying not to freak out, Pam made an educated guess and chose a direction to walk in. Two directions would lead her back to civilization. The other two were unknowns. That meant there was a 50 percent chance she'd wind up home or back at the church. However, that also meant there was a 50 percent chance that she was wandering into a wooded abyss. The forest was a large one—the largest in the state, in fact. A person could spend days hiking through its depths and still not see everything it has to offer. Pam tried not to think about this, and instead focused on the task at hand.

Denial was a lovely friend to have in the middle of the wilderness, but eventually Pam had to admit to herself that she was lost. She had been walking for far longer than it should have taken to get home or to the church, and her environment was beginning to look noticeably different. It was the same forest, but the trees looked bizarre and out of place. Not only that, but they seemed to have markings carved into their bark. As odd as this appeared, it did not alarm her. She was sure that she had merely stumbled into a deeper part of the woods than she should have, and the markings were just the product of people who had been there before. Perhaps hunters marking where they'd been. Knowing this was unfamiliar territory, Pam turned and began heading in a different direction in the hopes of more promising results.

Before getting too far from the marked trees, Pam heard a sound coming from deep in the bowels of the forest. It was an unnatural growl coming from the direction she had just turned from. It was subtle, but still quite loud. It sounded to her ears like the restrained snarl of a large animal. Chills traveled up and down her spine as she stood in shock. Her brain was telling her to run away from the sound, but she couldn't find it in her to move, at least not right away.

While Pam stood there, the sound continued—a grotesque orchestra of growls and groans with the occasional grunt. It was becoming noticeably louder, an indication that whatever it was might have been getting closer to her. Still, she could not budge. The sound eventually reached such a high volume that she could tell it was coming from directly behind her. She could almost smell its breath as it seemingly seethed. Her fight or flight response finally kicked in and Pam took off as fast as she could in the opposite direction of the sound, but not before turning around and glancing at what it was she heard.

She saw something, but fear coupled with darkness made it difficult for her to fully process what it was. Plus, she was too preoccupied with running for her life to dwell on it. Lucky for her, the sound faded. Whatever it was that resided deep in the forest had not followed her.

After sprinting in one direction for a solid twenty minutes, Pam found herself back at the church. She was delighted to be out of the woods, even if it meant taking the long way home. She was happy she made it out alive. That was the important thing. That was all she cared about. The dark and treacherous forest was behind her and she would never have to go back. She could once again partake in the normal routine that was her life. Or so she thought.

• • •

The next day at work, Pam was less than productive. She hadn't had a whole lot of sleep the night before and was out of sorts. She had thought about the beast all night, and was continuing to think about it at work. At least, that's what she convinced herself it was. Thinking back on the ordeal, she could swear she saw a massive shadow looming over her, as well as large red eyes when she turned around. It kept her up half the night and consumed her every thought while working. She ended up making several mistakes that day and even spilled coffee on one of her customers. Because of this, she was asked to leave early.

Pam accepted the situation and left the coffee shop, hoping the walk home might clear her head. This time she could read while walking, like she usually did. She hoped the book would take her mind off of the beast. And so, she escaped, back into the kingdom of Fereldor and the perils of Garrett the monster hunter:

Garrett awoke strapped to a chair in the witch's shack. Amber The Witchtress had cast a sleep spell that knocked him off his feet, then dragged him to her shack and restrained him. Garrett could surmise all of this, but felt foolish for falling into her trap. He wished he'd never summoned her to begin with. That's when he lost the element of surprise—something that he should have implemented on his hunt. He underestimated the witch's abilities.

The witch was nowhere to be seen. Garrett used this to his advantage and looked around the room for anything that might help him escape. What he saw surprised him. There were no altars, pentagrams, spell books, potions, or anything indicating that this was the lair of a witch. Instead, there was a fireplace, a small kitchen area, and bed. Words like "ordinary" and "cozy" came to Garrett's mind when giving the place a good once-over. He was baffled.

Amber came through the front door with a pile of firewood in her arms. She walked over to the hearth and set the bundle down. Garrett watched in confusion. Amber looked over and noticed the quizzical look on his face.

"What? It's getting chilly. Haven't you seen someone start a fire before?"

Garrett kept to himself, sticking to his rule of not conversing with monsters.

"Were you expecting cauldrons, chalices, and voodoo dolls, is that it? Well, I'm sorry to disappoint you."

Garrett looked at her blankly. Amber placed the firewood on the hearth. She then grabbed a match from her britches and used it to start the fire. Garrett was puzzled by this.

"I'm not like other witches, you know. I only use witchcraft when I have to. I use it solely to survive."

Garrett wasn't sure what to make of her at this point. He ended up giving in to his curiosity and listened intently to what she had to say.

"You're here to kill me, are you not? Probably hired to rid the world of me once and for all? Well, then I'm sure you've heard the local legend, the one that states that I kill people as a ritualistic recreation. Well, you should know that I fabricated this tale to keep people like you out of my forest."

Garrett could no longer bite his tongue. Her story had roused his curiosity.

"What do you mean?" he asked.

"He speaks!" Amber cackled a bit before speaking further.

"The fact of the matter is, I do kill. I need to in order to stay young. But I do not kill humans. Blood is blood. Any blood will do for my rituals. That's why I kill animals. It's true that human blood would work better, but I've decided to play nice. I don't want to be more of a problem than the locals already think I am. Truth be told, you're the first person to come all the way out here to kill me."

Garrett stayed silent, unsure of how to react.

"Look. If you want your payment, you can take my staff to the villagers and say that you've killed me. They'll be more than happy with that. I can make a new one."

Amber walked over to Garrett and undid his straps. He was free to go. Instead of leaving, however, Garrett walked over to the witch and asked one last thing.

"I came here to kill you. I am a threat to your very existence. Why just let me go?"

"It's simple, really. Like I said, I'm not . . ."

Before she could finish her sentence, Garrett thrust a blade deep in her gut, making sure to dig the sharp edge in where it really counted. He watched as the life left her eyes and she fell to the floor. Garrett knew that anyone could be convinced of anything, but he was not anyone. He wasn't about to buy the witch's act and let her pull a fast one on him. Even if she was telling the truth, Garrett's work relied on seeing his contracts through to the end. After all, leaving loose ends would be bad for business.

Before exiting the shack, Garrett grabbed the witch's amulet. He looked at it for a moment before smashing it on the floor. It broke apart into several tiny pieces. Garrett had dealt with witches before, and he knew that they all had a source of power. He guessed that the amulet was Amber's. If left intact, the witch's source of power could resurrect the dead witch. Garrett had learned this the hard way on one of his first contracts. Nearly got himself killed because of it. But now he knew better. He looked down at the blood-red fragments on the floor and smiled. His work here was done.

Upon finishing the chapter, Pam looked up to see where she was. To her surprise, she was behind the church, standing directly in front of the woods. She was taken aback by this, not knowing how she wound up there. She didn't remember walking in that direction, but then again she had been busy reading her book. She thought that perhaps it was muscle memory from the day before. She knew this was unlikely, but it was the best explanation she could come up with.

Content with her theory, Pam attempted to turn around and head back. Before doing so, she looked up at the forest again. For whatever reason, the scenery mesmerized her. In the daylight it looked surreal and otherworldly. She felt that it was calling out to her, beckoning her to once again enter its unsavory depths. She couldn't explain it, but she felt the insatiable need to go into the woods despite the beast that lurked within it. This sudden and powerful craving governed her movements. Pam walked back into the forest in a dazed stupor, unable to control what she was doing.

Pam wound up at a clearing in the woods. She remembered entering the forest, but could not for the life of her remember how she arrived in her current location. But that was the least of her concerns. The clearing, it seemed, was occupied. There were several cloaked individuals standing in a circular formation, each with their own black altar. They seemed to be chanting under their breath. At the center of this circular formation was none other than the beast. Pam knew those eyes anywhere.

The beast had been flailing about and growling ferociously, unable to move. But once it locked eyes with Pam, it stopped. The beast was docile. Pam noticed that the chanting had ceased as well. She looked around and realized that the cloaked individuals were now facing her. One in particular walked directly into her line of view and spoke.

"It's okay! Don't be frightened. You can come out, child."

Pam didn't know how to react. What was happening was unbelievable, but she sensed no ill intent. Slowly, she stepped into the clearing and up to the cloaked person.

"You're here! This is a glorious day indeed!"

It was a woman. A beautiful one at that. Long blonde hair, an elegant red cloak, and gorgeous red eyes. Pam was awestruck, though she didn't know what the woman was talking about. She was also a bit nervous as the beast was standing directly behind her. The cloaked woman noticed this.

"Not to worry! The beast will not harm you. It can't, in fact. You are its master."

Pam was dumbfounded. She didn't know what the woman meant, nor how any of this was possible. It all seemed like a weird dream to her. For better or for worse, it was all too real.

"I'm its master?" Pam asked.

"Yes. Perhaps I should explain. Come."

The woman gestured for Pam to walk with her over to the beast. Pam obliged, though still nervous. This allowed her to get a closer look at it.

The beast was enormous, the size of a small house. It looked like a bear, but not quite. In place of fur was a pelt of darkness—a black aura made up of a swirling energy of some sort. And, of course, there were those striking red eyes, not unlike the woman's. The beast was intimidating, though seeing it up close in daylight made Pam less scared. She thought it was cute, in a way. Especially considering it no longer wanted to kill her.

"You may call me Abaddon. I am the leader of the Clan of the Red Wolf. We have existed for many centuries. Our doctrine is simple. We seek divinity through nature, and to protect all wildlife."

Abaddon spoke for quite some time about the Clan, revealing all of its inner workings to Pam. She learned that they worship a deity called the "Red Wolf." His teachings had been passed down from generation to generation, allowing the Clan to flourish to that day. She also learned that the Clan used dark magic for various reasons. The black altars were used to help strengthen and direct this magic.

"We were trying to calm the beast before your arrival."

THE BEAST OF BATTERED GROVE

Pam was still confused as to how she fit into all of this. She waited for Abaddon to explain further.

"One of the Red Wolf's teachings speaks of an ancient beast; one that will one day awaken from its slumber and aid the Clan in protecting the Earth from further destruction. After many years of researching the word of the Red Wolf, we were able to unlock the secret to waking the beast in the form of an incantation."

"So why am I its master?" Pam asked, wanting to know more.

"Waking the beast does not make you its master. It's not that simple. The beast must choose its master."

Pam was noticeably perplexed by Abaddon's statement.

"It is my understanding that you were in our forest the other night and had a run-in with the beast. It has taken a liking to you ever since then. That is why the beast chose you."

A plethora of emotions and questions went through Pam's mind. She didn't know how any of this could exist. It was like something right out of one of her books. She was finding it even harder to come to terms with the fact that she, herself, was at this story's epicenter. Pam needed to know more.

"What does this mean?" she asked.

"We've learned a lot about the beast, but we are unsure of how it is to aid us in our endeavors. We do know that it possesses a powerful magic—far more powerful than the Clan's. We also know that as its master you are the only one who can command it."

Pam's heart sunk. Her world had drastically changed in a matter of mere moments. Dark magic was real. Supernatural cults were real. Monsters were real. By pure circumstance, she had stumbled upon a dark layer of reality that had apparently existed since the beginning of time. And in her hometown of all places. This greatly complicated her life, and she wasn't sure she wanted any part of it.

"What if I don't want this? What if I refuse to be its master?"

Abaddon looked bewildered when Pam asked this.

"It cannot be undone. You and the beast are one. You share a bond that cannot be broken. Did you not heed its call when it drew you out here?"

Pam looked up at the beast. It grunted in disapproval and walked away. It then proceeded to lie down like a dog would, at the edge of the clearing. Apparently Pam had offended it.

"You need to spend time with it. Get to know it. We'll meet you back here in one month's time. Hopefully by then we will have discovered the beast's purpose."

Abaddon began walking away.

"Wait!" Pam exclaimed. Abaddon stopped and turned around. "Yes?"

"How will I even find it?" Pam asked.

"This is where it lives. It will guide you here, just as it did today."

Abaddon and the other members of the Clan formed a small circle outside of the clearing and held hands. Pam could hear Abaddon speaking in another language with great conviction. After she finished speaking, Pam watched as the Clan vanished before her eyes. She looked around, shocked, as she noticed that the altars were gone as well.

Thinking that perhaps she somehow hallucinated the entire thing, Pam continued looking around. To her dismay, she had not. The beast was still lying at the edge of the clearing, pouting.

Pam began pacing around wildly. A million thoughts went through her head. She knew neither how to comprehend her new reality nor what her next course of action should be. As she paced, a wave of anxiety overcame her. She became frantic. Her movements were wild and sporadic, but she couldn't control them.

She also couldn't control the tears that began running down her face. It was just too much.

Noticing Pam was distressed, the beast walked over and nuzzled up to her. She could tell it was trying to comfort her and this took her off guard. All at once, her tears stopped. Her anxiety vanished. The beast seemed to have an effect on her, one that made her feel safe and relaxed. She reached her hand up and started petting it on the chin, noticing that it actually had fur underneath its black aura. The beast seemed to like this.

Having bonded with the beast, Pam decided that it was time to go home. She was mentally taxed after everything that had happened. She knew there would be a long walk ahead of her too. She looked up at the beast one more time to say goodbye.

"I'm going to go home now. Okay?"

The beast closed its eyes. Its aura became larger. A loud humming sound resonated from its pelt. Pam was confused. Within a matter of seconds, she went from looking up at the beast, to looking up at her house. She was no longer in the woods. She was home. Pam smiled. Her new friend could do amazing things. Feeling a little bit better about everything, she went inside to get some rest.

• • •

The next day at work, Pam was far more productive. She still couldn't get the beast out of her head, but this time she wasn't frightened. This time it put her in a good mood. Reflecting on the previous day, she realized how remarkable it was. She wondered how many people could say they'd seen dark magic at work. She wondered how many people could say they were a magical entity's master. Thinking about it thrilled her no end. She found the adventure of it all to be alluring and intoxicating. She was also growing slightly attached to the beast—like one would with a new pet. She couldn't wait to venture out to the clearing and see it again. Because of this, she worked to the best of her ability, keeping a fast pace in the hopes of leaving early.

While making a pastry a customer had ordered, Pam wondered: did the beast eat? If so, what would it like? After thinking about it over the course of the remainder of her shift, Pam whipped up a pastry of her own creation. It implemented all of the ingredients the coffee shop had to offer. She hoped there would be at least one flavor in there that it liked. She wrapped it up, placed it in a paper sack, and headed out the door.

Pam ventured to the edge of the forest, pastry in hand. She couldn't wait to give it to the beast. Before setting foot in the forest, however, she felt that strange feeling again. This must have been what Abaddon was referring to, she thought. It was the beast guiding her to the clearing. Understanding this, Pam gave in to the trance. Just as before, she arrived at the clearing having no memory of the walk there.

Gathering her senses after snapping out of the trance, Pam noticed the beast sleeping in the center of the clearing. Without giving it much thought, she ran over to it and began nudging it to wake it up. The beast did not budge. Pam decided that her next course of action would be to yell as loud as she could, giving the beast a nickname in the process.

"Oh, Mr. B! Wake up!!!"

The aura around the beast made it difficult to determine its gender, but Pam had a hunch that it was a "he." Its nickname reflected this, along with a "B" that stood for "Beast." It wasn't the most creative nickname in the world, but Pam liked it. To her, it fit just right. After she had screamed in his ear for a few moments, "Mr. B" finally arose.

The beast initially grunted at Pam for waking him but eventually nuzzled up to her. He was happy to see her. He was even happier when she pulled out the pastry. She unwrapped it and placed it near his nose. He sniffed it for a few moments before a behemoth of a tongue flew out of his mouth and grabbed it from Pam's hands. The beast swallowed it without chewing and began running around the clearing in delight. It was safe to say that he enjoyed Pam's creation very much.

Seeing the beast run about made Pam happy, and reminded her of the dog she had had as a child. It passed away when she was young, but she remembered playing fetch with it and having so much fun. This gave her an idea.

Pam looked around a bit and found a huge branch that had fallen from one of the trees. She picked it up with both hands and yelled across the clearing to the beast.

"Hey, Mr. B! Fetch!"

Pam threw the branch with all her might. The beast turned and saw it flying through the air. He immediately ran to it and jumped into the air, successfully catching it in his mouth. He then trotted over to Pam and dropped the branch at her feet.

Pam couldn't believe it. Mr. B looked like a giant, monstrous bear, but acted just like a domesticated dog. She didn't expect him to actually play fetch, nor did she expect him to jump through the air like that. She could swear he stopped in mid-air for a second when he caught the stick.

Knowing that the beast could understand her, and wondering what the extent of his powers were, Pam asked him a question.

"Mr. B, can you fly?"

As soon as she finished the question, the beast took off into the air. He flew all around the clearing before landing right back in front of Pam. She was stunned. Intrigued, she asked another question.

"Can I come with you?"

The beast kneeled before her so she could climb onto its back. Both nervous and excited, Pam did so.

The beast took off like a rocket into the sky. Pam held on tightly. She could feel the wind in her face and the speed as they darted through the air. It was exhilarating, a pure adrenaline rush for her. She could hardly contain her excitement.

The two of them flew for hours all around town. Pam was given a literal bird's eye view of Battered Grove. From a high altitude, she saw every last structure that made up the town. She even saw some of its residents going about their daily routines. Pam was awestruck.

After flying around for a good, long while, Pam and the beast headed back to the clearing. They played a few more rounds of fetch before the beast became tuckered out and laid down on the ground. All of the flying and running had gotten to him and he needed a break. Pam noticed this and laid down with him, up against one of his legs.

While laying down, Pam decided to pull out her book and start reading aloud like usual. She was on Chapter Four, "Fragments of Deceit." While reading, something weird happened. Out of the corner of her eye she saw a person. Looking up from her book, she noticed a man standing before her. It was Garrett. She couldn't be completely certain of this at first, but inspecting his features more closely led her to believe that it was.

He wore clothing accurate to the time period in which the book took place. He had black hair and facial hair, as well as a scar across the left side of his face. His eyes were mutated, looking like those of a cat. Hanging from his back was a large blade. These were all features that Garrett had in the book. It was exactly how Pam pictured him.

Pam looked at Garrett, who was just standing still, and then looked back at the beast. He was unfazed by Garrett's presence. This led Pam to wonder if he had something to do with it. She slowly looked down at her book and continued reading. While doing this, she kept a close eye on Garrett, looking up periodically as she read. In doing this, she noticed that more things and people started to appear. Garrett began interacting with them, acting out exactly what was happening in the book. Pam was bewildered.

She looked back at the beast and noticed that he was watching Garrett intently. She realized that the beast must have been doing it; he was listening to her read and bringing the book to life to watch the events unfold. Because of this, Pam started the chapter over. This time she made sure to read loud and clear, knowing that Mr. B was listening. She wanted to watch as much as he did:

Garrett reaped the rewards of the witch's death, happy to put another case to rest. Before moving on to his next contract, he decided to take a couple of days off. Even a professional monster hunter needed a break every now and again. As such, he stayed at an inn located in the town he had killed the witch for. Without the witch there to terrorize the town, he knew he could relax without any distractions. Unfortunately for Garrett, he was dead wrong.

Early the next morning, after a partial night's rest, Garrett awoke to the sound of banging at his door. It was the Innkeeper, there to inform Garrett that an angry mob had formed outside, demanding his presence. Garrett was not too thrilled about being disturbed at such an hour, especially after dealing with the town's problem for them. He assumed they had another job for him, and even though he had no intention of working that day, he decided to greet the townsfolk and hear their plea anyway. He preferred to turn down a contract in person.

Upon opening the inn door, Garrett was bombarded with accusations from the townsfolk. They threw names around like "liar" and "fraud." They accused him of not killing the witch like he had said he did. Garrett was not amused. He shouted for everyone to be quiet, and asked the person conducting the mob for an explanation. This happened to be the village leader, the same person who hired Garrett in the first place. Given Garrett's intimidating demeanor and brutal reputation, everyone shut up at once, allowing the village leader to speak.

"The witch has struck again! She left Mr. Abernathy dead on his own farm, lying in one of her pentagrams, constructed of his own blood. You told us that she perished at the end of your blade, but she lives! How can you call yourself a hunter?"

Garrett didn't appreciate the tone the village leader took with him. Noticing Garrett's displeasure, he took a few steps backward out of fear.

Garrett then replied, "Take me to her victim."

The mob, equally angry at Garrett as they were frightened of him, led him to Mr. Abernathy's farm. There, Garrett investigated the scene. Lying on the ground was none other than the old farmer the village leader had spoken of, completely drained of blood. Said blood was in fact used to form a pentagram around Mr. Abernathy. Garrett noticed that something else was amiss. There was a marking just below the man's neck, above the collar of his tunic.

Upon ripping the man's tunic open, Garrett discovered that Mr. Abernathy's entire chest had been carved. The markings spelled out a message in the language of Garrett's youth. The language of his people.

"Rah'diafh gie ess'eav naegiepe ah daeried ess'eav."

Roughly translated, this meant "Garrett the wolf, Garrett the fool." It was a message meant for him and him alone. Not many people knew this language, and even fewer knew that Garrett was fluent in it. The witch was somehow still alive, and she wanted Garrett to know that he'd been outsmarted. Her latest victim was a laugh at Garrett's expense, and not one that he would take lightly. He was determined to find Amber and kill her once and for all.

Garrett immediately left the crime scene and entered the forest. He headed toward the witch's shack, knowing that she would be there to greet him. She was a cocky sorceress, but apparently had the juice to back it up. Even destroying her source of power wasn't enough to kill her. Garrett knew she wasn't scared of him. She wanted to see the anger and frustration in his eyes, knowing that he failed. It was a first for him, and something that he couldn't let himself live down if left unfinished. He had to take care of her as quickly as possible.

Garrett found the shack in no time at all and waltzed through the front door. There, sitting in the chair Garrett had once been strapped to, was Amber, looking as pleased as ever. Unmoved by her presence, Garrett looked around the room. He was sure that the amulet was her source of power, but if that were the case, she'd be dead. He wondered if maybe he got it wrong and her true source of power was hidden in the room.

"Hello, Garrett. Happy to see me?"

Garrett turned his attention to Amber, knowing that after she gloated, she would move in for the kill. He wanted to hold off on this for as long as possible while he searched.

"Happy as ever. Killing you the first time was fun. I'm glad that I have the chance to do it again."

Amber, knowing that he was using wit to mask his feelings of failure, laughed at Garrett's sense of humor.

"Oh, Garrett, come now. Did you really think I'd die so easily?"

Garrett smirked at Amber, still combing the room for any clues. Nothing stood out to him.

"And the amulet. How dare you smash such an expensive piece of jewelry. I had to steal that from royalty, you know, and it was no easy task. Did you truly believe that I would be so dumb as to wear my source of power around my neck in the form of an eye-catching gem? Are the other witches you've dealt with that thick? How pitiful."

Amber's condescending words confirmed Garrett's suspicions, but not in time to do anything about it. Amber got up out of the chair and reached out her hand toward Garrett. His legs and arms stopped working as he froze in place. He was unable to move. While in this state, Amber grabbed his immobile body and threw it onto the bed in the corner. Amber followed suit and straddled him at the waist while holding his arms down with hers. He couldn't lift a finger to fend her off. All he could do was watch as the horror unfolded.

"I can do anything I want to you right now. Anything at all, and no one will come to rescue you. That's the downside of being a loner, I guess. But I'll never know that feeling. Because there's no one out there powerful enough to stop me."

Garrett looked into her eyes and felt nothing but dread. She had him right where she wanted him, and he was powerless to oppose her.

"I wasn't lying when I said I need sacrifices to stay young, you know. But do you know how I kill my victims? I devour them."

Amber proceeded to sink her teeth into Garrett's neck, tearing a chunk of his skin off using nothing but the strength of her jaw. She then swallowed his flesh whole and licked her lips upon doing so. Garrett let out a scream, but still couldn't move a muscle to help himself.

While groaning in pain, Garrett's eyes wandered. He noticed something leaning up against the wall in the opposite corner of the room. It was the witch's staff. In all of Garrett's years, he'd never seen a witch perform magic without their trusty staff, but Amber had just done this. Garrett knew that she was no ordinary witch, and perhaps this meant she could perform spells without the aid of a staff—but then that begged the question, why did she have one?

Amber went in for another bite and tore off another patch of skin from Garrett's neck. He screamed in pain and then stared at the staff again. He knew what he had to do. Focusing all of his might into one arm, Garrett began to move it. It was slow at first, but through sheer strength and determination, he was able to regain full control of it. Using that arm, Garrett pushed Amber aside. She fell to the floor with a loud thud, hitting the back of her head. She passed out on impact.

Garrett felt his limbs come alive when Amber hit the floor. Thinking quickly, he ran to the other side of the room and grabbed the staff. He placed it on the hearth in the fireplace and pulled out a match. Before he lit it, he looked back at Amber. She was beginning to come back to her senses. She looked up at Garrett and realized what he was doing.

"NO!" Amber shouted at the top of her lungs, begging Garrett not to do it.

This was his cue. He lit the match and threw it at the staff. In an instant it burned into a crisp. Amber's shouting ceased at once. Garrett looked back and she was gone. Only her clothes were left. She had truly been defeated this time. Garrett had succeeded in protecting his reputation as a no-nonsense monster hunter for hire. He had finally put an end to Amber The Witchtress, the woman of the woods.

Pam finished reading the chapter, as well as watching the events of it unfold before her very eyes. She was amazed. Truly amazed. She had never enjoyed reading a book so much, and that was saying something considering what an avid reader she was. She looked back at the beast and noticed that he seemed satisfied as well. He also appeared to be very tired. Pam was too. Her eyelids were growing heavier by the second.

"Mr. B, it's time for me to go home."

Much like before, Pam was transported to her house within a split second. She stood there for a moment before going inside. Thinking back on her day and all the wonderful things she was able to do with the beast, Pam smiled. He could do anything; the possibilities were truly endless. She couldn't wait to spend more quality time with her new friend. Pam was content.

The weeks passed and Pam and the beast enjoyed many more adventures together. They played fetch, flew around town, and read some more books. They even went off and explored the forest a few times. Everything was going well, but it couldn't last. Eventually, the pair's routine would be disrupted, and that day came sooner than Pam thought.

One day, upon reaching the clearing after a long day's work, Pam saw a familiar sight. Inside the clearing was the beast, as he usually was. In addition to him, however, were the members of the Clan, back to test the beast's power. Abaddon stood in front of him, waiting for Pam's arrival.

Pam's heart sank. She had almost completely forgotten about the Clan and Abaddon. She got so caught up in bonding with the beast that it nearly slipped her mind. Had it been a month already? Pam had lost track of time, surprised her month was up already. For some reason, the presence of the Clan left her worried. According to Abaddon, their intentions were good, but Pam couldn't be certain. Still, she walked over to greet her.

"Hello, child. I take it you've bonded with the beast?"

Pam nodded in approval, still unsure of how to go about conversing with Abaddon. She was intimidating.

"Good, good. We have some great news to share. In doing further research on the Red Wolf's word, we were able to uncover an incantation that will allow the beast to aid us in our endeavors. I have it here."

Abaddon pulled out a parchment from her cloak and handed it to Pam, who looked at it in confusion.

"It's in Latin, but don't worry. I can help you with the pronunciations."

Pam remained silent, still confused. Abaddon noticed this.

"Child, you need to cast the spell. You are the beast's master and only you can command its magic. We need your help in order to complete the task. Worry not. It is all we will ask of you."

Pam was reluctant, but gave in to Abaddon's wishes. After going over the language for a bit, she was ready to recite the incantation in its entirety. Before doing so, Pam wanted answers.

"What will happen when I've cast the spell?" Pam asked.

"To be completely honest, we aren't sure. The only thing we know for certain is that this will help immensely in fortifying our ideals. Protecting the boundaries of nature, once and for all."

Pam wasn't sold just yet. She wanted further assurance.

"Will he be safe?" she asked.

"You mean the beast? Yes, of course. No harm will come to it."

Still hesitant, Pam chose to believe her. She convinced herself that it was her environment making her uneasy, what with the red cloaks and black altars everywhere. It looked like the Clan was getting ready for war. But Pam knew they were just there to observe. They were ready to help if anything went wrong. At least, that's what she hoped. Without further ado, Pam took a stance in front of the beast and began reciting the spell.

While enunciating the words of a dead language, Pam looked up at the beast. He seemed to be a tad restless. She wondered if it was the incantation doing this and stopped. Abaddon chimed in.

"Don't stop now. You're doing so well!"

Pam continued, chalking up the beast's demeanor to the same reason she felt off—all of the people staring at them. Pam also felt a great pressure. She felt like she was saving the world, and one little screw-up could cause the whole thing to backfire. That's why, after uttering the last word, a wave of relief washed over her. That relief was quickly replaced with a sense of all-encompassing trepidation.

A swirling vortex of black energy shot out of the beast's aura with great force. It was a frightening tornado of pure darkness. It spiraled toward Abaddon, who, with arms outreached, gladly accepted the gift. As her body surged with dark magic, she cackled in delight.

Pam was petrified. She had no idea what was happening and stood still, making sure to avoid the blast of energy that was connecting Abaddon and the beast. After the initial fear tapered off, she was able to compose herself and think clearly. This is when her fear was replaced with anger. Abaddon lied. She knew what the incantation would do and it was hurting the beast. She was stripping him of his power and retaining it for herself. She was a conniving, power-hungry woman who needed to be stopped.

Pam ran over to Abaddon while screaming in disgust. Abaddon, with the flick of her wrist, cast her aside. Pam fell over onto the ground, unable to move.

"You don't understand, child. This is the power we need. Stopping humanity is the only way to protect nature. They are the one true evil in this world. They need to be ended."

As Abaddon said this, several more spirals of energy shot from the beast and into the black altars surrounding the clearing. Pam noticed that the other members had their arms reached upward. She guessed that they were reciting spells of their own and collecting the beast's energy. The Clan was harvesting his power, one drop at a time. Pam felt sick.

Looking over at the beast, Pam saw how badly he was struggling. Just like her, he could not move or free himself from the clutches of Abaddon or her henchmen. Tears began rolling down her face. She wished she could help, but she could not. All she could do was scream in dismay.

"Mr. B! Mr. B!"

The beast looked over at Pam and groaned loudly in distress. The bond they shared was strong, and he felt the need to help her. But he was in the same predicament that she was. Neither one of them could lift a finger to help the other. Instead, they were forced to watch each other's undoing.

Pam continued to scream out at the beast, wishing she could help. Eventually, the torment became too much. In tears and out of luck, she succumbed to her mental exhaustion. Pam lost consciousness while still screaming at the top of her lungs.

While out cold, Pam dreamt. In her dream, she found herself in the witch's cabin—the one from her book. It was empty, but there was a fire crackling on the hearth. Almost immediately, panic set in. Pam was well aware that she was dreaming, and knew what was happening around her lifeless body in the real world. She had to wake up. Even if she couldn't help, she had to at least try.

Before Pam could attempt any of her usual methods for waking up, someone came through the front door of the cabin. It was Amber the Witchtress. She was bringing in firewood. She set the wood down by the fireplace and looked over at Pam.

"I hope you're not catching a cold. It is fairly drafty in here."

Pam didn't know how to respond. Amber was, after all, a creation of Pam's mind, not to mention a bloodthirsty witch. Almost as if she could tell what was on Pam's mind, Amber addressed these concerns.

"Oh, don't worry. I'm not going to eat you. Though, you do look delicious. I am here to answer your questions."

Though in a hurry to wake up, Pam felt the need to stay and unravel the mystery of her dream. It felt to her as if she needed to.

"What do you mean you're here to answer my questions?" Pam asked.

"Well, what is it that you need to know? There must be some pressing matter on your mind."

Pam was perplexed by the plot of her dream, but continued to converse with Amber.

"I need to help my friend."

"Good. Let's start there. Maybe I can help."

Amber seemed confident in her reply, which made Pam a bit angry.

"No, you can't. You're nothing more than a figment of my inner psyche."

"That's just it, isn't it? You need to help your friend, and I'm you. Together we can come up with a plan."

Pam was taken aback by this response. It was unorthodox, but Amber was right. Perhaps some good could come of her untimely slumber after all.

"I'll ask again, what is it that you need to know?" Amber asked.

Pam thought for a moment before responding. "Do all wielders of magic have a source of power?"

Amber looked delighted when asked this question.

"Now we're getting somewhere. Yes, all magical entities have a source of power."

Just then Garrett came through the front door with some more firewood and placed it by the hearth.

"She's right, you know."

Garrett put some logs on the fire before walking over and standing next to Amber. Pam found it odd seeing these characters side by side, not at each other's throats. Garrett then explained further.

"All mages have a source of power. Including Abaddon. As an expert in identifying these weaknesses, I can help you find hers."

Amber looked over at Garrett and laughed.

"Expert? You couldn't even identify my source of power and I practically handed it to you on a silver platter."

"Lay off, would you? I was having an off day. Let's help the girl out, here. Maybe the source of her power is her cloak. That makes sense, right?"

"A cloak? Really, Garrett, and you call yourself a monster hunter."

"Her shoes, maybe?"

Pam listened as the two of them squabbled back and forth, coming up with more and more ridiculous guesses as to what Abaddon's source of power might be. She cringed at every guess, knowing that not one of them made any sense. Not a single one.

That is when it hit her. The two characters from her book failed to help Pam directly, but instead inspired an idea that she hoped would work. As soon as this idea sprang to mind, she woke up.

Gathering her senses, Pam looked up at the beast. It was still being drained by Abaddon. Without even thinking about it, she put her plan into action.

"Mr. B! We need Garrett! Bring him here!"

The beast looked over at Pam and understood. With what little power he had left, he conjured up Garrett's character, just as he had when Pam read to him. Pam shouted again, this time at Garrett.

"Abaddon needs to be stopped! Go for her heart! Kill her! Kill her now!"

Pam knew that there was no source of power for Abaddon. This was not a work of fiction—it was real life and she was a human being. A blow to the heart would do her in just like it would anyone else. At least, that was the hope.

Garrett immediately drew his blade and ran after Abaddon at full speed. Noticing this, she attempted to fling him aside like she'd done to Pam. It didn't work. Perhaps it was because he wasn't real, or perhaps it was because, even as he was being drained, the beast's magic was still more powerful than hers. Pam couldn't be certain, but she certainly wasn't complaining.

Pam watched as Garrett ran up to Abaddon and delivered the final blow. He thrust his blade right through the left side of her chest before completely vanishing. The dark storm of energy cleared up and Abaddon fell to the ground. She was dead. As soon as her disciples noticed this, they swiftly retreated into the forest. Their altars vanished into thin air. The ordeal was over.

Free from Abaddon's spell, Pam got up and ran over to the beast. He was trying his best to stand up, but his legs gave way, causing him to fall to the ground. Too much energy had been drained. His aura of energy had disappeared, revealing a gray fur-like substance underneath. The beast was dying, and Pam knew it. Even still, she couldn't accept it.

"Mr. B! Get up! You have to get up!"

She pounded on his fur, pleading with him to produce another miracle, but he didn't have it in him. She stopped pounding on him and began crying. With the last of his strength, the beast rested his head up against Pam, then drew his final breath. He was gone.

Before she could mourn the loss of her friend, a dagger was thrust through Pam's heart from behind, killing her instantly. The attacker was none other than Abaddon, alive and well. After pulling her blade out of Pam's lifeless body, the other members of the Clan came out of hiding, pleased that their master had not succumbed to death. As they gathered around her, she opened up the front of her cloak, revealing the wound on her chest healing at a rapid pace, as well as a red amulet that hung from her neck.

"That was a close one. A few more inches to the left and I'd be a goner."

The Clan kneeled before Abaddon out of respect, thankful that she was not hurt.

"The Ritual has been completed. The beast of Battered Grove has fallen, and its power is ours. Now our work may continue. We must show the world who we are. We must show them our strength. The trials are almost complete, but there is still much to be done. Let us venture on to our next task."

SLUMBER PARTY

Ashley Franz Holzmann

I couldn't take any of it back. It was a night of dreams and death. Thomas was the one with the idea.

It wasn't that we had all grown apart, so much as we had just grown up.

Dan used to be the glue for us all. He was the outgoing one who made the decisions and we all followed him. Thomas was sort of the second in charge, but he thought it was always the Thomas Show when we were together.

We had grown up together and gone through all of grade school as a group. It was cool until we got to middle school. That's when Thomas became the popular kid in school and he had too many friends to balance, so we were relegated to intermittent contact.

It wasn't a sudden thing, either. It just sort of happened.

Randy was the fourth member of the group. Randy was the paranoid one and I was the quiet one in the group. Randy got beat on by his mother a lot. She was really hard on him and had a million rules. We were the only guys that she would let Randy hang around, so whenever we wanted to do something he was almost always on board. It got him out of the house and away from his mother.

I was sort of the guy along for the ride. Looking back, it's hard to figure out why I was ever there. It's funny to think about friendships from those days and how so many of my friends were simply friends solely because they were my age or based off of proximity.

When Thomas suggested that we all get together to celebrate Dan's birthday, we all thought it was an awesome idea.

Dan was the oldest and he was the first of us to be turning thirteen—which we all thought was a huge deal back then. He was going to be the first of us to be a teenager. We all knew he'd also be the first to be able to drive and the first to do basically everything else in life. That was Dan, though. He was the leader and he always did everything first.

Thomas promised it would be a night to remember. Of course, we would all go over to Thomas's house. It was the place we always hung out.

Thomas was always the type to try and go all out. If it wasn't a night to remember it wasn't a night worth doing in Thomas's book. He was always trying to get us to experience things that would be "movie worthy," as he'd put it.

We could never just hang out. We had to do things that were totally epic. Outside-the-box sort of stuff that he'd then tell everyone about the next day at school. Thomas was good at making things sound cooler than they really were. He was a good storyteller.

We lived in the suburbs. It's hard to describe the neighborhood and my childhood as anything besides that. You've probably seen the movies of kids growing up in places like that. That's how it was. We could ride our bikes down the sidewalk or the road, walk to school, and play in the street until the streetlights came on. Everyone I knew was only a twenty-minute bike ride away. That was life.

All of the streets had sidewalks with trees. Some of the trees along the streets had been there for decades and began to connect with each other over the road.

The houses weren't extravagant. They were simply American.

We had all four seasons.

Sometimes the winters would go long, but we were young back then and didn't care about that. It was the early fall and all we cared about was having fun. We were still young enough to make that our priority.

The night of the party was all planned out by Thomas. He had insisted on planning everything himself. He wanted it to be a special night for Dan. Despite him not hanging out with us as much in those days, he was still a really good friend. We had a lot of history with Thomas.

When we hung out, everything went back to the way it had always been. We were a team. The four of us felt like we could accomplish anything if we really wanted to. It was that sort of group of kids. We rarely fought, and we always enjoyed each other's company.

We were the type of kids that could all sit in a room and just chill together. No cellphones, no TV. We could just be cool and hang out.

I was the last one to show up at Thomas's house. The other guys ragged on me for a moment about being late. I was surprised that Randy had arrived before me. He was always the last one because of his mother, but he was there before me, so it was hard to say anything to counter the slams.

Thomas's dad was an alcoholic. He wasn't abusive, really. He sort of talked down to Thomas sometimes when he was really drunk, but for the most part Thomas's dad was just absent. He would go to the closest bar a few blocks away and stay there until after Thomas had gone to bed.

It made Thomas into the type of kid who could get by on his own. Really, it was probably one of the reasons Thomas had become as popular as he had. Thomas simply had a confidence about him.

It was something that I never really understood at the time. It was more than I was capable of.

I was the type of kid who sort of just existed. I'm sure you also had a few people in your life growing up that skirted life without ever really doing anything. That was me. I was there, and I existed, but I was pretty forgettable. It didn't feel like that at the time.

Once we were all together again at Thomas's house, it felt like old times. We were the type of friends who always picked up from where we left off.

Thomas went through his normal rituals of briefing us on the locations of everything. He had always taken his hosting duties very seriously and felt it mandatory for us all to hear the spiel every time. He showed us the bathrooms, the basement, and the exits to the house.

Then he took us upstairs so we could see his father's room and where his dad kept the gun and ammo. Just in case.

We were then told that the gun was off limits and that the upstairs was off limits. That we wouldn't have to go back up there again. There were some old porno mags and whatnot around the room. We used to find those fascinating when we were a little younger, but we had grown up enough to not care about that as much. Not that we didn't still look at stuff like that, but it was easier to get away with it with a smartphone than to try and sneak the dangerous peek at Thomas's father's stash. We were smart enough about that stuff.

Seeing the gun was normal. Again, we weren't kids anymore, and we had no desire to mess with stuff that we knew was dangerous.

We walked back down to the kitchen to prep for the evening of epic events.

Thomas immediately gave us all massive gallon-sized containers of sweet tea. He had a large bowl of popcorn for each of us and he had already set up his basement as a dungeon of epic potential activities: board games, video games, movies, blankets and sheets to build forts—everything awesome.

We decided that we wouldn't watch any movies. It would be too tempting to pass out, killing the evening. Instead, we started with some retro games on the old N64. Mario Kart came first, followed by a couple rounds of Star Fox, GoldenEye, and then Smash Brothers. A perfect game-a-thon.

Thomas tried to cheat by using all of the shortcuts in Mario Kart. Dan kept using the bombs in Star Fox and messing us all up. GoldenEye was my game and I forced everyone to play with Proximity Mines as the only weapon. Randy had always been better at Smash Brothers. He picked Kirby and he was not fun to play with. Thomas was a good host. He knew to pick games that we could all enjoy while also picking the stuff that each of us was good at. We played Star Fox last, since it was Dan's favorite and the wins at the end of the game-a-thon could be fresh in his mind. It was his birthday, after all.

We decided to take a break after that. It wasn't too late, and the night was full of potential. We could transition to board games, or start watching Jerry Springer reruns, or catch up and gossip about school. It felt good to be hanging around each other as a group again.

The kitchen was our primary reset spot. Dan had already finished his gallon of sweet tea.

It was in the kitchen on that break that the night shifted.

Thomas's father was a pretty late drinker and his mother wasn't in the picture anymore. When his dad went out, he stayed out until the early morning hours.

So when we heard tapping on the glass doors in the kitchen that led to the backyard, we all looked at each other with expressions of hesitation.

Dan was the first person to hear something. "What was that?" he said.

"What?" said Randy, who quickly put his drink down.

"Glass," said Thomas.

I waited to see what would happen.

We all stood there in the kitchen, not hearing anything for a minute.

Then the tap, tap, tapping started again.

Small. Inconsequential. Except that it shouldn't have been happening.

Dan was the one who put down his drink and moved over to peek through the curtain.

That's when everything started to get weird.

Dan pulled the curtain back from the glass door and there stood a figure about our size, except that he wore a strange, brightly colored puffy coat. His expression seemed sincere, and something about him made all of us feel at ease.

We weren't dumb kids. We knew all about strangers and the dangers of letting someone randomly into a house, but the sense of safeness that seemed to glow from the figure—the Man in the puffy coat—was somehow rewarding.

No words were exchanged between us, and no eye contact was made. The sensation must have been universal, because there was no lasting hesitation.

I was the first one to move toward the glass door, but Dan was the closest one. So he moved to open the door.

"Thank you for letting me in, Dan. You deserve a candy bar," said the Man in the puffy coat. He thrust one of his hands in between the buttons of his coat and pulled out a large bar of chocolate. The Man's face was odd. It was as if we couldn't truly see his face. It wasn't blurry, or covered, and we all knew there was a face there. But if I had to tell you right now what it looked like, I couldn't. It was simply there.

"Thank you," said Dan.

"You can be my favorite, Dan. Would you like to be my favorite?" said the Man.

"Sure," Dan said. He was excited about the attention. It was all over his face.

Then the Man smiled and reached out to touch Dan's stomach with a single finger. "Oh, good. That deserves a tummy tap." The finger wiggled and Dan laughed a little, knowing it was lame. But a chocolate bar is a chocolate bar and a little extra attention because of it seemed perfectly reasonable.

"How did you know Dan's name?" asked Randy.

"Oh, Randy. I know all little boys' names," said the Man.

"We're not little boys," said Randy.

"Hm. Too right, Randy. Would you also like some candy?" said the Man.

Randy seemed to snap out of the rationality and nodded his head. The Man reached within his puffy coat and then pulled out another massive bar of chocolate. Then the Man briefly touched Randy's stomach with one of his fingers. "Tickle tickle, little tum tum," said the Man. And we all giggled a little at how ridiculous the whole situation was.

"We're playing games next," said Thomas.

"Games? I cannot wait," said the Man.

We filled up on sweet tea and popcorn before heading back down to the basement.

First we played some Monopoly, but that got really boring quickly. The Man stopped playing after a few minutes and he started to dance around the room and throw his Monopoly money everywhere. At first we all laughed at him. Then we realized he had run out of fake money and had pulled out real dollars and was tossing them all over the room.

Dan was the first to get up and start scrambling around after the Man, picking up the real money that had been dropped. Thomas and I followed right after. Randy paused briefly, but also picked up a few dollars.

The Man ran around the basement tossing money everywhere. Eventually, he went up the stairs and we chased him all over the house, picking up money.

At some point, the Man turned around and smiled with his empty hands out in front of his face. "No more tonight, little boys."

Dan was the first to try to coax more out of the Man. "Well, what if we did something to earn the money?"

"Well, I don't know. I don't have that much left, Dan," said the Man.

"But you have more?" asked Thomas.

The Man let his hands drop and then slide behind his back. "Maybe." He slowly backed up into the living room, maintaining eye contact with us with his blurry eyes. We followed him with some hesitation and he carefully sat on the couch.

Then the Man jolted up and tossed the pillows from the couch at us. A pillow per boy. The Man picked one up for himself and ran out of the room, screaming "Pillow fight!"

We must have played for an hour. Glasses were shattered, plates were thrown, TVs were brought down to hide behind and even mud was tracked inside from the backyard. All of the photos were off the walls. Most of the frames were shattered.

It was only once we got tired from the battle that the security began to fade.

Dan had switched sides halfway through and started to fight against us on the Man's team. The Man didn't seem to mind and we had seen him slip Dan the rest of the cash he had.

Favorites are favorites.

It was around then that the Man found Thomas's father's liquor cabinet. There were cheap bottles and expensive looking ones. The Man took one of the more expensive bottles and started carrying it with him, sipping straight from the bottle regularly.

He did that with two bottles before the fun began to dissipate.

We had ended the pillow fight in the basement. Thomas flopped down on the couch, sweaty from the activity. Randy laid down flat on the floor, Dan sat next to the Man, and I sat down on the steps to the basement.

I looked over at the Man. Maybe it was the lack of activity, or the upsurge of movement, but I could almost see the Man's face clearly. He didn't look like a person without the blur. His face looked like that of a goat. He had yellow eyes.

Something must have shifted in the room, because then the Man looked back at me and the blur was back and any uneasiness we were experiencing went away. He took a sip from the liquor he had been holding.

"We should play hide-and-seek next," said Dan.

"No, we're too old for that," said Thomas.

"Who cares? We're too old for a pillow fight," said Randy. He seemed to be gaining confidence with the Man around.

"Randy's right. And we haven't played that game in forever," I added.

"Oh! He speaks!" said Thomas.

We all laughed.

"I don't think that's a good idea, boys. I'm not the only tum tum tickler here, you know," said the Man.

Our smiles went away.

"What?" asked Thomas.

"Well, there's the other Man. The Gray Man. He isn't colorful like me. He enjoys things that I don't. We should have fun instead of thinking about him, though. Who wants to play Twister? I'm really flexible. I bet all of you are too. Wouldn't you all like to play?" The Man smiled. Then he took another sip of Thomas's father's liquor.

Something about the mentioning of another Man around—maybe even in the house—seemed to make the spell that was over us fade enough for us to think rationally.

I caught Thomas zoning out and then slowly coming back to reality. I saw his eyes as he started to understand the depth of the mess we had made. Ruined pillows, shattered glass, the works.

Randy stood up suddenly. He was always the neat freak of the group and he seemed to be taking the emotions very seriously. "I'm going to refill. Would anyone like to refill with me?" asked Randy.

Thomas stood up and I followed the other two boys up the stairs. The further away from the Man we got, the clearer our heads seemed to become.

We stood in the kitchen very briefly, looking at each other. The lights of the house were all turned off except for the glow that was filtering in from the basement door attached to the kitchen. It was a calming moment. Even in the darkness, we could sense the amount of chaos in the room. Drawers opened, spilled flour, more shattered glass. It was a good thing Thomas's father didn't care about us wearing shoes in the house.

"What the fuck is going on?" asked Randy.

"Something," I said. Randy nodded his head. It was hard to figure out the words to use.

"Shh, let's go outside to the back," said Thomas.

We closed the glass door behind us. We started walking slowly away from the house.

"What do we do?" asked Randy.

Thomas was quiet. There was enough land in Thomas's backyard for us to walk for a few minutes before hitting his chain link fence at the back end of his father's land.

"Something," I said again.

"It's not a Man," said Thomas.

Randy and I nodded in agreement.

"What is it?" asked Randy.

"Something terrible. Like a Venus flytrap for guys like us," said Thomas.

"We need to do something. We can't just sit around and keep doing this. And when he's nearby it's like . . ." Randy started.

". . . a cloud is in the way and it makes you feel good," I finished.

"Yeah," said Randy.

The neighborhood wasn't very active during that time of year. It wasn't cold out, but it also wasn't warm. It was that time of year when everyone stayed inside and relaxed. Not because they had to, but because they wanted to.

It made the night air seem like it had more room to move around. The wind tossed about and blew goose bumps onto our skin. The clouds left the sky alone, and the stars were bold enough to show themselves.

"Wait. Where's Dan?" I asked.

Randy's eyes went wide. Dan's presence hadn't occurred to us. I think we had all assumed for some reason or the other that he had come with us.

But he hadn't.

"Holy shit," said Randy.

"What next?" I said, looking to Thomas.

Thomas looked at us with a stern face. He had something to say. He had an answer to the question, but he wasn't saying it. He waited with that look on his face until Randy and I got it, then Thomas turned around and ran to the house. We followed him.

As soon as Thomas was inside he slammed his hand against the wall and the lights in the kitchen turned on.

Thomas stopped moving further into the room and Randy and I bumped into him in the doorway.

"What's going on?" I asked.

"Why'd you stop?" Randy asked.

Thomas didn't say anything in response. He was frozen.

I peeked over his shoulder.

The kitchen was spotless.

Glowing.

All of the broken dishes were gone. No glass on the floors, no spices or flour or anything.

I looked at Thomas and he was breathing quickly. It made me feel anxious and realize that my heart was racing.

The whole house was silent.

Thomas slowly stepped into the kitchen with us. We looked around the room. It looked perfect. Better than before we had come over.

The only thing that was out of place was one of the drawers. I walked over to it and saw that it was the drawer they kept the knives in. I closed it.

Thomas waved to get my attention—he and Randy were near the other side, ready to go up the stairs to get the gun. They motioned for me to join them. Sticking together would be the goal.

We ran quietly up the stairs and reached Thomas's father's bedroom door.

The door creaked a little. Every sound seemed to echo. Thomas hit the light switch.

The room was cleaner than it had been earlier in the night, and even though it was empty it felt like someone else was in the room with us. That weird television static sensation clung to the back of my neck and upper back.

The porno magazines were stacked in a nice pile. Randy whispered something about them and how he'd never seen them in a pile before.

Thomas went over to his father's bedside and put his finger on the little gun safe. It read his thumbprint and he pulled out the gun, pausing only for a moment.

There was an empty tequila bottle next to the gun safe that hadn't been there before.

Thomas quietly closed the little gun safe and tried to ignore the bottle.

That's when I looked down by the window to the room and saw the feet underneath the curtain. I decided not to say anything. Something about the feet felt different. Dark, dark boots came to mind. Not the colorful blue shoes of the Man in the puffy coat. The black boots seemed more industrial. More forbidding. More out of place—and I didn't want to confront the wearer. I felt a great urge to leave the room and run away.

I was the first person out of the room and down the stairs. Thomas caught up and put a finger over his mouth to make me slow down.

"We're going to go room to room. Turn all the lights on. Make sure the house is safe. You take this. Start loading and hand them to me as I need them. If that type of stuff happens," said Thomas. His father had spent time in the Army and made sure Thomas was ready for the type of moment we were experiencing. It was time well spent. I immediately listened to him and trusted his judgment.

"Is there anything else to grab? For protection?" I asked.

"No, just stay behind me," said Thomas. It was brave of him. Genuine bravery. "Randy, try to pick up something big in the basement. There's baseball bats down there and the other sports stuff in the house is all there."

"I'll take the ammo. I'm a Boy Scout now and learned about this stuff at summer camp over the summer. Can't be the scaredy cat of the group forever." Randy gave a nervous smile and took the ammo from me and the magazines.

We all made eye contact.

The tension was high.

I swallowed and Thomas turned around. We had to finish going through the upstairs rooms first. He started to move and we followed him.

The bedrooms were empty. I made sure to look behind all of the curtains but the boots were gone and no one was hiding up there. We managed to get a system in place and kept Thomas by the door with Randy, and me moving around the room to make sure it was empty. We turned on the lights, opened the closets and threw the curtains to the side while Thomas stood ready.

The second floor was finished.

The first floor went nearly as quickly.

We stood at the door to the basement. All of the lights were on in the entire house.

"Should we call the police or something first?" asked Randy.

"What do we tell them? That a strange being without a face came and cleaned the house; then he gave us candy and money? Dan's probably playing Twister down there with him right now," said Thomas.

"He's right. Everything's in its place. Nothing really abnormal. That. And we let him in," I said.

"Right," said Randy, accepting the logic.

We were in a weird position. If nothing else went wrong, we wouldn't have to worry about anything. We could toss around the porno mags to make them not tidy and, if anything, Thomas's father would probably be too drunk to notice the house was cleaner. All we had to do was go downstairs and point a gun at the Man and tell him to leave and never come back. Then we'd be able to live the rest of our lives and not talk about anything we had seen.

Thomas took a breath and then cracked the door. Randy went down first. The lights were out, so his goal was to hit the switch as fast as he could. I knew my job was to run for the near corner and grab a bat. There were no windows with curtains and no closets to check. We would just run down and save Dan.

That's not how it ended up happening.

We swung open the door and Randy ran down to the bottom of the steps to turn the lights on. I was right behind him, ready to go for the closest corner to get a bat.

The lights went on and that's when I realized we should have called the police when we had the chance.

The entire contents of the room were stacked into one massive pile in the shape of a chair. A throne for Dan, whose body was sitting atop the pile, slouching and lifeless, covered in a red blanket.

We were all still, taking in what we were seeing. We had only been outside in the backyard for a few minutes, but it looked like we were gone for days. The detail to which the throne was arranged was horrifyingly magnificent. The television, the sports equipment, and other contents of the room were perfectly fused together.

Dan's body was so white. It took a moment for me to register that he was stripped of his clothes. He wasn't wearing a red sweater or covered in a blanket, his stomach had been torn open and his insides were stringing out of him like a red spider web.

The hairs on my entire body stood on end. My eyes filled with tears of self-pity.

I looked over to Thomas and Randy, who were equally shocked. Randy had sat down and pulled his legs into his chest. Thomas had lowered the gun and made his way down the steps.

The silence stood there with us as if it were a truly sympathetic presence in the room.

There was no Man in the room. No boots hidden somewhere or waiting behind any curtains. Just us and Dan.

We waited for a moment, considering our options. The paths we could take. Our escape. The Hell we had found ourselves surrounded by. It was a lot to take in. There was no reason for what was happening. We weren't bad kids.

That's what made everything all the more unbearable. We were victims of luck; of a selection process that we were never told existed. Chosen by creatures that existed for reasons beyond us and the realities that had shaped our world only a few hours previous to that moment we shared with the corpse of our best friend, Dan.

No one had been brave enough to speak. We were too young to understand how to say something meaningful in a moment like that. Maybe adults aren't any better at stuff like that.

Then we began to hear footsteps from upstairs—from the kitchen above the basement. It was sporadic. As if someone was dancing and hopping around.

Thomas began openly crying. He didn't whine or sob. He was simply crying. Almost uncontrollably. Thomas was the bravest kid I ever knew and he was just as scared as I was.

Randy had stood up to listen to the steps and he was visibly shaking. Almost violently shaking.

I tried blinking away the tears, but it seemed completely useless to care about that sort of thing anymore. Not when we knew we were about to enter a fate we had no control over. There was no help for Dan. We were stuck down there.

I have never wanted to run away more in my entire life. To spirit myself off into another dimension or anywhere. Anywhere else in the entire world.

But it wasn't that type of basement. The only way out was the stairs. The stairs that led to the kitchen. We gathered at the foot of the stairs and we could hear joyous singing accompanying the footsteps. The dancing. A celebration.

I tried to remember to keep breathing. My face was warm from crying.

"Stay behind me, guys," Thomas said. He held the gun a little tighter and tried to sniffle away what he could of his tears. He wiped his eyes on his shirtsleeve.

The singing from the Man got louder as we got closer to the kitchen.

The Man's singing went from mumbles to something we could slowly start to understand. We moved slowly up the stairs. Trying to be as quiet as possible. ". . . Tummy tums and little bums and chocolate for the singing. Running on for wanting ones that wiggle giggle's pleasing," the Man was singing.

We reached the top of the stairs. The door was open and the Man was dancing around the kitchen, twirling his body and his arms and singing gaily. There was another liquor bottle in one of his hands: half empty.

Thomas raised the gun. "Get out of my house or I'm going to kill you," Thomas said.

But the Man didn't stop dancing or singing. He barely even turned in our direction, only glancing from the corner of his eye, "And tummy tums can be the ones who attract all of the meaning. I'm not the only one in town who tickles boys' beginnings."

It was a never-ending song. It kept going on and on. There didn't seem to be any choices. I tried to be small and thought about how many steps there was between the kitchen and the front door.

I looked around and that's when I saw the boots again.

The black boots were sticking out from under one of the sets of curtains in the living room. We could barely see the room from where we were in the doorway, but the lights were still on and I could see the boots clear as day.

There was a massive bulge behind the curtain. Something incredible was crouching there, wearing the boots and waiting.

". . . Tickle tickle, tummy tums . . ." the Man dancing in the kitchen started to dance over toward us. Everything that happened after that was so fast.

Randy had already finished loading the additional magazines. He was the first person to move and he shoved the magazine toward Thomas's hands. Thomas began firing immediately. I could see the Man getting hit by the bullets. It seemed as if every single shot jerked the Man in one direction or the other.

Thomas quickly ejected the magazine and grabbed Randy's first extra to reload. Thomas pocketed the other magazine and Randy then sprinted across the kitchen. It was the bravest thing I had ever seen Randy do. He managed to get to the landline phone while the dancing Man in the puffy coat was on his knees, slowly falling the rest of the way to the ground.

I saw Randy dial 911. It seemed like everything was going to be all right, but then Randy glanced over to the living room from where he was and then turned quickly to us with his wide eyes.

Two things happened in that slow moving moment. First, I saw that the Man in the kitchen was not bleeding. In fact, he had started to giggle. Second, a mass of blacks and grays moved toward Thomas and me at an incredible speed from the living room.

Thomas died almost immediately. He was nearly pulled out of his clothes from the violent tug at his abdomen from the Gray Man. Guts flew against the kitchen wall in a sloppy spray. I heard a small gasp from Thomas, like the wind had been taken out of him. He fell to the ground and the gun slid across the kitchen.

I almost passed out from the shock of it all.

Randy dropped the phone and tried to run to the front door. He didn't make it outside and he screamed while the Gray Man did horrible things to him in the living room. Randy kept asking for help, but I couldn't move. I just listened, frozen; knowing I was next.

"Help me, God. Please, help me. Please, stop. I won't tell. Please, God, I don't want to. I won't tell. I can still . . . no. No, no, please, no," Randy was crying hysterically. I'll never forget that moment or the things Randy said. How ashamed and afraid I was.

My eyes stayed focused on the giggling Man in the kitchen. The Man in the puffy coat. He slowly stood up and continued to giggle. He had never let go of the liquor bottle he was holding. He took a long draw from the bottle and that's when I saw his face un-blur again.

Alcohol.

It was the drinking that took away the Man's power. The blur surrounding him faded slightly. I could see the fur and the outline of his face start to look more and more like a goat.

My body unfroze. I stopped thinking and ran to the liquor cabinet. There was hope.

As soon as I went into motion I knew both of the Men were behind me. The back of my neck was cold from the sensation of being followed.

I grabbed two bottles of liquor from the cabinet and turned around as quickly as I could.

Both Men stood there. Eyes fixed upon me.

They smiled at the idea of drinking more.

I wish I could tell you that I made it out safely without any additional trauma. I'd like to be able to tell you that the liquor saved my life or that it was all a dream or an allegory or some movie-esc form of insanity.

But that wouldn't be true.

I was found the next day, alive, but mostly catatonic. My stomach was red from the Men touching me. I remember them goading me and threatening me and telling me what they were going to do to me.

I had stood there and taken it with no intention of ever speaking of that night. No thought of telling my parents or the police or Thomas's father. No one would ever find out about the Men.

The only reason they kept me alive was because I scared them. They had been very absent-minded with the amount of alcohol they were drinking. I started talking to them and telling them about their faces and their furry hands.

It made them defensive and it startled them to know I could see them for what they really were. Goat heads on the top of human looking bodies.

There was a lot of screaming and they thought about doing more horrible things to me. They talked about it with me sitting right there. In the end, they decided the night was full. They left, making sure I was scared enough to never talk about it.

There was a lot of fallout over the night. My clothes were missing when the police finally reached the house. It felt like an eternity before they responded to the 911 call that Randy had made.

I wasn't able to speak for a year. No one blamed me.

The things Randy said while he was being killed; the realization of Dan's evisceration, Thomas's brave tears—it all has stayed with me.

Sometimes I wake up in the middle of the night and feel as if I can hear the humming. Songs about tickling little boys and making sure they never talk about it.

NEPTUNE'S FANCY

Vincent V. Cava

Upon my soul, she was a lovely thing—pale-skinned, dark hair entwined with the green weeds of the sea. A pity she looked dead. We hauled her up in the tuna nets, along with dolphin heads and fins. Those warm-blooded bastards would trail the fishing fleet and try to steal our catch when they could. Cunning they were too. But the dead ones're not as smart as they might be since the razor edges of our nets would slice them up if they weren't quick enough.

Aye, but she was whole I saw, as we laid her on the deck. Perhaps she'd fallen from some rich man's pleasure vessel in a drinking party out at sea. A whore more likely than not, and naked she was as on her born'in day. But as I leaned over to touch those blue tipped breasts, I was surprised to feel her move beneath me hands.

"Hai! Cap!" I yelled, "She be not altogether dead, I think!" And the others came closer then to take a look. Those turquoise lips, they parted in a gasp and she opened up her eyes, as red as blood.

Of a sudden, she sprang up and dashed across the deck! She crouched amongst some boxes there and we could see she weren't no human girl at all. How lithe she was! How lean! Her lips drew back to show her teeth, small, white, and sharp like a barracuda's. Moisture beaded, shining on her face and arms. The muscles in her thighs were taut, but scratched deep by our razored nets. Her breasts were large and pointed. Her fingers and toes were webbed.

Rainbow-colored scales speckled her body in places, growing over her skin like the heavenly sores of some angelic leper. She was an apparition of a sailor's blackest, sweetest dreams.

Antony, our ship's first mate, was the first to break the trance induced by them round red eyes. Cautiously, he gazed about as he forced himself to venture closer to the thing we'd just caught by chance. Antony was the most respected sailor on our boat—a Scot, tall, red, and broad at the shoulders, who had once served in the Queen's Navy. The monster girl was silent as she eyed him from her fortress-nest of boxes. Then she made some sounds down in her throat—a seal or dolphin maybe like was how it rang inside my ears.

The Cap clutched his brother's arm and shook his sister's son and roused the rest of us to wakening. The shock of our first finding her then dripped away like spindrift against a boat's hull. Now we was all just curious as hell, and Antony was standin' closest to the girl. He took another step and held his hands out so as to let her get the scent of him by way of introduction. She didn't seem to take too much to that 'cause soon as he was near enough she bit off a piece of his finger.

"Ayeii!! Ya poor dumb animal!" Antony hollered and waved his damaged finger in the air—it was bleedn' horrible. He pulled a kerchief from his pocket and wrapped it tight 'round the tip of it. "Ya needn't a' be afraid, gal!" he called out. Antony was a godly man and wouldn't curse the devil himself. "I did not intend ta harm ya!" The rest of us set up a general roar, but the mate said "Quiet down ya fools, or else you'll frighten the girl or fish or whatever that thing is! And ya wouldn't be wanting to scare a wild animal when it's cornered and hurtin' and female ta boot!"

"Aye," the Cap agreed in a soft voice, parroting Antony, as was his wont. "And I'm bettin' if she's scared enough to dash for it, she's primed and able to tear the insides out of anything that's got in her way!"

That's when some sailor said he feared she'd slaughter us all!

"Kill her, Cap," another cried, "before she comes at us with that shark-toothed mouth of hers!"

Then Antony, who had the most reason to wish her harm, raised up his bandaged hand and bade us to relent. "Ya gents're being hasty here," said he in a peaceful voice. "Mayhap she's not so vicious as we might suppose." And he hid his bloody hand behind his back. "Mayhap she be a gentle thing when she's at home beneath the sea."

"Aye," the Captain interrupted, a gleam came to his eye. "She's not a monster come into our midst lads, but a treasure rare! And beautiful she is too! A valuable oddity! A priceless curiosity! Boys, we could peddle her in any port for coins enough to last us years to come!" He put his arms around the shoulders of those men closest to him, and went on. "Fellow sailors! Brother merchants! Relatives and friends! If we handle this thing correctly here, we'll all come out as rich as kings!"

And then the eyes of all of us glistened with that golden light. The Cap had hit upon the thought that each of us had been afraid to see. A treasure trove indeed, she was.

But what to do? How to proceed? Once caught, how did ye keep such a ken of the sea? It was my thought then to give her tuna. Why else would she pursue the nets? A poor dumb thing I thought her to be. Human in form mayhap she was, but without a soul she were no more than a beast. And beasts were such that man was commanded to rule in those first days of the creation of the world.

She would'na take the tuna from the deck where I'd tossed it, but she took it soon enough from the bleed'n hand of Antony.

THE CREEPYPASTA COLLECTION, VOLUME 2

And when she made her noises then again, a light struck up across the first mate's face.

"I hear her, brothers! She speaks the queen's English!" He sputtered and looked around at each of us, but seeing that we did not hear nor understand the words of the female gave him pause. "But it's as plain as milk!" he offered toward the Cap. "As clear as me mother's words when I sat upon her knee!"

"Are ya daft man?" the Cap inquired. "Ya say there's words inside them chirps and whistles?"

Antony turned around, gazing wide-eyed at the creature as she went on with them noises, those blood red eyes of hers staring back at him just the same.

"She says it was me blood that done it. The bit of me flesh that she consumed," he turned to look at the Cap. "She says that's why I can hear her in me head."

He pulled the rag from his torn finger and we could see the white tip of the bone as he dripped his own blood onto a piece of tuna in his other hand. The girl-thing sparkled her bloodshot eyes at him, but reached for his injured digit instead of the fish. Gently, slowly, she seemed to move as she raised the bloodied finger to her lips and nipped at his damaged flesh.

"Have ya gone mad?!" cried the Cap. "Feedin' ye'self to this sea beast?!"

The creature pulled Antony's finger, which by now had been gnawed halfway to the second knuckle, from her mouth and began to yammer once more. We stood in awe while he nodded his head as if he were understandin' her yips and yaps.

"She be tryn' ta get back to her home, gents," he said with certainty.

"And where would that be?" laughed the Captain. "A thousand leagues below the ocean's surface?"

"Nay, it be off the coast of an isle 'bout a week's sail west of here," Antony replied. "She told me so herself. She said she was makin' her way home when our nets snatched her up. This jewel of the ocean be royalty, Cap'n. Her king rules the sea and she's his favorite wife."

"You sayn' this thing, this fish-woman, this web-toed female, be Neptune's fancy?" asked the Cap.

But Antony kept right along as if he hadn't heard him. "Our nets've done too much harm ta her legs," and he gestured toward the gashes running up and down the merwoman's thighs. "Now she's ask'n for our help. Her kingdom's built of gold and pearls and precious rubies. And she swore to me, on the sanctity of her husband's throne, that if we return her home, then we'd be paid in all the priceless gemstones this barge can haul."

"Aye," responded the Cap. "Why be as rich as kings when we can be as wealthy as gods?"

There was a low rumble from the crew when he said that. Visions of golden underwater towers jutting up from the ocean's rocky floor danced and twirled through our heads like barmaids in a tavern when the grog is flow'n heavy and the music be merry and the drunks be clapp'n along, encouraging 'em.

"Bah!"

From amidst the crowd arose a voice—hoarse and graveled it was—that broke us from our fantasies. It was Old Man Job—a half-blind, half-drunk scoundrel that had joined our crew 'bout three years prior. Job wasn't much use for sail'n and he wasn't much use for whalin' or fish'n either, but the Captain kept him around 'cause he mopped the deck and cleaned the heads for a bottle of rum, a place to sleep at night, and a little bit of food to go in his belly. When we wasn't out at sea, Job slept under the stars and begged for his meals. I'd have felt sorry for the old vagabond if it wasn't for his nasty demeanor—cold and hostile, calloused from years of livin' in the gutters with rats. Couple that with the fact that he'd been caught a number of times stealing from the crew and you can see why I thought so little of the wretched bastard. Truth be told, none of us cared for him, but we tolerated Old Job 'cause he took on the duties nobody wanted.

Every sailor on the ship then turned his head toward the elderly old man. He was sneering at the girl still crouching amidst the stack of crates, a trail of Antony's blood trickling from her turquoise lips.

"A fool's errand ya be suggest'n, Antony!" said he. He snorted like a pig then spit a thick wad of phlegm from his mouth. It landed at the first mate's feet and a bit of it caught the toe of his boot. "And a dangerous one at that! We haven't the rations fer such a voyage and what've Salle Rovers? Have ya not considered such things?"

"We can restock off the coast of Portugal," Antony replied. "From there our destination is only three or four days out depend'n on the wind," and he once again began to bandage his bloody finger. "As for pirates, my vote says the risk is worth the reward."

Job pulled a flask from his coat and took a swig, then fired an eye at the fish-girl so sharp it could've pierced her scaly skin. "I don't like that thing, Cap'n," he said, his voice grinding like a stone pestle being put to work. "It's an abomination of God and we shouldn't be a' trustn' it."

And then the Cap's voice erupted into fire. "Shut your vile trap, old man!" he shouted. "Did you forget your place on my ship? Next time you think to instruct me on anything, I'd suggest you bite your tongue 'less I'll be cutting it out with the blade I keep in me boot! Antony, set course for the port of Lisbon so we can restock. Friends and brothers, I aim to get rich. In a week's time we'll never be need'n to pluck another fish from the briny blue again!"

And with that, we raised the main sail and changed course, setting off west toward our dreams of wealth and fortune.

⚓ ⚓ ⚓

Morale was high amongst the crew three days into our voyage. The men sang shanties 'bout mermaids and treasure when we was work'n, and when we weren't they talked of the extravagant things they aimed to purchase with their share of the loot. You could feel a buzz throughout the ship as every sailor was excited to see what treasure lay at the end of our journey—every sailor 'cept Job, that is. He hadn't spouted off since the Cap had put him in his place, but I could see—even with me bad eye—that the old man's heart had yet to thaw when it came to the web-toed female.

Antony, on the other hand, had grown as close as heat to a flame with the girl. She was moved to the first mate's private quarters, away from the curious eyes of the men on our vessel. The door was kept closed for privacy, but remained unlocked as per the Captain's orders. Periodically, Cap would send a sailor down to check on 'em so as to make sure the Scot and the fish-girl weren't engaging in any perverse, ungodly acts onboard his ship, but as I said before, Antony was a man of the book and I have my doubts that a deviant thought ever crossed his mind.

That isn't to say our first mate wasn't actin' strange 'round the girl though. He took to feed'n pieces of himself to her nightly and I had the dubious honor of assisting him on those first couple evenings when the Cap had ordered me to pay them a visit.

First, Antony would instruct me to fetch a tuna from the deck—a big one—as it turned out the girl had an appetite on par with a that of a horse. When I returned, he would unsheathe the

269

knife he wore on his belt and roll the sleeve of his shirt up around his elbow. Much to the displeasure of my eyes, Antony would then dig the blade's edge into his forearm and carve free a small sliver of flesh. Inside the mouth of the tuna is where he'd place the lump of skin and muscle so that she could eat it with her supper.

The girl devoured her fish raw, like I hear the heathens of the Orient do—head, bone, and tail, all with the bit of Antony's flesh inside it! I'd watch her eat it while I helped him dress his wound. The smacking of her lips as she savored the uncooked tuna in her mouth was difficult on my ears—every bite, accompanied by an abundance of nauseating noises. Slurp'n and suck'n sounds would fill the first mate's cabin while she licked at the poor dead fish's eyes and grinded its bones between her pointed teeth. A gruesome sight it was indeed, but I came to reason that Antony was lett'n the she-thing consume him for a purpose. It was explained to me through my discussions with the first mate, however limited they might've been, that over the course of each day Antony lost the ability to understand the fish-girl's tongue. Only when his flesh was inside the merwoman's stomach could he make heads or tails of her high-pitched whistles. And how clever of him it was, I did believe, to continue their discussions and gain her trust, so as to ensure she did not go back against her word.

I was glad that it was he and not I that had bonded with the creature. She appeared almost human at passing glance, but moved and acted like a wild animal. Gaze into her eyes and all you'd see was a feral beast staring back at you. This I found to be unsettling. I wondered too how the Scot felt safe sharing his cabin with her, but alas, men have done far stranger things for the promise of wealth.

On the final night before Lisbon the she-thing even managed to bite me hand as I was offering her a fish. An accident is what I believed it to be. Mayhap I should've paid more mind when delivering a hungry animal its meal. Nevertheless, her teeth had broken the skin and drawn blood enough that I needed to bandage myself. Happy to oblige I was, when Antony dismissed me from his quarters for the evening following that encounter.

By the time we docked in the port of Lisbon the next day, our rations had run bone-dry. The Cap sent only his most trusted men out for supplies and ordered the rest of us to stay onboard. He feared that turning us loose in the city might've lead to some unwanted queries from locals 'bout the special cargo we was haul'n. When sailors reach dock, sailors tend to drink. Now, a boozed-up sailor can still be of use to a captain in a lot of ways, but keep'n a secret ain't one of 'em. All this was for the best as I was not wanting to take on any extra responsibilities that day anyhow. From the moment I had woken that morning my joints had ached terribly and my head had felt misty and muddled.

Antony had locked the girl away inside his room while he was out leading the Cap's chosen few through Lisbon. I along with most of the crew stayed on the ship and waited for he and the rest of the men to return with provisions so we could be on our way. Without the freedom to leave the boat, there wasn't much to do 'cept drink myself to sleep and hope my joint pain passed so that's exactly what I aimed to accomplish that afternoon.

I was takin' a catnap in me hammock when I felt a cold, clammy hand wrap around my forearm. The sensation shocked me something fierce, but a sudden feeling of dread kept me from opening my eyes right away. For ya see, I was sure as birth and death it was the fish-girl that had snagged me. With Antony out acquiring rations, my groggy mind reasoned she had come to me looking for a meal. After all, it had been I alone who was assisting the first mate during her grisly suppers. Those icy fingers were gripping me tight and the damp hand had me certain I was 'bout to wake and find her stand'n over me, grinning down with that mouth full of daggers, and staring through me with those blood red eyes.

But when I finally mustered the courage to look I saw that it was Job who had stirred me back to the waking world. I sat up in me hammock and readied myself to crack 'em with the back of my hand for rousing me from my nap. There weren't a lot of men on the boat that I would strike, but Job was the lowest in the pecking order, and a known thief at that, so I had no qualms with belting the old bastard, especially after catch'n him sneaking around the berth when he should'a been topside scrubbing the ship's heads. To top it off, the pain in me joints was throbbing worse than ever and I had attributed that to my sudden wakening. But the look of distress on his face gave me pause long enough for him to speak and I lost the urge to strike him once he opened his yellow-toothed mouth.

"Ya needn' a' be upset 'bout me risin' ya from yer slumb'r," he said. Even the sound of his whisper'n grinded awful-like inside my ears. "I came ta talk 'bout that monster we pulled from tha drink a few days back. Tha thing that's got our first mate wrapped 'round 'er scaly finger and our cap'n fantasiz'n 'bout a treasure that may 'r may not be real. There be not someth'n altogether right 'bout the journey we're embark'n on. Ta me, it stinks ta hell and back! Last eve' I hid behind the Scot's door an' listened to tha things he was say'n to tha creature. Well, he weren't talk'n of no jewels or kingdoms, I can tell ya that! I can't say fer sure, cause I could'na understand the monster's tongue, but his words, they sounded treacherous! She put a spell on him, I be think'n—one that somehow gives 'er tha key ta his mind. Mayhap, her power lies in tha fact that she be eat'n little bits of him nightly. I watched ya help 'em feed her and that's the only reason me head can fathom why he'd collude with such a beast in tha first place. Witchcraft it is! Now, I be think'n he and she may be lead'n us ta our deaths!

We must be wary, you and I. For ta blindly trust a soulless creature such as she is as mad as takin' the Devil for his word!"

I yanked my arm free from his grasp and told him he was lucky I wasn't the type to rat him out to Antony 'bout his eavesdropping. He tried to plead with me, but my bleary mind had been made up and I was in no mood to listen to the ramblings of a dirty old thief.

"Ta hell with ya!" he shouted at me. "Yer just like tha rest of 'em then! Just like the Cap'n! So blinded by yer greed ya can't see tha danger right b'fore ya eyes! Well, if ya don't believe me, then I'll prove it to ya!"

Job then stormed from the berth with the fury of a tempest while I strained to forget the old man's warnings long enough to fall back to sleep. We was puttin' a lot of trust in Antony to lead us to the Promised Land. True it was, the first mate had never given any of us a reason to doubt him, but I wondered then, as I lay in my hammock, if that was *cause enough* to follow his lead without question.

We raised anchor and set off from the dock the next morning. Once the shore had disappeared behind the horizon the Cap called every able-bodied sailor up to the deck for a meeting. When I arrived I was surprised to see the fish-girl stand'n beside Antony and the Cap. It was the first time she had been topside since we caught her. She was dressed in a garment so as to cover up her lady parts. More animal than woman she might've been, but the Cap had insisted that keep'n her covered was the Christian thing to do so he made sure to have her garbed in front of the crew. It was the first mate's sleeping shirt she was wearing, and it hung from her thin frame, swallow'n up her figure—like a young boy sport'n his father's coat.

"Friends and brothers," the Cap sang out. "Our stern is to the coast so there'll be no turning back now. The next time we drop anchor we'll be doing it at the bay of this fair sea queen's kingdom." He waved a hand toward the girl, but she paid him no mind. She was still act'n skittish and feral—just the same as she'd been since I first laid eyes on her. "Our first mate, Antony," continued the Cap, "has been communicating with the female. It is he and only he who she has trusted with the coordinates to her kingdom so follow his orders, sailors, and we'll all be wealthy men by the week's end."

Antony took a step forward to address the crew. He may not've been the Captain, but he had the ship's reverence just the same—maybe more. "Ahoy, fellow sailors. When we set off on this vessel four days ago, we did so as fisherman, and whalers, but when this voyage is over we'll be returnin' home as men with influence, men of means."

"Hear, hear!" cheered the crew.

"In a few days we'll be a' reach'n our destination," he explained. "The entrance ta this girl's kingdom lies within a place her people call the Golden Grotto." And when he said that, I saw an eager smile stretch across the Captain's face. "It's a place plucked straight from the fables we read as children. A cavern where the water's liquid gold and the walls are encrusted with diamonds. When we find the Golden Grotto, we'll be so close to the treasure we'll be able ta reach out and touch it." He pulled a piece of paper from his jacket. "I've takin' the liberty of drawing us a map based on me conversations with tha girl. Now if ya be needn' me, don't hesitate to call down ta my quarters. I'll be in there with the lass discussing the customs and diplomacy of her people. Such things will come in handy upon our first encounter with the royal party."

Antony and the she-thing then departed from the group. Most of us went back to crack'n jollies and laugh'n bout our good fortune after that, but not Job. I spotted him hovering in the back of the crowd all by his lonesome. He just kept right on starin' at the Scot and the girl until they disappeared below the ship's deck. Only now do I think I know what he was gapin' at.

He had spotted something wrong regard'n those two, something I believe that I had spotted as well, but had been too afraid to admit. And now that these events are behind me, I can permit meself to recognize the signs that I had so willfully ignored. It wasn't Antony that had broken free from the group first once the meeting had adjourned; it was the girl. He had followed her all the way below deck and not the other way around—like a child tail'n his mother on an afternoon stroll through the marketplace.

Job saw it then and I see it now.

※ ※ ※

Illness would befall me not long after the meeting. By that very evening I had come down with a sudden fever that set my skin ablaze, sent throbs of pain coursing through my muscles, and left me confined to me hammock. And so I slept, soaked in sweat and shivering from the chill running through my veins as the crew carried on their duties topside without me. It was during my malaise that I began to experience horrific nightmares—visions that buried themselves so deep inside my head they torture me to this day.

I dreamt of a city beneath the ocean, looming up from the seabed like the unholy mecca of Lucifer. So real these visions seemed throughout the duration of my delirium, that I could'na tell the difference between reality onboard the ship and the fabrications of my ailing mind. There were castles built of black jagged coral, so razor-sharp that the barbs and spines jutting from their immense bastions would rip a man's skin open upon contact. Spires standing hundreds of feet high, erected from the bones of sea-creatures more massive than any whale were scattered about the place. Each underwater structure was enormous and intricately decorated, adorned with thousands of seashells or draped in colossal curtains of kelp. I had no body during these bizarre fever dreams; instead I moved about the sunken city like an ethereal specter.

In the center of the district was a church with pointed steeples. Its walls were sculpted from one large piece of smooth black rock, extending upward from the earth. Its roof, a dark, sea-green mass of repulsive projections, wriggled as if it consisted of millions of monstrous worms. At first I thought it was made of seaweed and the moving parts were simply a product of the ocean's influence, but as I ventured closer to the wicked house of worship I found this not to be the case. Nay, I fear the truth is far more unsettling. For, to my dismay, I discovered that the thing draped over top the church was in fact alive and conscious!

It was like no creature I'd seen b'fore—at sea or on land. It had no head or tail and I could not for the life of me tell you where the beast ended or began, but it writhed about and moaned loud and deep as though it were suffer'n horrible. The moving bits were tentacles of some kind, the tips of which were flat and white, each as long as a full-grown man. An enormous green slug covered with feelers is how I'd describe the unfortunate thing. Foolish it may sound, but I could'na help but feel sorry for the monstrosity. To my eyes it seemed as though the slug was a prisoner of that church. The unhallowed cathedral's steeples rose up through the beast's flesh, skewering it alive so that it could not swim away.

Closer to the terrible place I journeyed, unable to stop myself. I realized then that I was not in control of my actions. A chanting arose from the black church, drowning out even the cries of its monstrous captive. The voices were not human; they sounded of singing dolphins, but unlike the girl, there was some semblance of language in their words, albeit ones I could not understand.

Through the doors I traveled, ever nearer to the chants, and there I witnessed horrors that could warp a sane man's mind. The underside of the slug-thing above the church was now visible. The creature had no eyes or ears, at least none that I could recognize, but its enormous oval maw, large enough to swallow a merchant ship whole, spanned half its body. Every one of its teeth was as big as a baby humpback and as sharp as the devil's tongue. Columns arranged in a circle ascended up, piercing the creature's pink spongy belly so as to pin it in place.

The interior walls were carved in runes the likes of which I'm certain no man has seen since before the time of Christ. There were no pews inside the structure and aside from the pulpit and the columns, the chamber was completely bare, but I was not alone inside the church. There were hooded figures in black robes as well. They floated between the pillars in the center of the room and I knew then that they were the origin of the strange chants I'd been following. The shrouded beings were busy performing their depraved religious ritual and did not acknowledge my presence so I watched in silence as they worshiped and sang their ominous incantations. In response, the immense slug above cried and moaned throughout the strange ceremony, but never did the dark monks react to its bellowing.

When the chanting came to an end, all but one of the worshipers removed their robes and dropped them to the floor. They were males the same race as the fish-girl and bore the same sharp teeth and webbed fingers as she. Colorful scales even speckled their bodies in a similar fashion. They formed a circle 'round the one figure still cloaked and lowered their heads in what I assumed to be prayer. This monk was bigger than the lot of 'em—at least twice as large. I had'na noticed 'til the others removed their garments, but now the size difference was palpable.

It was their leader—the Archbishop of their ungodly congregation. It turned to face me and I realized then that I wasn't as invisible to these things as I had thought. From the sleeves of the high priest's robe emerged a pair of gigantic webbed hands, though they were unlike those of the merpeople surrounding it. More monstrous in appearance were these, with grayish-green skin and talons in place of nails. On its wrist it wore a golden bracelet of a strange unearthly design. Mesmerizing I found it to be—both stunning and frightening at the same time, and unique to any piece of jewelry I've ever seen in my life. I feared with all my soul to look upon the face of the horrible being, but as I said before my actions were not mine to control. The thing then raised its claws and removed its cowl, revealing its awful features to me.

There would be no mistaking the priest for human as one might the girl or the other worshipers of that sinful underwater temple. Nay, this creature was no more man than the beast imprisoned on the church's roof. Its head was a swollen, misshapen mass of blue-gray scales and I'm not ashamed to say that I still shudder when I think of it. A dark green fin ran down the middle of its skull, disappearing into its robe. I found meself somehow grateful that it was still wrapped in its ceremonial garments 'cause the sight of its naked, bloated body may have been enough to break my psyche. Nevertheless, so hideous was the priest's face—froggish and fishlike in appearance—that I'm sure even the most courageous men would scream aloud if they were to lay their eyes on it. A series of gills flapped on the sides of creature's neck and tusks extended from between its flabby gray lips. Its glassy eyes, yellow and unblinking, sat too far apart on its face, protruding outward like a pair of rotten cabbages as they studied me.

Without doubt, the unhallowed congregation was the most appalling vision I've ever seen. I attempted a scream, but alas I could not, though the slug expressed enough displeasure for the two of us. It started to thrash above our heads and cry at a deafening pitch. The other worshipers then started up their dolphin chants again, but this only seemed to trouble the sea monster more. It shook the foundation of the building, yet even that did little to cause the priest to break its awful stare from me. My mind was swirling with the horrid sights and sounds occurring inside the submerged church, but just as I started to believe that they would drive me mad, my vision began to darken and the blare of the creature's screams faded away to nothingness.

When my sight had returned I was again lying in my hammock on the ship. I had my body back and no longer did my skin burn to the touch. For the first time since Lisbon the fog that had settled inside my head had started to disperse. My fever had recessed and with it the visions of that wicked temple and the city beneath the sea. Though the images I bore witness to managed to stay with me, as I could still recall those terrible dreams whenever I closed my eyes.

☸ ☸ ☸

I would come to learn that I had been laid up for three days and in that time things had changed aboard the ship. The merriment that'd been buzzing through the crew just days prior had vanished only to be replaced by nervous whispers and a sense of trepidation. Out at open sea, surrounded by nothing but the deep blue depths, sailors tend to gossip just as females do, and, once my strength had returned to me, a few of the fisherman made it their duty to catch me up on what I'd missed while I was wrought with fever.

The recent trouble seemed to be stemming from an altercation that occurred the night the illness took me. As I slept—so sick that I was well-nigh dead to the world—an incident occurred that had rattled many of the men on the boat, and not surprisingly it was regarding Job and the girl.

The story as it was told to me is that Antony had been topside that evening, navigating the ship through a patch of stormy weather so as to ensure the winds did not blow us off course.

When the sea had calmed he returned to his cabin to find the old man, dagger in hand, harassing the fish-girl and declaring that he aimed to kill her. The old man was bleedin' awful from the side of his neck. The merwoman had taken a bite out've him after he'd made an earlier pass at her with his blade. Gushing his wound was too! A crimson pool had collected at his feet, but despite the loss of blood, Job had a fire burning so bright inside him that night he had moved beyond all reason.

Antony ordered him to halt, but the old man refused to yield to his commands. He wanted only to bury his dagger into the merwoman's heart and there was no threat the Scot could make that would deter him from his mission. Aye, all else had become trivial to the old man. Job backed the girl into a corner, raised the knife over his head and readied himself to come down on her with the point of his blade. But the Scot was quicker and stronger than he. B'fore the gray-haired beggar could drive his dagger into her chest, Antony dashed across the room and sunk a knife of his own between the blades of his shoulders. The men who had witnessed this said Job then folded like a book, crumpling to the floor an instant later. As it turned out, the first mate's knife had delivered a fatal blow, but the old man did not pass quietly into the afterlife. He groaned and howled for minutes. Some of the crew tried to tend to him, but the beggar's injuries were too severe. Antony's knife was buried down to the hilt. In time, Job's breathing shallowed and his eyes began to dim, but just b'fore his soul would leave his body and travel to the heavens—or down to hell, where I believe it may've been destined—he raised a finger toward the first mate and uttered his final words.

"She's *his* master now."

The Cap did not reprimand Antony for killing Job. After all, he was only a beggar and as I said b'fore, the old man did not have many friends aboard the ship. Nevertheless, he was given a proper eulogy the next morning and his body was buried at sea. The Scot, however, was absent from the ceremony and it was then that the rumors began. Those who witnessed what happened did not believe that lethal force had been necessary. Antony was one've the strongest sailors on our ship and could've easily subdued the frail old man without the use of his knife.

The girl we was harboring was an unnatural, frightful thing—strangely beautiful though she was—and with the death of Job, much of the crew was beginning to grow nervous 'bout her presence on our vessel. Mayhap the old man's final words was getting to 'em. This is something I cannot say for sure, but a bit of mild panic had broken out amongst the men and it seemed to have spread like a plague while I was ill.

The lot of 'em knew little 'bout the feeding practices I'd been assisting Antony with in secret b'fore my fever struck. I'm sure their fears would've swelled considerably if privy to that information, so I thought it best to keep me mouth closed when they started prodding me about such things during our discussions. No need to fan the flames, I thought, especially when we were so close to our destination.

Antony might've been able to quell concerns himself had he appeared on the deck now and again following Job's death, but for much the time I was sick, he'd been cooped up in his quarters, battling an apparent fever of his own. Word amongst the men was that the Cap had checked on him and upon seeing his condition, feared for his first mate's health. He ordered Antony to relinquish the girl so another sailor could mind her while he recovered, but the Scot had somehow talked him out of it. Ill he may have been, but Antony was still a persuasive and powerful speaker. He managed to convince the Cap to send him a hand instead, so as to help him feed the girl since I was too delirious from fever to offer my assistance.

The man's name was Jacob. He was a young fisherman from a poor village, who had learned everything he knew 'bout sailing while working aboard the ship. He too had been questioned by the others 'bout Antony and the girl, but refused to talk of them. However, once he heard that my fever had passed, he sought me out to converse about our shared experiences. Jacob approached me the afternoon I woke from my watery nightmares and requested that we speak in private. We found an isolated spot at the hull of the boat. It was only there, where he knew others would not hear our discussion, that he felt secure enough to open up to me. The young fisherman spoke in a hushed tone and I knew from the cadence of his voice and the way his hands gripped me tight around my shoulders that he was very troubled.

"Antony has mandated that I do not speak of my chores outside of his cabin," Jacob whispered to me. His silky blonde hair had fallen over his face and for a moment, he looked almost mad. "He knows his practices are unconventional and he fears it would upset the crew if they were told how he goes about the girl's feedings." I nodded in agreement, for in the many years I've walked this Earth I've come to recognize that even a fool alone in distress is far more rational than a collection of great thinkers when danger's hanging over their heads. "But you've been present for them too," he continued. "You were helping feed the girl before the illness fell upon you. Before I was chosen to take your place."

I remained silent as it was not yet my turn to speak. Something was weighing heavy on the young man's heart—a secret he felt a need to disclose.

"The only thing that kept me sane during the time I spent with the Scot was knowing you had not run screaming from his cabin after witnessing those horrors." Jacob paused for a moment and bit his bottom lip. His face was rife with terror. I bade him to carry on so he took a deep breath and glanced over his shoulder.

Once he saw no one was in earshot he resumed his account. "The things he did. The way he fed himself to her . . ."

But his voice trailed off again and his dark brown eyes fell to his boots. It was difficult for him to relive those moments. I placed my hand atop his shoulder to soothe the young man's worries.

"Aye, friend," I replied with a smile. "It is a dreadful habit he's developed."

I assumed that Jacob was speaking of the very same practice I had witnessed Antony partake in with the merwoman. His disgust was something I found reasonable. Watching the Scot carve the flesh from his arm was a sickening sight to behold, but Jacob was acting as if he'd just crossed paths with the devil himself. When he spoke, his voice quaked with fright and his lips quivered like the plucked strings of a lute. I thought mayhap his fears were overstated, but when the young man opened his mouth again, I began to reconsider that notion.

"Dreadful?!" he cried. "If only one could describe such things with a word as modest as dreadful! Nay, there is no way to express the horrors I witnessed inside of that man's chamber. Tell me how you managed to keep your sanity?! I saw you those first few days. When you weren't assisting him, you walked about the ship as if nothing were the matter. How did you keep your conscience clear, knowing full well what he was allowing that creature to do to him?!"

I shrugged my shoulders, but b'fore I could answer him Jacob started up again.

"He said it was for the good of the ship, but I won't be a part of it anymore! Now that you're well, I'll be informing Antony that I no longer wish to aid him while he feeds himself to that terrible thing. If it doesn't frighten you, then I beg you to take my place. *God*, how he allowed her to eat him alive! The way she sank her teeth into his chest and stomach! The awful hymns he would

THE CREEPYPASTA COLLECTION, VOLUME 2

recite! They burned my ears! He sang them aloud with a smile on his face as she devoured him—as she sucked the blood from his veins!"

I tried my best to calm him, but Jacob had worked himself into a frenzy. His face bore the desperate look of an injured animal and all of my words appeared to fall on deaf ears. It seemed as if he was losing his mind b'fore my very eyes. Of a sudden the young fisherman spun around and ran off. He stormed below the deck and I knew he was heading to the first mate's quarters. I didn't try to follow him though. The last few things he'd been yammering on about had made me hesitate.

From what I could gather, Jacob's time with Antony sounded far different than my own. Never did he let the girl bite directly into his flesh while I assisted him. And the part 'bout her drinkin' his blood sent a chill through my body. I pondered too about the hymns the young man spoke of and found myself thinking back to the dark monks of my dreams, wondering if they and the first mate's songs were one and the same.

Moments later I would hear a scream rise up from the berth and I knew at once that it came from Jacob.

✸ ✸ ✸

By the time I arrived below deck, a dozen men had already gathered around the first mate's quarters. Jacob was shout'n and holding his arm and I could see the sleeve of his shirt was stained a deep red.

"Ya blasted beast!" he shouted. "Ya Godforsaken animal!"

Antony was in the doorway. He had put himself between the crew and the girl. Blood was smeared across her face and it looked as if she was still chewin' a piece of the young man in her mouth. I peered back at Jacob and realized then just how much muscle she had torn from his arm. Jacob's wound was spilling like a waterfall.

284

I could see the bone of his forearm; a flap of his flesh, attached by only a single piece of skin, dangled loosely from the mangled limb. The young man screamed again—harsh and shrill it sounded echoing off the walls.

"Ahhh! It burns! Like fire! Like a flame to my flesh!"

The men were trying to console him, but the young sailor had fallen into full panic. The Captain had entered the berth by now, having been lured by all the commotion. He instructed some of the crew to take Jacob topside and help him dress his injury. It took four men to pull him away, kicking and screaming, from the first mate's door. I stayed behind; Jacob was bucking like a wild horse and though my health had improved I was still weak from my fever's lingering effects. Once he was gone, Antony stepped outside his cabin and closed the door behind him to address the Cap.

"He burst in like a madman, Cap'n," Antony explained. "No fair warning at all. Not even a single knock. It startled the girl."

This was the first time in days that I'd gotten a look at the Scot and I understood then why the Cap had been so worried 'bout his well-being. Antony looked to still be suffering from what had been ailing him. His face was as pallid as a phantom floating through the fog and it seemed as if he'd lost considerable weight. His movements were sluggish. Each of his steps demanded the will of the world. Even his curly hair that had been such a vibrant, fiery red just days before had dulled to a drab orange. Antony gazed out at the remaining men through a pair of glossy, tired eyes set deep in the sunken sockets of his face and a strange thought then crossed me head that he had the look of a man waiting for death to take him.

"How much further, Antony?" asked the Cap. "The crew is restless and I can't be having anymore of this nonsense on my ship."

"We'll be a' reach'n the grotto b'fore next eve, Cap'n," the Scot mustered out.

And when he said that the Cap's eyes glimmered for the briefest of moments. Driven by the promise of riches, he was. So much so that he'd begun to let the treasure consume his every waking thought. The Cap scratched at his beard while he contemplated the first mate's answer.

"Good then," he finally responded. "And how're you feeling?"

"Aye, strong 'nuff ta make the journey, but I need me rest."

The Cap turned to face the rest of us.

"Well, you heard him," he barked. "Let him rest! Tomorrow we drop anchor and there'll be no more disturbing him 'till then!"

Fever struck Jacob that night, just after dusk had begun to settle in—and by the time the sun had fully sunk below the edge of the sea, the young fisherman had been reduced to an unconscious, babbling, sweat-soaked mess of a man. The crew was in an uproar. Their fears had more than doubled once word of poor Jacob's condition had travelled through the ship. I pitied him, knowing full well how terrible my own illness had been and prayed that he made a swift recovery. I believed that our fevers had been connected. After all, the only three men who had fallen ill on the ship had each felt the merwoman's teeth pierce their flesh. Mayhap her bite was venomous. This is something I now know to be true, though I would have no idea just how potent her poisonous mouth could be until a good deal later.

The Cap himself stood guard outside of Antony's door that night so as to prevent a repeat of the Job incident from earlier. This worked well enough to suppress any budding unrest. The night passed along without a skirmish and before I knew it the sun had begun to reappear over the eastern horizon.

The morning passed by easily enough. Though tensions throughout the ship were still high, I found myself sharing laughs with a few of the men as we waited to hear word from the Cap. It wasn't until midday that he made his way up topside to speak to us. His eyes were red and swollen from lack of sleep and his arms hung loose and heavy like pendulums from his shoulders. When he spoke I could hear the fatigue in his voice, but his eagerness for adventure and hunger for wealth was still apparent.

"Today is the day we make our fortune, men," he said to us. "Today we become rich."

And then, in a moment so timely that it must've been orchestrated by The Fates themselves, the excited shouts of a crewmate called down from the crow's nest above our heads.

"I see it! I see it! Land ho!"

※ ※ ※

By the time we drifted into the bay, the late afternoon sky was beginnin' to rust and it looked as if the heavens were cast from copper. The island was so small a man could set out on foot at dawn, explore every nook and crevice of its terrain, and still return back to where he started b'fore evening came about. The beach was littered with palms; birds with bright feathers and hooked beaks grazed its sandy shores. Beyond that was a lush garden full of ferns, colorful flowers, and exotic trees.

Antony appeared topside with the girl shortly after the beaches first came into sight. He navigated the ship to a cove tucked away in a rocky corner of the isle. Here is where we were told we could expect to find the Golden Grotto. The mouth of the cove was too narrow for our ship, so we lowered three whalers into the water and rowed out. There were six of us to a boat. Mine brought up the rear while the boat with Cap, Antony, and the fish-girl led our modest procession. Most of the crew stayed onboard the ship and I'm not ashamed to admit that I envied them for it as my trust in the Scot had been waning since the prior day's incident with

Jacob. The other men in my whaler must've felt the same way for their faces were grim and cheerless. There was gloom hangn' in the air and I felt less like a treasure hunter and more like a doomed soul embarkn' on a one-way voyage down the River Styx. Our boats were rigged with harpoons, but we were fisherman not soldiers, and the Cap was the only one among our three vessels carrying a pistol.

At a glance, the grotto was by no means remarkable. After hearing Antony talk of it, I had been expecting marble statues and jewel-encrusted archways, but the mouth of the cave was small and ordinary and our heads nearly touched the ceiling as we paddled inside it. We used torches to light our way through the darkness. I thought my nose had grown numb to the stench of fish, but the smell inside that cave was so harsh and overpowering that it caused my eyes to water. Black rock formations rose out from the water's surface like tentacles of the kraken and our voices bounced hollow off the walls.

Aye, the grotto was a peculiar place indeed, but peculiar for all the wrong reasons. The Scot had promised us a wondrous vault full of precious emeralds and rubies, but the deeper into the cave we travelled, the more I felt my dreams of riches drift away. The walls were made of stone, not diamonds, and even the slightest hint of gold was absent from its murky waters.

A steady unease was growin' throughout the group as we snaked our way down the grotto's narrow canal. So deep we had journeyed into the treacherous cavern that the mouth of the cave was no longer in sight. The flames from our torches were casting strange shadows on the walls. They danced and frolicked across the rocks like ghastly spirits. A feelin' of dread was beginning to swell inside me like a rising, black tide and I feared I might never again gaze upon the sky. Eventually, our party came upon a dead end, but this only gave my worries even more reason to flourish. Now the promise of treasure seemed farther away than ever. I know that I was not alone in this thought because after some time it was the Cap himself who turned to Antony and began to question him.

"Where are the rubies, Antony?" he demanded. "Where are the pearls and the emeralds you spoke of?" His words were full of rage, but the Scot said nothing. His only response to the Captain's interrogation was a stare so cold and distant that I briefly thought he might've been dead. "Answer me!" shouted the Cap, and when he said this, he lowered the barrel of his pistol between the first mate's eyes. "Where is the gold? Where are the diamonds?!"

The girl leaned over the edge of the boat and dipped her webbed fingers into the water. Aloof and childlike was her demeanor, as if completely oblivious to the ruckus the Cap was raising. The torchlight reflected red off her scaly skin and I remember thinking she looked like Hell incarnate. The Captain cocked his pistol so as to impress his point upon the Scot, but Antony sat in silence, never flinching, only breathing.

"Captain!" one of the men called out. "There be somethin' in the water!"

The lot of us then spun around and saw six heads breach the water's surface. Now I know you may think me mad, but I recognized the creatures from my nightmares. I was now face to face with the very same wretched monks that had tormented me during my fever-dreams. A chill ran through my body once this realization came to pass. That fishy smell had somehow grown more potent, so much so that it left its foul flavor in my throat every time I drew a breath. Time seemed to stop as we stared in awe at the horrid things treading water before us.

A scream rose up from behind me, sharp and jarring, it pierced the moment like the tip of a dagger, and when I turned in its direction I saw that it was coming from the Cap. The fish-girl had ambushed him from behind while his attention had been diverted. Her arms were wrapped tight around his shoulders and those shark teeth of hers had burrowed themselves into the side of his neck. He fired a desperate shot, but alas, the Cap was too far-gone. The bullet missed completely and when he tried to cock his pistol again his fingers betrayed him, and he dropped his weapon into the dark waters. The blood running down his throat looked black against the glow of the torchlight. Again and again, she tore away at his flesh, opening his wound larger with each bite. Antony did nothing to stop her. The other men in the boat pulled at her arms and legs, but the girl's grip was strong and they couldn't pry her loose.

I glanced back toward the mermen just in time to see the last of 'em dive out of sight. Seconds later our boats were rocking back and forth and I knew then they intended to tip us over. Out of instinct I snatched a harpoon and jabbed it into the water, though I could'na see a thing beneath the surface and my spear came up empty each time. A mate in the second boat did the same, but the mermen lunged up and grabbed hold of his harpoon's shaft, then pulled the poor bastard overboard. He breached just long enough to let out a horrible cry before the creatures pulled him back under.

The girl continued to feast on the Captain, but his screaming had sunk to a pitiful groan. No longer did he have the strength to struggle. His throat was red and gnarled; it looked like raw meat.

My boat was the last to capsize and by the time I hit the water the wicked things were already swarming the sunken sailors just as piranhas do. They glided through the water with incredible speed and grace, attacking from every angle, and tearing into the men with ease. The cave was pitch-dark now. The torches had been extinguished, but I could feel the creatures moving all about me. My crewmates' garbled cries told me just how deadly those waters were, but even the sounds of the slaughter didn't disturb me as much as Antony's voice when I heard it chanting out amidst the madness. Flat and colorless it sounded, as if the first mate was under the influence of a spell. He recited those blasphemous prayers—the very same I had heard in my nightmares—as the creatures massacred our friends and brothers all around us.

I shut my eyes and began to swim. The fish-people were faster than I—this I knew—but I reasoned that fleeing was my only chance to survive. I couldn'a see a thing in the darkness so I used the screams of my fellow sailors as my guide. I swam from the carnage as fast as my arms and legs would allow me. So sure was I that I'd soon be meeting my death that I had already begun to make my peace with the thought of their teeth shredding my flesh. I could hear the blood-soaked cries of my crewmates even after I emerged from the cave.

I gazed out over the cove as my eyes adjusted to the twilight and saw the ship still anchored in the bay. The sight was indeed a relief, but I knew I was far from safe. As long as I was in those waters, I was nothing more than prey. I felt myself growing weary. My heart was pounding inside my chest like the stampeding hooves of a hundred horses. My muscles were aching terribly and my vision was growin' blacker by the minute. Once or twice, as I made my escape, I thought I caught the fishy stench of that cave, but every time I peered over my shoulder expecting to see those things chasing me down, I found that I was still alone.

My mind was fading fast and I feared if the fish-people didn't kill me then the cove's warm, tropical waters would, but just before darkness grabbed me, I felt myself plucked from the sea, as if by an angel, and pulled aboard a boat. When I opened my eyes I saw the worried faces of my crewmates staring down on me. One of them attempted to ask me questions, but I'm afraid to say, my memory completely leaves me after that.

❀ ❀ ❀

Next thing I recall, I was back in my hammock aboard the ship. I had awoken from yet another deep sleep. So long I napped, that we were already more than halfway home. Many days had passed since that bloody afternoon.

I was told by the crew that they had lowered a rescue boat into the water when they heard the crack of the Captain's pistol, but the screams pouring from the grotto had deterred them from entering the cove. And so they waited until they spotted me making my escape. The men said that my eyes were wild when they pulled me from the drink and that I yelled and blathered like a madman, but my warnings had frightened them enough to turn back and leave the rest for dead. I passed out by the time they brought me aboard the ship. Not long after, they raised the main sail and decided to make a hasty departure.

I spoke to Jacob while I recovered below the deck. His fever had left him and he was eager to talk about the nightmares he suffered through. When I told him of the grotto, he said the scene I described unfolded just the way he experienced it in his dreams. He saw that awful city as well, and witnessed those monks and that wicked high priest performing the same depraved rituals that I observed.

❀ ❀ ❀

That was all many years ago. I left the fishing business and moved as far inland as I could. Jacob too retired early. He travelled back home to live and care for his elderly mother. But even though we went our separate ways, the two of us made sure to keep a correspondence. Ya see, we shared a mutual bond. Those awful dreams still haunted us and they were often the main topic of conversation in our letters. We believed it was the fish-girl's bite that induced it, and that mayhap her venom still flowed inside our veins.

I looked forward to hearing from him because he was the one person I felt I could speak freely to about my nightmares. Through our discussions, we tried to decipher hidden meanings in our dreams. We researched the ancient runes we saw carved inside the dark church and tried our best to translate the monks' language, though we made little progress in this endeavor. In his letters, Jacob often spoke of a book that he was searching for—an ancient tome written by a mad Arab that he believed would hold the answers to our questions. To my knowledge he never tracked it down, but I wonder if the book could have helped him once things took a turn for the worse.

I started to worry for my friend a little over a year ago. His words began to sound paranoid and I noticed a rapid decline in his penmanship. He told me his dreams were now unbearable and that they had been weighing heavy on his thoughts. This concerned me most of all. Then a few months later, I stopped receiving letters from him altogether. I wrote him many times, inquiring 'bout his well-being, but never received a response. And so, after some while I decided to pay him a visit.

His village was out on the coast. It was the first time in years that I had seen the ocean and I was surprised to find myself undisturbed by the sight of it. Nay, in fact, I found comfort in its rolling blue waves. His mother answered the door when I arrived at Jacob's home. I introduced myself as an old friend, but a look of grief struck her face when I uttered his name and right away I knew my fears had been confirmed.

She said that a terrible tragedy had occurred. It seems as though Jacob's final letters only revealed a small sliver of his tormented soul. His mother told me just how much he'd changed over the past year. He had become detached and standoffish. She said he was full of angst and that he often woke up screaming in the night. The man I knew was a devout Christian, but she said he had renounced the church, and when she asked him why, he would only talk of crazy things—as she would say—like ancient beings and sleeping gods. His behavior too had begun to scare her, but she was old and feeble and feared if she spoke out then he might strike her.

And then, early one morning while his mother still slept, he stripped himself bare, walked naked through the village, and threw himself from a pier. He fell like a stone into the sea. A few fisherman setting out for the day witnessed the whole thing unfold. They said he was ranting and speaking in tongues and it seemed as though he was talking to the ocean itself. His body was recovered and a memorial service was held in his honor. At the time I felt pity for him. I thought mayhap his dreams had worn away at his mind like waves do against the face of a cliff, but this I now know is not entirely true.

Mayhap it was my proximity to the coast, but soon I too began to have new, vivid dreams and they haven't stopped since I ventured out to Jacob's village. Each nightmare seems more real and frightening than the one that came before it. In them, I see more underwater cities filled with monstrous creatures like the high priest from my fever dreams, but now their history is told to me as I sleep. These Deep Ones have lived for millennia below the ocean's surface. It is they who rule the fish-girl and her carnivorous brethren. They view these merpeople as abominations—an early failed attempt to breed with the human race—but they tolerate their existence and let them worship in their sunken temples.

They are used in religious rituals, sometimes given up as a sacrifice to Father Dagon or Mother Hydra. Other times they are utilized by the Deep Ones to manipulate man.

I am sure now that there never was a Golden Grotto, nor was the girl really a queen of the sea, but the venom of her bite was powerful and I think I can feel it taking effect even today. The thought of land now repulses me. For a week I've been in this village on the coast and have not been able to peel myself away. I want to go home, but the ocean won't allow it. It beckons me. I can hear its voice calling in the wind, gusting over the water, begging me to take the plunge just as Jacob did. It wants a sacrifice.

And the more I dream, the harder it is for me to fight these urges. There is a realm of wonders that is unknown to man, dark cyclopean cities beneath the sea—magnificent, inconceivable spectacles. The Deep Ones build churches there and worship all-powerful gods—sleeping gods that will return, and when they do it will mean the end of the world.

I used to think man ruled the sea—that the creatures dwelling in its depths were ours to hunt and kill, but the venom in me blood has pulled the veil from my eyes and revealed the harrowing truth. We are nothing in this world. Its true kings will show themselves soon enough. I can hear the prayers of those monks now, even when I'm awake. They haunt me and remind me of this fact. *He sleeps*, they tell me, *he sleeps*, but I know that he will not sleep forever for the day will eventually come when he rises from his slumber!

Ph'nglui mglw'nafh Cthulhu R'lyeh wgah'nagl fhtagn!

CONTRIBUTORS

K. Banning Kellum

Banning is a lifelong resident of New Orleans, Louisiana, a husband and father, and a U.S. Army veteran. Banning started writing short stories as a child and the passion has evolved since. He finds sources of inspiration in all walks of life, from the esoteric lore of his city, and the love of his family, to his devotion to creating the perfect horror masterpieces.

CreepsMcPasta

Creeps is the British voice of creepypastas on YouTube. If you're a fan of Top 10s or a fan of smooth-sounding voices with British accents, you definitely know CreepsMcPasta. He's been a great friend of mine for many years now and I'm extremely happy to have him as a part of this collection. For many years he's been creating, writing, and recording creepypastas for YouTube and his audience has exploded as his popularity soared. To join that ever growing group of fans, check him out at: youtube.com/creepsmcpasta.

Max Lobdell

Unsettlingstories.com has the most insane update schedule. Max, owner and operator of the website, can pop out disgusting, exciting, and oftentimes lewd horror stories at an incredible pace. He keeps his website of short horror functioning at a speed that most people would expect from a full team of writers. Best of all, each story is unique and different from the last, and every one is guaranteed to leave you with a sleepless night.

TalesOfTim

Tim reads creepypastas on YouTube, with a twist. Tim is an artist that animates his original stories as well as other online material using digital and traditional mediums. His artwork and his voice have become known throughout the community as a charming and unique addition to horror. Find more of Tim at his YouTube channel of the same name.

Madame Macabre

This wonderful writer, voice actress, and musician is a triple threat. Madame Macabre's channel has become a staple in the creepypasta community and includes her comic "The Seer" as well as her wonderful music with macabre themes. In addition, Madame Macabre also works as a voice narrator and an actor to complement the horror writing she does. Some of her larger and well-known pieces can be found in this book and on her YouTube channel.

WellHeyProductions

Old Man Murphy, as he's known in the creepypasta community, is back once again for this volume. Murphy has always had a sense for creating interesting horror shorts and his inclusion in this book is no different. And most interestingly, his stories all seem to serve as a small cautionary tale. Wellhey.com, home of WellHeyProductions, is a great place to find more of his wonderful short stories.

Aaron Shotwell

Aaron Shotwell debuted on the creepypasta scene in 2012 with his first piece, "The Owl," narrated by YouTuber TheCreepyDark. Since then, he has been a regular writer for several popular YouTube channels dedicated to the subculture, and is best known for his ongoing scifi-horror epic trilogy, "The Twin Paradox." He has contributed to several viral marketing campaigns and collaborations, and is currently aspiring toward a career in screenwriting.

His first anthology, *Pleasant Nightmares*, is available on Kindle. Hard copies can be found on Amazon.com.

Jagger Rosenfeld

Known for his YouTube videos and writing, Jagger Rosenfeld (also known as DeadPasta) has made quite a name for himself in the online horror community. He's worked with many names in the community and is frequently a featured writer on the CreepsMcPasta channel.

BleedingHeartworks

Maja is an artist known for not just creating the Puppeteer but also bringing so many creepypasta monsters to life. Maja has gone from creating prints and fan art for characters to being the main artist for the stories in the *Creepypasta* comic book. In addition to her artistic talents she also has writing talents as well. The first Puppeteer story is included in this book and more can be found on her DeviantArt of her name: BleedingHeartworks.

Chris OZ Fulton

Chris is a famed artist from the entertainment circuit with a great love of the creepypasta genre. If you find yourself venturing into any avenue of horror, from "Silent Hill" to "Stranger Things," you're almost guaranteed to find an image that Chris has had a hand in drawing and that includes creepypastas. Chris has created artwork for the MrCreepyPasta channel as well as prints and designs for every creepypasta monster you can imagine. Some of his most famous images are from the story he penned himself, "Hobo Heart." Hobo is a brilliantly drawn and designed character that pulls at the teenage heart strings and feeds us enough gore to keep our bellies full for weeks. To see Chris's images including Hobo Heart, you can find Chris at: chrisozfulton.deviantart.com.

Jaime Townsend

Jaime Townsend is the author of many wonderful short stories that can be found around the Internet. Most popular of her stories, however, is a novel by the name of *The Darklings*. The Darklings are an army of demons, ghosts, and spirits just on the edge of shadows. In her book Jaime describes a woman's life as she grows up seeing, living with, and oftentimes witnessing murders by the hands of The Darklings. To read *The Darklings* for yourself and find more of Jaime's work go to Amazon.

Michael Whitehouse

Michael Whitehouse is by far one of the farthest-reaching authors from the creepypasta community. Michael has been around for almost as long as the genre has and certainly longer than the MrCreepyPasta channel. Now starting his own storytelling and horror shorts channel, you can find Michael Whitehouse at Ghastly Tales on YouTube, as well as on Amazon with *The Horrors of Christmas* and *The Face of Fear*.

Isaac Boissonneau

Isaac or HopefullyGoodGrammar is the youngest of this group of handpicked authors but that in no way holds him back. Isaac has shown himself to be one of the greatest of the community when it comes to writing and has much promise for the future. More of his work can be found as the most popular picks on the creepypasta Wikia.

M.J. Orz

M.J. Orz started *HorrorFictionBlog* in June 2016. He is a horror writer and blogger. His writing has been featured on podcasts such as The NoSleep Podcast, MrCreepyPasta, Phantom Librarian, and

Night Fears Podcast. You can also find his stories published in places such as Thought Catalog and EveryWritersResource.com. His debut horror novel, *Don't Kill the Pretty One*, is available now on Amazon.com. His second novel, *Andrew*, is now available on Amazon as well as at: http://horrorfictionblog.com.

Leonard Petracci

This author is very well known across Reddit's NoSleep community, however his name is slightly different. Leonard Petracci is known around YouTube and Reddit as LeoDuhVinci, creator of books and tales such as "The Lucienne Twins" and *Til Death Do Us Part*. As MrCreepyPasta, I've had the pleasure of working with him on both books and short stories as well as many, many other projects and each and every one has never come short of incredible. To find more from Leonard you can always check out his website: https://leonardpetracci.com.

The Right Hand of Doom

Doom has been a YouTuber and talented voice actor for many years. Doom has worked on many projects including charity streams, writing websites, and of course, he has become well known for his range of voice work. You can find more from Right Hand of Doom as well as hear his magical range at his YouTube channel of the same name.

Christopher Maxim

Publisher of quite a few horror books and anthologies, Christopher Maxim has made a name for himself online and on the shelves. His calling to the horror page is to take real life events and twist them to include the supernatural. Often this leads to a beautiful blend where you can't tell where the truth ends and the fiction really begins. It's always a pleasure seeing Christopher Maxim's work, and if you'd like to see more, you can always find it online at his website: www.christophermaximwriter.com.

Ashley Franz Holzmann

Ashley Franz Holzmann was born in Okinawa, Japan, and raised in a variety of countries while his parents served in the Air Force. He considered attending art school, but is instead a graduate of West Point, where he enjoyed intramural grappling and studying systems engineering and military history. He majored in sociology and is currently a captain in the Army. He has a published collection of short stories titled *The Laws of Nature*, and several other projects in the works. You can visit his website at www.asforclass .com, or check out his other works on Amazon.

Vincent V. Cava

If you know creepypastas, you know the name Vincent V. Cava. Vincent started as a Redditor for NoSleep and shortscarystories and rocketed his way to fame on both boards. From that point he's become a huge name in the creepypasta community. Many of those stories can be found in Volume 1 of *The Creepypasta Collection* and on the channel MrCreepyPasta, but more are in Vincent's collection of books available on Amazon. A good friend and a talented author, be sure to check out Vincent V. Cava's newest book, *Pastel Colored Dreams & Human Flavored Nightmares* for more of his stories.